SUSAN WRIGHT BEARD

I0547881

AT LAST?

Patten-Miller House
Salisbury, NC

i

Patten-Miller House, LLC
P.O. Box 1624
Salisbury, North Carolina 28145-1624
susanwrightbeard@gmail.com

ISBN 978-0-9911079-5-7

Library of Congress Control Number: 2020947475

Beard, Susan Wright.
At Last? / Susan Wright Beard.
pages cm
LCCN 2020947475
ISBN 978-0-9911079-5-7
ISBN 978-0-9911079-6-4

1. Progressive Christianity--Clergy--Fiction.
2. Women pastors--Fiction. 3. Southern--
Literature--Fiction. 4. Romance--Fiction.
5. Christian fiction. I. Title.

Dedication of this book by James M. Beard
to
Susan Wright Beard

This book is dedicated in memory of the woman who inspired it and without whom it would have never been written. Susan was my wife of 32 years before she died in 2018. The characters in these novels became over the years a part of our family as she worked and developed them. These novels reflect her Christian faith and her devotion to women's rights, LGBTQ rights, racial justice, justice for immigrants, and the basic equality of all people. Although she was unable to write this third novel, she was able to leave an outline that it is based on. Although Kayla Dunigan was hired to write this third novel, Susan did actually write the first three pages.

Acknowledgements

This like many projects has been a collaborative effort and could not have been carried without the help of many. Of course, Susan herself created the characters and the church on which the novel is based.

Our son David Beard was instrumental in helping to move the project along. He was a key advisor all along the way.

My daughter Kelly Berry suggested the Upwork organization through which we hired Kayla Dunigan to do the actual writting of the novel.

I cannot thank Kayla enough for her ability to pick up on Susan's ideas and to write in a way that was compatible with Susan's writing style. Her writing was well-done and timely. Again my thanks to her.

After having gone over the manuscript by Kayla, David, and I several times, it was time to hire a professional to line edit the novel. Again through Upwork we hired Rachel Mitchell to do the editing work.

My thanks to Mike Wilson of the Catawba College Modern Foreign Language Department for his checking of the small amount of Spanish in the novel.

I cannot say enough in thanks to Maegen Worley who donated her appropriate and well-done book cover in memory of Susan. In spite of her full time job at Catawba College she always came through for us.

My thanks to the Rev. Stephen McCutchen, Presbyterian writer and retired pastor for taking the time to read through the manuscript and to write a review on it. Also, my thanks to the Rev. Dale Walker for her review of the book as well.

Finally, my thanks to Lois Hinson for her support and reading the manuscript along the way. Lois is now my wife as we married in July of 2020.

Jim Beard
Salisbury, North Carolina

Forward

I never had the opportunity to know Susan Wright Beard personally. Yet I did know her: when you are a queer Black Christian who refuses to give up your relationship with Jesus, despite a chorus of brethren insisting that the Kingdom of Heaven is not for you, you, as Fred Rogers' mother suggested, "look for the helpers." If you search wide enough, you will find them, allies who put their reputations, relationships, and livelihoods on the line to publicly proclaim that people like me are loved and accepted by God. Susan was a helper. I found comfort in her first two books as Annie and the members of Covenant wrestled with long-held traditions and the question of who is allowed to come to Jesus. Susan knew me also without knowing me, and she stood up for me in her stories. She knew I needed help. Susan was also a realist in her writing: as in our actual world, not every character in her novels was able to accept people like me into the family of God. And I am still searching for Susans, for helpers.

It was an privilege, an honor, and a blessing from the Lord to help bring Susan's series to completion, and I thank Jim and David for allowing me to be a part of this special project. When I finished the draft earlier this year (2020), I, like the rest of the world I imagine, had no idea all that the year would ultimately bring. And when I see the protests across the U.S. and the world, when I look into White, straight faces with fists raised high as they march alongside People of Color and queer people, when I see a fellow Christian online challenging the exclusion of specific groups from the Gospel of Jesus Christ, I think of Susan. And I am grateful.

Kayla Dunigan
Nashville, Tennessee

Chapter 1

I think I might be the worst person ever. Here I am, pouring sweat, my t-shirt soaking wet, a sore thumb that I accidentally hit with a hammer, and paint all over my new shorts. I want to go home and be in air conditioning, but I'm twenty-nine, and almost everyone else working around me is in their sixties or seventies. Why am I such a wuss? Actually, I don't really care why. I really do want to go home.

As the pastor of a Southern Baptist church with these incredible members who always want to live their faith as well as speak it, I'm always having to try to keep up with them. Right now, we are finishing building a small home for a friend of one of our deacons whose home burned to the ground, taking everything she owned with it. It's really a great thing to do, and the seniors have worked hard and recruited a lot of help from the community. I'm here today because I felt guilty. I haven't done much on this project, and I thought I should make an appearance.

Now as pastor, I work very hard and stay busy, doing pastor stuff. Writing sermons, preaching, attending committees, visiting the sick and other members, counseling members, representing the church to the community and the community to the church. But physical labor is not my thing.

We started at six o'clock this morning, and it is now eleven-thirty. It's ninety-four degrees. Did I mention I was hot?

Edna Allen, chairperson of the deacons, appeared beside me.

"Annie, for pete's sake, why don't you take a break? We all take a ten minute break every hour and a half or so. It's hot out here, and you haven't stopped at all."

"Y'all take breaks? How come I didn't know that?"

"I don't know, but you need to go home now. We all usually go home about noon, and some of the professionals we have hired come in later in the day to do their part."

"Ok."

"You know, Annie, we're getting close to getting this finished. I can't believe it's really happening. It won't be long before Lizzie can be back in her own home."

1

I stopped a moment and appreciated what these church members had done. It was amazing how this group of senior Christians could lead the way for such a major project. When they announced what they were planning to do for Lizzie, I wanted to bang my head on a table because we were already in the middle of another project that involved seniors as well. I couldn't help but wonder what they were thinking.

But as usual, I learned that this church I was so blessed to serve somehow came through on following God's guidance in their projects. This house building started right after Memorial Day, and here it was late August, and they actually were working on the inside of the house to finish it up in the next few weeks, maybe a month or so. While they were doing that, admittedly with a lot of help from younger people in the community and people from other churches, Covenant was also involving more and more seniors in the area in speaking out about what services and events they wanted to see happen locally. We started out as a small group of twenty or so, surveying seniors as to how they saw needs in the area, and then actually recruited many of those seniors to help us survey others. It kept building as we added workers to the group, and now we had about fifty seniors meeting and continuing to work on these surveys and the collection and analysis of the data gathered.

Even saying all this made me tired. But to be honest, the members did most of the work, and I watched them do their thing. I haven't figured out yet whether I'm the luckiest and the most blessed pastor in the world or the unluckiest.

Since I'd been given permission, I gladly headed for my car, looking forward to turning the air conditioner on high.

"Annie, don't tell me it's quittin' time already? I thought noon was when all the action started."

Recognizing the voice, I said, "What a surprise to see you, John. It's been several weeks since we talked so I wasn't even sure you still lived in the area."

I was being petty, and I knew it, but John and I had been kind of seeing each other a little more regularly than earlier in our relationship, and then all of a sudden, three weeks had gone by without a call from him. I'm sure from John's point of view, the fact that I was also still dating Greg Barrow, a state trooper, made him feel justified in ignoring me for so long. I didn't feel that way.

"Come on, Annie, give me a break. I told you I had a case coming up that was going to take all my time for a while. Don't be mad."

He stepped closer to me and not only was I hot, but now I was having trouble catching my breath.

"I've missed you too," he said, "but I can tell you guys have been working hard. This house is actually going to be finished soon, isn't it?

"Looks like it. One day I'll learn to stop underestimating this group. They truly are something special."

"They sure are," John said, now leaning against the car and directly next to me, so close that I could smell his cologne. Even though I was still dating Greg, it had indeed been a long three weeks of not seeing John. Greg was a sweet man, and I was truly enjoying getting to know him. But there was something different about John, a sort of connection that I couldn't quite articulate clearly. They were both wonderful men, and I knew that the time would soon come when I'd have to make a decision about who to continue dating.

"I was wondering if we can get together tonight to catch up now that my case is finally over," John said. "Maybe grab some dinner at—"

"Reverend Adams?"

A middle-aged man in paint-splattered carpenter pants and a purple t-shirt approached John and me and stuck out his hand. "I'm Clint, Pastor at First Presbyterian. I've been working closely with Ben all day, and he was telling me a little about himself and all the great things going on at Covenant. I just wanted to catch you before you left to introduce myself and commend you. Ben seems to have found quite the support system, which is important with everything he has going on right now."

"It's nice to meet you, Clint, and thank you, but I try my best to lead the Covenant congregation only where they want to go, so they are the ones who really deserve all the credit."

Ben had seemed a little happier and in his element while serving as the site manager for the rebuilding of Lizzie's home

3

over the past several weeks. A former pastor, Ben Merriweather had contacted me by phone several months earlier after being disowned by his family after revealing to his wife that he was gay. After a terrible incident at a homeless shelter where Ben was beat up and admitted to the hospital, the Covenant congregation had allowed Ben to stay in the fellowship hall of the church until he was able to get a job, save money, and secure his own apartment in Bakerstown, three miles away from the church. But, he still had not been able to get in touch with his wife and kids, nor his parents since being kicked out of his home and church.

"Well, this is a special group you have here," Clint said.

"Thank you, Clint. As you know, trying to lead a progressive church, especially in the Southern Baptist Convention can be very challenging. I do have a few people that I lean on regularly for support, but I also know that the Presbyterians have been walking this road for a while. Maybe I can reach out to you for advice if I need it?"

A wide smile spread across Clint's face. "Well, you're certainly welcome too, Annie. If you ever need anything, I'm just a phone call away. But from the looks of things here and from what I've already heard about Covenant, it sounds like you all are well on your way down the path to making sure every person is included in God's Kingdom. Keep up the good work."

"Well, look at you, superstar," John said after Clint excused himself and walked away. "You look exhausted. I'll let you get back to your escape."

"Well, I certainly am tired, but I thought you were in the middle of inviting me to dinner tonight?"

"Yes," John said. "If you feel up to it after you get some rest. Pick you up around seven?"

"Sounds like a date."

I climbed into the car and finally cranked it, then sat for a minute and soaked up the cool air blowing from the vents as I watched John walk over to the construction site, kiss his mother Edna on the cheek, and pick up a hard hat. I desperately needed a shower and a few hours of uninterrupted rest, but I was already looking forward to seeing John again that evening.

4

Chapter 2

My date with John the night before had been wonderful, and was a nice ending to the long day working on Lizzie's house. Now I was back in the office and preparing for a visit. It was Wednesday afternoon, and I was headed to meet the others at Mr. Ryan Woolworth's house, an eighty-two year old widower who didn't attend Covenant, but had agreed to a visit by the group to participate in the survey. After the visit, I had a deacon's meeting to attend at 6:00 o'clock pm, where for the first time I'd share with them Dawn and Heather's request to have their wedding at Covenant. I'd been immediately nervous when the couple—one of two LGBT couples who were now attending Covenant—first met with me to ask if it was an option. I had spent the time since praying and asking God to give me courage to not fear, trust Him, and seek His direction as to whether to allow the wedding or not. Ultimately the decision was up to the deacons, but regardless of what they decided, I was the pastor of the church, and the person on whom most of the consequences, blame or guilt would fall.

I'd blocked out a couple hours this morning to work on this Sunday's sermon, and Elizabeth, a young mother and Covenant member who helps out around the church office in the mornings before her classes at UNC, held all the non-emergency calls and took messages until the two hours were complete. We then had lunch together in the office around noon before Elizabeth set off to her classes. Now I was ready to join Charlotte Wilburn and Elinor Bigsby on their visit to Mr. Woolworth. I checked my phone to make sure I had the correct address, and fifteen minutes later, pulled into Mr. Woolworth's driveway directly behind Charlotte's car. Charlotte stood outside the house with Ms. Bigsby, who glared at me for a few seconds through the windshield as I parked the car, then looked away. I glanced at the clock on my dashboard: I was seven minutes late.

"Hi ladies," I said as I hurried out of the car. "Good to see you both, and sorry I'm a few minutes late."

"If you're going to be joining us on these visits, Reverend Annie, it's important that you're on time. Early even."

"I agree, Ms. Bigsby. I'll make sure I arrive early for any future visits."

I wasn't really offended by Ms. Bigsby's hard, drill sergeant-style demeanor since meeting with her in the Spring and learning more about her missionary life in Liberia and her unfulfilled desire to be a pastor at home in the United States. And, I *was* late, and I definitely wanted to be respectful of everyone's time, including the seniors we would be visiting. I couldn't assume that just because they were elderly, they'd have all the time in the world to wait on me.

Mr. Woolworth must have seen us in his yard, because he opened the door before we got a chance to ring the doorbell and welcomed us inside his home. At eighty-two, he still possessed a full head of snow-white hair, and he wore a crisp, buttoned-down white shirt with baby blue pants with a sharp crease down the middle, and since I knew from the information we'd collected on some of the seniors, his wife was deceased of five years. I wondered whether he ironed his clothes himself or sent them to the dry cleaners to be pressed.

"Thank you for agreeing for a visit and participating in our survey, Mr. Woolworth," I said as we all sat down in the living room. "As Charlotte may have mentioned when she called you to ask if we could visit, we're a small group of people who have come together to survey the senior community here and around Bakerstown to gather knowledge about what issues you might be facing, and what we at Covenant could possibly do to help with those issues."

"Well, I've been thinking about this since you called," Mr. Woolworth said. "I'm still pretty mobile and independent, even in my old age. I do get lonely since my Kathryn passed away, but I spend a lot of time at my own church, First Baptist, where I've served as an usher for the last twenty-two years. I get to see people the few times a week that I'm there, and that helps. I'm a retired railroad engineer, so sometimes I go down to the yard to hang out and mentor the younger people. You'd think some of the technology would be more advanced now and that I wouldn't have much to offer, but the rail industry is surprisingly slow to adapt. A lot of the methods I learned and tools I used when I started at the old Southern Railway some fifty-plus years ago are still used today. Of course, I'm a lot slower and weaker than I used to be, so I let them do all the work, and I mainly just talk them through it. Keeps my mind sharp. But one thing I reckon I struggle with is getting a proper dinner at night. I never was the best cook, and my wife was an excellent cook and took very good care of me. But I'm afraid I never learned a thing from her. I make myself a sandwich for lunch most days, but my dinners are pretty pitiful. Of course, I'm not starving to death, just wish I'd learned to make myself a proper meal."

"I think that's one we haven't heard yet, Mr. Woolworth," Charlotte said. "What do you normally do at night for dinner?"

"I make another sandwich or warm up a tv dinner sometimes, but some nights I just don't eat at all."

My heart ached at the thought of Mr. Woolworth going without a meal some nights because he wasn't the best cook. I wasn't sure how much more the church could take on, but maybe we could get together at the next meeting to discuss some of the needs they'd identified and what they could do about them.

We presented Mr. Woolworth with a gift bag filled with coupons, fruit, and other small items that Charlotte had been so grateful to put together. Then I prayed for Mr. Woolworth and the group before we left his home, asking God to continue to watch over Mr. Woolworth, and provide us with a solution to his dinner needs. Outside, I bid Charlotte and Ms. Bigsby goodbye and drove back to the church to pray and prepare for the deacon's meeting.

All of the deacons were already milling about by the time I made it to the fellowship hall where we met once a month. Jesse Akin, one of the three newer deacons and who was expecting a newborn with his wife Lorraine any day now, waved at me as he sipped from his cup of coffee and sat down amongst the others.

Edna, our chairperson and strict timekeeper, erased the whiteboard and opened the meeting in prayer. "God, thank You for another day and another opportunity to come together and seek Your will for our lives and this church. Help us as we discuss how we may continue to take action and live out the Gospel, and not just talk about it. Please forgive us our sins and guide us along the path you would have us take. Amen."

"I guess we can start with an update on the survey visits," she said, "and then Annie has asked for time to speak with us about a request."

Edward Anderson, who had come up with the ideas for Covenant's last three major outreach initiatives, spoke first. "So far, the surveys have been going very well from what I've seen myself and heard from the group," he said. "At my last count, which doesn't include any visits so far this week, we've visited forty-two seniors and spoke with them about what issues they may be dealing with. Of course, we still have a lot more people to visit, but it looks like loneliness and loss of mobility and independence have been the main two issues to emerge as problems that elderly people in our community are facing.

"The group met here last week and started to draft some possible solutions to what we are discovering from the preliminary data. One popular idea that Carlita Alvarez presented to the group was a sort of resource guide that contains all of the information about groups and services in the area that are available to the community, complete with phone numbers, websites, addresses, and so forth. Even what day and time the groups meet, things like that. So, if an elderly person finds that they are lonely and would like to go be around other people, say on a Thursday around lunch time, they can pick up the guide and see if anything is going on that day and have all the relevant info right there in their hand. Now, I know the younger people are able to quickly access that type of information within seconds by just picking up their phone and typing in a few words. But a lot of seniors don't have smartphones or may have problems typing in the info on such a small screen, so we thought a book would be better, maybe written in large print and organized by day of the week or by month. I guess the most tedious part of that would be gathering all of the information, but again, we haven't gone too far down the road just yet. Just tossing around ideas. I'll keep you guys posted when there's something more concrete to share."

"Thank you, Edward and please do keep us posted as the group goes along," I said. "Also, I tagged along with Charlotte and Ms. Bigsby today on a visit to a Mr. Ryan Woolworth, and he shared with us that sometimes he skips dinner because he doesn't know how to cook. So please add that to your list as identified concerns and think about how we might can help there."

"I've known Mr. Ryan my entire life," Danny O'Reilly said with a look of shock on his face. "I had no idea he was not having dinner every night. Please keep him on your list Edward, but in the meantime, me and my wife will make sure he has a proper meal if he wants it."

"Thank you, Danny. I'm sure he would love that."

"Yes, thank you, Danny," Edna said. "I think your stepping up to fill in, also reminds us that although we are meeting here to discuss what we can do as a church, often times God doesn't want us to wait on something formal or organizational to be established to help those in need. He is depending on each one of us as individual Christians to be His hands and feet and representation of Jesus Christ here on Earth. I know in my own life, often times it's easy to see someone in need and think 'someone should do something,' when a lot of times, we are that someone who has the capacity and resources to help if we would only stop, take the time out of our busy schedules, and do it."

"Thank you Edna, for sharing such poignant wisdom," I said. "I think that's something I'll share with the entire congregation this Sunday. Let's all make sure we take the time this week, and beyond really, to identify needs that we can meet for someone else as individuals without waiting on someone else."

Edna smiled and winked at Danny. "Okay, if there aren't any more updates about the survey, I think we're ready for you Annie. What do you have for us?"

"Well," I said, standing up from my chair while Edna took a seat in hers. "I'll just jump right in: Vivian Art's daughter Heather and her partner Dawn have decided to get married, a Spring wedding, and they have asked if it is possible for them to be married here at Covenant."

The room was silent. Too silent. It was like no one knew what to say, either for fear of how they might sound or being the lone voice to support Heather and Dawn's request, or the lone voice to not support it.

Finally, after about two minutes, Jesse Akin spoke up. "Well, I realize I may be the only one, but my vote is yes, to allow it. I know most of you might not be there yet, officially having a gay or lesbian wedding in the church, and I can appreciate where you're coming from, at least biblically, considering this is a church. But I've been in their shoes not once, but twice before, being looked down on and rejected for who I loved. It wasn't right then and it's not right now."

Jesse was married to an African American woman. Edward, who's wife was Vietnamese, patted him on the shoulder. Jesse, in turn, reached over and softly double-tapped Edward on the knee.

"I think your experience of being discriminated against for being married to a woman of another race was a little different than if you were wanting to marry another guy," Alan Emerson said, with Fred Miller staring at the floor but nodding in agreement beside him, his arms crossed. The two men had both been a lot more hesitant than others about some of the progressive actions the church had taken since my arrival as pastor. But to their credit, they hadn't outright left the church—which of course was an option—but had stayed and tried to be open-minded and really get to know some of the new members who Covenant had sought to welcome and include.

"How so?" Jesse said. "The Bible has been used to justify a lot of evil in the world. "Wars, slavery, racism. Now homophobia. One hundred years from now, Christians will look back at our times and wonder what the heck we were thinking."

"That may be true," Alan said. "And while I also have generally—albeit somewhat reluctantly—supported where this church has positioned itself lately and some of the initiatives we've done to reach all different kinds of people, I'm afraid something like this may be too much too soon for the congregation."

"If not now, then when?" Jesse asked. "We say no to Dawn and Heather, but if Donnie and Steve want to get married two years from now, will we say yes? And if we say no to them also, then all of these initiatives are really just for show."

10

"This is still God's house," Fred said, speaking up now, "and the Bible still says what it says. Now or two years from now, I can't support it."

The room fell awkwardly silent again as everyone tried not to make eye contact with each other as they thought about the ramifications of having a lesbian wedding at Covenant. Although I couldn't know for sure until it happened, I began to guesstimate how each person would most likely vote: Fred and Alan would probably both vote no, with Jesse voting yes.

"How soon do we need to tell them of our decision?" Anita Fleming asked. If I had to guess, based on some of Anita's past comments about not-wholeheartedly agreeing about some of the initiatives the church was taking on, she'd probably vote no also. I had no clue how Edna, Edward, and Danny would vote.

"They had originally anticipated a fall wedding, but later decided that Spring suited their schedules better. But you know it can take a long time to plan, and venues are often booked up to a year in advance, often times longer. So, in order to be fair to them, I think we should tell them something soon. Maybe we can give it a couple weeks to think on it, then agree to meet again two weeks from now to vote."

"That sounds good," Edna said. "Give us a little time to pray about it."

"Also, I don't know this for sure," I said, "but as deacons, you should also probably consider what a possible yes vote would mean and if that would jeopardize Covenant's membership in the Southern Baptist Convention."

"Oh boy," Edward said. "I know we've made a point to actively be more inclusive recently, but this is where the rubber meets the road, huh?"

"Yes, I'm afraid so, Edward."

Edna rose from her chair and began to pray. "Father, thank You for our time here today, and for empowering us to continue to take action to take care of Your people. Thank You for revealing the needs of the seniors in our community, so that we can provide for them as You have provided for us. We have what looks to be a difficult decision to make regarding Dawn and Heather's wedding and the future direction of this church. Please help our hearts to be

11

as Yours and show us what path to take in the coming weeks. Regardless of the outcome, thank You for Dawn and Heather's commitment to each other and to You. We thank You for your guidance in advance. Amen."

Jessie gathered his things, nodded to Edna, and walked out of the fellowship hall without acknowledging anyone else with a goodbye. I felt a tinge of sadness of what this group may go through in the coming weeks, and what the group's decision would mean for the future of the church.

Chapter 3

Two days later, I was looking forward to my bi-monthly Friday appointment with my mentor Reverend Brian Stanley, a Southern Baptist minister who had been advising and counseling me since my arrival at Covenant. Brian was hesitant to support a female pastor—as they are virtually non-existent and not allowed in the SBC—but had agreed to mentor me anyway. He had really been helpful in helping me work through the stress and responsibilities of being a pastor. When I sat down in the chair in front of his desk, the first thing he asked me was whether I'd been continuing to write down my task list, prioritizing it, and only doing what I can do.

"Yes, I have. And I've tried not to stress over problems I can't solve or lament that I can't fix everyone's problems and solve every issue in the world."

"Good," he said. "But I can tell you're concerned about something. What's been going on?"

When I told Brian about Dawn and Heather's request to have their wedding at Covenant, and the deacons' reaction, Brian exhaled a whistle and leaned back in his chair.

"I also warned the deacons about what this might mean for our membership in the SBC," I added.

"Yes," Brian said. "That is a very real possibility Annie, so I'm glad you alerted them to it. I have admired everything that you have done since you accepted the position at Covenant, and I can see now how important the work is. But unfortunately, the larger organization is just not there yet. In fact, they may be moving in the opposite direction. So, not that you and the deacons aren't taking this request seriously, because I know that you certainly are, but this is indeed the fork in the road, and most likely the point of no return when it comes to the SBC. They've...tolerated...having a woman pastor in one of its churches, but hosting and officiating any kind of wedding that is not between a man and a woman will probably be the last straw before they feel forced to step in."

I slumped in my chair and looked out of the large window besides Brian's desk, and thought about the past almost two years at Covenant and what would happen if the deacons voted to allow the wedding. Brian had just pretty much confirmed the church would get kicked out of the SBC. Would I lose my job and have a scarlet letter on my resume? Would I ever be able to pastor another church again? I immediately regretted only thinking about myself, when I should be thinking of what a no vote would do to Dawn and Heather. Dawn had said they'd understand if the church voted no, but would they really? Would they still want to worship at Covenant with their kids? And what about Vivian Artz, Heather's mother and longtime member of the church. How would she feel?

Brian's voice broke through my thoughts of doom. "I have to admit that I'm a little shocked at the look of worry on your face. You had to know something like this was coming, right? The road that you and Covenant have been on recently was always leading to this. It was only a matter of time."

"You're absolutely right, and I can see that now. When I first interviewed for the position of pastor at Covenant and learned that they'd always been a little different than other Southern Baptist churches in the embrace of progressiveness, it excited me, considering I'm a woman in a position that has been traditionally held by men. I felt grateful at the possibility of finally getting to live out what I consider God's calling for my life, a calling that I wasn't sure would ever be fulfilled in my lifetime. Dawn, Heather, and everyone else who attended our Family Day event and have been worshiping at Covenant since must have had that same hope blossom in them when they saw our ad in the paper and came to our events. I just hope that we make the right decision, even though I know we can't and never will be able to please everyone."

"I firmly believe that you are built to lead this church wherever it wants to go," Brian said. "Speaking of marriages, did you ever choose between those two guys?"

"I haven't yet, Brian. But I will soon. I know it's not fair to continue to see the both of them, especially if either or both of them want to work on developing a more serious relationship— which neither has expressed to me yet, by the way."

"Sounds like you could use a date."

"I think you're right. A night out and not thinking about what to do about Heather and Dawn's wedding will do me some good."

14

"There you go," Brian said. "And remember, you are a pastor. Go to God, as I'm sure you've done and continue to do, and let His peace be your guide. You've handled these type of situations before and came out fine. I'm sure you will do it again. Have faith."

I thanked Brian for his encouragement and time and drove back to the church. After checking the phone for messages and returning one call, I took Brian's advice and texted Greg to see if he was free for our usual Sunday night date this week. *"Sure am,"* he responded.

Chapter 4

The next morning I slept in, silently congratulating myself as I nestled into the comforts of my bed for making it through the week and having already finished my sermon for tomorrow. Of course, I'd look over it again tonight for good measure, but I had most of the day to rest or go out and do whatever I wanted. I was also already looking past the morning service to tomorrow night's date with Greg. It had been a while since I'd seen him since we'd both been quite busy lately: me with church and the responsibilities that come with it, and Greg with his regular duties as a State's Trooper, and also caring for his dying father. Thinking of Greg's dad being ill reminded me to make a definite plan to visit my own parents in the coming months, hopefully before winter, so I wouldn't have to deal with the snow and ice. I desperately needed the break away from all church related things, even if it was just for a couple of days. My next semi-annual vacation wasn't scheduled until late Spring, so until then, I'd have to look out for opportunities when the church wasn't too busy to sneak away for a day or so for a quick refresher.

After dozing off again and waking up a couple of hours later, I finally made my way out of bed around one o'clock p.m., showered, and sat down with a cup of coffee in front of the television. A couple of mindless episodes of a comedy was just what I needed: something entertaining and not too heavy or traumatic to invoke my feelings or emotions. I had enough of that in real life. Just as the third episode in my binge-watching session was beginning, my cell phone rang on the end table beside me. The caller ID read *Linda Wilburn Sanchez*, whom I'd been chatting with occasionally when she'd call the office to check in on her mother, Charlotte. But Linda had never called my personal cell before, so I answered immediately.

"Reverend Annie, I'm sorry to call your personal line and on a Saturday," Linda said, panic in her voice. "I just got a call from CMC Main in Charlotte. They found Mom in her car in the parking lot of the grocery store. They said the car was not running, the windows were rolled up, and that it's ninety degrees there today. I don't know if she fell asleep or what, but at some point she was alert enough to push the panic button around her neck and summon help. By the time police arrived, she was unresponsive, and they had to break the window to get in the car. They rushed her to the hospital. I'm so sorry to bother you on a Saturday, I just don't know who else to call."

"Don't apologize Linda," I said. I'd already begun walking to my bedroom to throw on some proper clothes. "Is she okay?"

"I'm not sure, the call came from a nurse who found my number in her purse. She asked if there was someone close by who could come to the hospital."

"Okay, I'm on my way. Call me back if you hear anything before, I get there. It will take me about thirty minutes. And I'll do the same for you and call when I get there and know more."

I prayed for Charlotte the entire way to the hospital, unsure of what I was about to walk into. Had she had a heat stroke? I hoped the paramedics hadn't gotten to her too late. Charlotte had been having memory lapses, and Linda had asked Charlotte to come live with her and her family in Mississippi. Later she changed her mind when they'd discussed Charlotte's need to remain independent as a senior so that she didn't feel worthless or feel like her life was over. Linda had gotten Charlotte a panic button to hang around her neck, which made Linda feel better and made Charlotte feel old. It had been my idea, and I was the one who had encouraged Linda not to worry that something tragic would happen to her mother. Maybe Charlotte should have gone back with Linda after all.

I shook away the pangs of guilt rising within me as I found a parking spot in the visitor's lot of the hospital and rushed into the emergency room. I signed in at the front desk, noting that I was there to visit Charlotte Wilburn, and after forty-five minutes of waiting, was summoned to the back by a young nurse who'd emerged through a set of double doors. "Are you Ms. Wilburn's daughter?" she asked as we walked.

"No, I'm her Pastor. Her only next of kin, her daughter, lives in Mississippi and asked me to come here."

"Oh," the nurse said, just a slight look of surprise on her face. "Well, we think Charlotte is going to be okay. She was extremely overheated when she arrived, and had passed out, but thankfully the paramedics got to her before she had a full out stroke. A few more minutes in that car, and she probably wouldn't be here."

"Thank God," I said, exhaling a sigh of relief as we approached a door across from the nurses' station. "Is she awake?"

"Yes, you can go in and see her now. She's a little upset and tired, but she's okay. We'll keep her for a day or two just to monitor her to make sure she's okay."

I gently tapped on the door, loud enough for Charlotte to hear, but soft enough to not alarm her or the other patients, and opened the door slowly, peeking inside.

"Come on in, Annie," Charlotte said. "Linda told me you were on your way."

"Oh Charlotte," I said as I walked over to her bedside and placed her hand in mine. "How are you feeling?"

"Better now," Charlotte said. "But I'm pretty disgusted with myself. I just don't know how I could have fallen asleep in that car! One minute, I was parking at the grocery store. I had a small list of items to get to make some meatloaf tonight for dinner. And the next minute, it seemed like I woke up and was so overwhelmed with heat that I literally couldn't move. It felt like one of those dreams, where you're conscious of what you need to do, but your body is moving in slow motion, or you can't get it to move at all. Thankfully, I put this alert button on a very long necklace, so it was laying on my belly, close to my hand, and I was able to push it. The next thing I know, I woke up here."

"I'm just glad you're okay, Charlotte. Every summer we read the stories from around the country about parents who have somehow forgotten their small children were in the car and left them in there by mistake. I can't imagine the pain and guilt those parents have to live with."

"That's exactly what I keep thinking about, what my poor Linda would feel if I'd convinced her that I could remain living here by myself and getting along well, only to die in a hot car a few months later. Maybe I need to rethink her request to move to Mississippi."

"Maybe so, Charlotte. But right now, let's just focus on getting you well."

18

The nurse came in and pressed the recline button on Charlotte's hospital bed so that she could take a nap and get some rest. I called Linda and she had already hit the road, but with a ten hour drive ahead of her, it would be well into the night when she got to Charlotte. Thankfully, I'd grabbed my book bag and sermon notes as I rushed out the door, and I placed a call in to Edna to let her know what was going on. She agreed to come to the hospital around six o'clock p.m. to take the "night shift" of staying with Charlotte until Linda arrived, which would probably be about one o'clock a.m. Soon after hanging up with Edna, I got a text from John. *Praying. Let me know if you need anything.*

I thanked John, then decided it was a good time to grab lunch while Charlotte was sleeping. I caught the elevator back down to the main level of the hospital and searched for the food court. I settled on a small chicken Caesar salad, an orange, and my second black coffee of the day, and as I paid for the food and turned to find an open table, I spotted Greg rising up from a table, waiving to get my attention.

"What are you doing here?" I asked after I reached him. Greg was in his full officer uniform.

"Dad's been admitted here. Had a bad bout last night, scared Mom to death. There's not much more they can do for him at this point."

"Oh, I'm so sorry, Greg."

"Me too, and thank you for your support, prayers, and for just being around for me. I think I should still be good for our d— oh, hi Stacy!"

I turned around to see who Greg was speaking to, a medium height, very fit woman in pink teddy bear scrubs waved and walked over to the table.

"I'm sorry, I didn't mean to interrupt," she said.

"You aren't interrupting," Greg said, and the genuine smile that spread across his face was hard for me to ignore. There was even a little light in Greg's eyes, where before they'd seem very distant and sad as he spoke about his father's condition. "Stacy, this is Annie, my good friend I was telling you about. She's a pastor in a church right outside of Bakerstown."

"Nice to meet you, Stacy."

"You too," Stacy said back to me before returning her focus to Greg. "How's your father doing today? I'm just arriving for my shift and stopped in here to get a snack."

"Not too well, actually. But I'm sure he'll be happy to see you."

"Well, let me get upstairs and see if I can brighten his day a little. See you in a few. It was nice to meet you, Annie."

"She seems nice," I said, trying to fight off the tinge of jealousy I was feeling at seeing Greg light up for another woman. But who was I kidding? Greg must have felt the exact same all this time knowing I was also dating John.

"She is. Dad's really taken a liking to her, calls her his favorite. But wait—what are you doing here?"

I told Greg about Charlotte and how I'd be hanging out for a while. We ate our lunches and caught each other up on what had been happening in our lives and after about an hour Greg brought up tomorrow's date.

"As I think I started to say earlier, I think I should be still good to go for our date tomorrow, if you are not too tired after being here all day and preaching a sermon tomorrow. The Panthers have a four o'clock game versus the New Orleans Saints, first game of the season, and my dad has season tickets. Of course, he can't use them, and offered them to me tomorrow, if you'd like to go with me."

"I'd love to," I said. "It's been a while since I've been to a game, and it will be a nice distraction."

"Great. Let's make a plan on where we will both park and then walk over to the stadium."

After we decided where to park, Greg said "Well, I'd better head back up. I'd invite you up to meet my parents but meeting a woman pastor might be just the shock to send my father on over to the other side."

I shook my head and smiled at Greg's dark humor and gave him a hug, and he kissed me on the cheek as we broke our embrace. "I will pray for him anyway," I said.

"Thank you. You know, being in a hospital is so humbling," he said while looking around at all the families around

20

us. "We always get wrapped up in our own little worlds, but this makes you realize everyone is going through something."

Chapter 5

Sunday morning was another hot one, having already reached eighty degrees by the time I left the parsonage and walked over to the church around 8:30 a.m. The sound of the organ greeted me as I walked in, and I made a point to peek into the sanctuary and lay my eyes on William, Covenant's music director, if nothing but to make sure he looked okay. The scare with Charlotte yesterday had my nerves slightly on edge about the older members of the congregation. Yes, they were a savvy and able group, but I knew there would come a time when some of them would not be able to keep up with their current pace. William sat at the organ, eyes closed as he played with his face tilted toward the ceiling, in the middle of what looked to be very personal and intimate worship with God. I softly let the door to the sanctuary close and backed away.

Two hours later, after some alone time in my office to look over my sermon notes for the final time, I walked down the hallway and stuck my head in on Pete Stoudamire's adult Sunday school class, then headed back to the sanctuary to greet worshippers as they arrived for service. Donnie and Steve made a point to walk over and say hi, with little Isabella in tow, as well as Mary LeBlanc and her son Damien. Lucille Smith, Elizabeth, and Elizabeth's two kids Lacey and Jeremy followed close behind.

Linda had sent a text this morning thanking me again for rushing to Charlotte so quickly. She let me know that they wouldn't be at the service since Charlotte was still in the hospital, but that Charlotte was feeling better and ready to go home. I said a silent prayer for the mother and daughter, thinking of the difficult conversation that the two of them would most likely have in the coming days.

Taking a cue from Edna's message to the deacons about stepping up individually to help others in need, my sermon was rooted in Matthew 25:35-40: *"For I was hungry and you gave me something to eat, I was thirsty and you gave me something to drink, I was a stranger and you invited me in, I needed clothes and you clothed me, I was sick and you looked after me, I was in prison and you came to visit me.....The King will reply, 'Truly I tell you, whatever you did for one of the least of these brothers and sisters of mine, you did for me.'"*

After the service, I shook more hands and was close to wrapping up when Heather and Dawn and their two kids Cody and Kami were the last people in line to say hello. "Great sermon today, Reverend Annie," Heather said.

"Thank you." I lowered my voice and stepped in close to them. "I haven't had a chance to tell you gals yet, but I want you to know that I presented your request to the deacons last week. They asked for two weeks' time to pray about it and make a decision. Is that okay?"

"That's fine," Heather said. I thought I saw a slight change in the expression on Dawn's face, but I wasn't sure. "And again, if the answer is no, it's okay."

"I'm not sure which direction they are leaning, but there will be a vote, and as soon as I know their decision, I will call you asap."

They thanked me and walked down the aisle, and I noticed Jesse and a still very pregnant Lorraine waiting for them by the door, smiles on their faces as they all grouped together and exited out into the sunshine. "Everything okay?" a man's voice said from behind me. It was William, his eyes also on the group.

"As of right now, yes. But put that bottle of cognac on standby," I said.

William was a gay man in his late sixties who had never gotten a chance to live a life being his true self, and I'd confided in him early on about Heather and Dawn's request. He winked and patted me on the shoulder, and I said goodbye and rushed out of the sanctuary and across the yard to change into my Carolina Panthers gear.

Greg stood waiting for me as I pulled into the parking lot we'd agreed to meet at about a mile from Bank of America Stadium. "Hey there," he said, and greeted me with a long kiss after I exited the car. "So good to see you."

It felt good to kiss him again, especially since for the past twenty-four hours, all I'd been able to think of was Greg's change in attitude when Stacy, the oncology nurse, had stopped by the table yesterday. Maybe he wasn't into her after all?

We walked the mile to the stadium in a sea of blue and black and black and gold, and I noticed the sizable amount of people wearing New Orleans Saints jerseys. Once inside, Greg said our seats were in the middle of the row, so it would be a good idea to get any refreshments now if we wanted to not miss any part of the game. I settled for a beer and pretzel, while Greg chose a beer and a hotdog, and we made our way to our seats in the lower level.

"How long has your dad had these seats?" I asked.

"About twenty or so years actually, from the very first season," Greg said. "One of my favorite memories I'll always have with him is coming to or watching these games every Sunday." Greg shifted his eyes and didn't say any more. I reached over and rubbed his knee.

"Thanks for coming with me today," he said after a few minutes. "I needed to get out of that hospital for a minute."

The stadium filled, and the game started, with the Panthers scoring two quick touchdowns in the first quarter. The Saints added one in the second quarter, and by halftime, the score was 21-7 Panthers. I stood in a long line to use the lady's restroom at halftime, as everyone had the same idea to relieve themselves while there was no action on the field. On the way back to our seats, I bought two bottled waters for Greg and me. The sun had been high in the sky and beating down on us for the entire first half. Greg was grateful and had completely finished his bottle in two long gulps.

The Panthers were in the middle of another scoring drive with the crowd on its feet in the middle of the third quarter when Greg reached into his jeans pocket, looked at his ringing cell phone and answered it, sticking a finger in his opposite ear to drown out the noise.

"Okay, I'm on my way," he said to the person on the other end, then ended the call. "Annie, I'm sorry. We have to leave."

"Okay. What's wrong?"

"It's my dad. He's taken a turn."

24

I didn't ask any more questions, and Greg held my hand tight as we worked our way out of our row and up the lower level stairs. I kept up with Greg as he ran through the concourse, out of the gate, and flagged down a cop and asked for a ride to the hospital. We didn't have time to walk back to our cars.

I climbed into the back and Greg sat in front with the officer as the policeman switched on his emergency lights and sirens and sped down the street. Within fifteen minutes, we'd arrived at the hospital, rushed inside, and tried to wait patiently as the elevator took us up to the oncology wing on the tenth floor. Greg gave me a quick hug as we separated at the waiting room, wiped the sweat away from his forehead and straightened his Carolina Panthers t-shirt over his jeans as he power walked the rest of the way to his father's room.

This time, I waited in the small waiting area down the hall and around the corner from where the patient rooms were. There were two kids also in the room: one teenage boy with headphones in his ears, who reminded me of my nephew Derek, and a smaller boy, who was sitting across the room watching cartoons on the television mounted high in the corner. I stretched out my legs and settled in for my second hospital stay in as many days. This time, I had no sermon to look over and nothing else to read as I waited, so I focused on praying silently for Greg and his family.

When I had first met Greg, he'd shared with me about how getting a divorce had caused a rift between him and his Baptist preacher father. I didn't know what Greg was feeling at this moment, or if he and his father had ever made up since they'd discovered that he was dying. Of course, as Christians we believe that dying is never the end, but the doorway to an eternal life in Heaven. Greg's father was going to meet Jesus. But his family would still be here, missing him and holding on to memories of him, and I could only imagine how terrible it would be for Greg to live with the pain of having fallen short of his father's expectations. I prayed for peace and reconcilement between them before it was too late.

I was casually watching the television in the corner as I drifted in and out of prayer for Greg, and before I knew it, two

25

hours had passed. Just as I stood up to stretch, Greg appeared in the wide doorway, his face red and damp. "He's gone," he said.

I crossed the room over to him, enveloped him in a big hug, and tried to hold on to him as his body heaved with the pain of loss.

Chapter 6

I sat in the sanctuary on Tuesday morning before anyone else arrived for the weekly prayer meeting, closed my eyes, and let the silence and stillness envelope me. It felt good to just sit for a minute. What I'd thought would be a restful weekend had turned into a very busy and emotional one. I hadn't been naive when I'd grown up wanting to be a Southern Baptist preacher; I'd known that leading and caring for God's people would not always be a walk in the park, if ever. But, I'd be lying if I said I hadn't imagined myself in the pulpit delivering awe-inspiring sermons and having illnesses miraculously healed more than I'd imagined dealing with death and funerals, being pulled in several different directions at once, and making decisions that could possibly get me removed from my position. I caught myself in my selfish thoughts and pushed them away. Regardless of the difficulties of the job, I was grateful that God had blessed me with this responsibility, an opportunity that most Southern Baptist women had not been afforded. I asked God to give me strength equal to my days and rested in the promise of Deuteronomy 33:25: whatever God placed before me, He'd also provide the strength for me to get through it, including supporting Greg at his father's funeral later that afternoon.

After a few more minutes of having the sanctuary to myself, I turned on some peaceful music just as Vivian Artz and Mary LeBlanc walked through the doors. Before long, about fifteen members of Covenant sat scattered throughout, and per our usual routine, I greeted them as a group before we all sat in silence for the next several minutes. I then stood up and asked the group if anyone had any prayer requests or anything else, they'd like to share. No one said anything before Edna turned around to the group.

"Charlotte Wilburn was admitted to the hospital over the weekend after having a scare at the grocery store," she said. "But she's okay now and back home, and possibly even up for a few visitors and phone calls if any of you would like to check on her."

"I will call her as soon as I leave here," Pete said. "Thanks for telling us."

I looked round at everyone to see if anyone else had something to share and noticed a big smile on Mary LeBlanc's face. I smiled back at her. "Well something certainly has you happy this morning, Mary," I said.

Mary grinned. "Ya know, sometimes in my daily prayers, even when I have a laundry list of things I need God to fix, I have to remind myself that if God knows how many hairs are on my head, surely He also knows everything that's going on in my life. So, instead of going down my list, I simply say, 'Thank You' and just praise Him, and trust that He knows and that He will work everything out."

Earlene Williams smiled and nodded beside her.

"Thank you, Mary. Although God wants us to come to Him for all of our needs, it is important that we remember to stop—often—and just thank Him for who He is and what He's already done for us. That is a pertinent reminder that I especially needed today.

"Before we dismiss, I know we have also used this Tuesday morning time to loosely discuss ideas about our next church initiatives. Does anyone have any thoughts about that, or anything the senior survey group has going on?"

Earlene spoke up. "I don't know about anyone else, but after spending the last couple of months building Lizzie's house in the summer heat, I could really use a break to enjoy the coming autumn season. I love helping others, but that last project just about wore me out."

I saw a few heads nod in agreement, including Alan's, who'd made the same observation in the deacon's meeting when discussing whether or not to allow Heather and Dawn to be married at Covenant; maybe he'd been right.

Pete offered to close the group in prayer: "Heavenly Father, as Mary reminded us, we won't ask You for anything this morning, although we know it's perfectly okay with You if we do. We'll just say thank You for another day here on Earth and another opportunity to fellowship with you and to enter Your gates with thanksgiving and Your courts with praise. Thank you that Charlotte Wilburn is well and back home recovering. And finally, thank You for the work and the mission You've given us to serve

Your people, but also thank You for the periods of rest and rejuvenation, so that we can continue to do Your works with a positive spirit and not grow weary. In Your Son's name, Amen."

I arrived at Shiloh Baptist Church in Charlotte in just enough time to grab a seat on the back pew: the place was packed. I could see Wilson Barrow lying in the open casket in the front of the pulpit, while others hurried to view the body before the family's procession into the church. Several people dabbed their eyes with white handkerchiefs as soft music played from the speakers. Wilson had been only sixty years old and had been the pastor of Shiloh for twenty-five of those years.

The pianist began the opening chords "It Is Well With My Soul" as a line of about thirty preachers in black suits entered the sanctuary and walked down one aisle, filling the choir stand as they snaked up the steps of the pulpit. Five older pastors stood in front of each of the large brown and red chairs behind the podium, and that's when I recognized a familiar face: Brian Stanley, my mentor, was sitting directly behind Shiloh's interim pastor. Seeing Brian reminded me just how small of a world we live in, and how tight-knit the local Southern Baptist Convention churches were as a group. I secretly wondered if I'd ever be allowed to sit in a Baptist pulpit outside of Covenant or amongst other respected pastors at a funeral like Brian was now.

The family walked in next, down the center aisle, with Greg leading the way, holding his mother's hand on one side and holding Anthony in his arm on the other. Three women, who I assumed were Greg's younger sisters, were next in the procession, followed by a large group of other relatives and close friends. Greg's mother, whose name was Lynn according to the obituary, stood in front of the casket for several minutes before taking a seat on the front row. Anthony took one solemn look at his grandfather lying in the casket before turning away and burying his face into Greg's neck. Greg reached into the casket and lay a hand on his father's chest for a split second, then took a seat beside his mother.

The order of service was as with any other traditional Baptist funeral, beginning with an opening scripture, invocation, music, and reading of the obituary. As everyone sat quietly thumbing through the pamphlet filled with tributes and pictures of Wilson and his family over the years, I saw something move in my peripheral vision. Stacy, Wilson's oncology nurse, sat on the opposite end of the pew and offered a quick wave. I intuitively smiled and waved back before my mind went into overdrive again. Wilson and Greg must have made a quiet an impression for her to show up at Wilson's funeral.

The eulogist spoke glowingly about Wilson, how he loved his family and what a great man of God he was. "Remember first Thessalonians friends, 'But I would not have you to be ignorant, brethren, concerning them which are *asleep.*' Paul didn't say 'dead,' friends. He said 'asleep.' Another verse: 'To be absent in the body is to be present with the Lord.' We know where Pastor Barrow is. Yes, it's alright to be sad. Of course, it is. But deep down we're happy. Pastor finished his race. Even after he found out he was sick, he still came here and encouraged us, preached until he just couldn't stand anymore. And when he couldn't stand anymore, he still made his calls, checked in on all these preachers you see sitting behind me. Each and every one of them heard from Pastor in the recent weeks, encouraging them while saying his goodbyes. He also spent precious times with his grandson. So, when you feel like giving up, let Pastor Barrow be your example of how not only to live well, but to finish well."

After the interment, I hovered just outside of a small group of people waiting to give their condolences to Greg and Anthony. When the crowd finally thinned, Greg hugged me and bent over and picked up Anthony. "Hey Buddy. This is my friend Ms. Annie. Can you say hi?"

Anthony thought about it for a few seconds, then burrowed his face into Greg's neck again, where it had lived all day. "Sorry," Greg said. "Tough day for him."

"Of course, it is, don't apologize."

"Thank you. I better get going. Thanks for coming. I'll call you later in the week."

On my way back to my car, I spotted Brian saying goodbye to some of the other men who'd been sitting in the choir stand with him before heading towards the parking lot. I caught up with him and tapped him on the shoulder.

"Hey there," he said, turning around. "What are you doing here?"

I was a little embarrassed to answer, even though I'd already told Brian about John and Greg. I lowered my voice. "Remember my being interested in two very nice guys, John and Greg?" I nodded my head toward Greg, who was talking with someone by the church.

"Ah. I had no idea that your Greg was Greg Barrow. Good kid."

"He is a good man. I'm guessing you and Pastor Barrow were friends?"

"Yup, went to seminary together. Known him a long time." Brian looked past my shoulder back towards the church. "Looks like we have an audience."

I turned around to see what Brian was referring to: the group of fellow pastors that he'd just said goodbye to were staring in our direction and talking amongst themselves.

"They know who you are," Brian said.

"Oh." I had never considered what counseling me may do to Brian's standing amongst other Baptist ministers in the area. "Do they know you're advising me?"

"Yes, of course. Of course, everyone has their opinions and a few of them don't agree with it, while others trust me to not be influenced by your progressive ideas. But the real reason they're probably looking this way is because somehow, word has gotten out and traveled fast concerning Covenant potentially performing a lesbian marriage in the church. I'm not sure how, because I haven't spoken with anyone about it but you. But I've heard whispers, and it looks like my suspicions are correct. If your deacons vote to allow the wedding, there will be a motion raised at the next local association meeting to revoke Covenant's membership from the association, which effectively removes Covenant from being a member of the Southern Baptist Convention. I was going to wait to

31

tell you on Friday, but since we crossed paths today, now's a good of time as any. I'm sorry, Annie."

"Thank you for telling me, Brian. I suspected it, but I guess it's good to know for sure. I'll let the deacons know."

I walked back to my car and just sat for a minute before leaving, watching the same group of ministers mill about, talking and laughing with each other, seemingly without a care in the world about how their spiritual beliefs directly and negatively affected the lives of other people. Yet, I could not vilify them, for the group of men before me were the same as some of the members of Covenant: the Alans and Freds who wanted to love and accept all people, but not at the expense of abandoning everything they'd been taught about their faith. How had word gotten around so fast? I wondered if there was a happy middle that everyone could meet at, loving each other and Jesus without judgement or prejudice. One thing was clear as I buckled my seat belt and shifted the car in reverse: I no longer wanted to break any barriers by being accepted by the group of ministers or sit among them in the choir stand at a funeral. Covenant could have hired any traditional Southern Baptist preacher to lead their ministry, and they had not, so I decided to no longer be concerned about what the Convention or other churches thought. I'd continue to lead Covenant wherever they wanted to go.

I felt a sense of peace, even after I noticed one last thing before pulling away: Greg walking out of the church with Stacy by his side.

Chapter 7

The next morning, I was back into my daily routine of working on the next sermon, returning calls, and the general business of the church. I felt like I hadn't been doing a great job of visiting with church members, so I made a few calls to see if I could set up in-home visits. The first person I called was Linda Sanchez, to see if Charlotte was feeling okay enough for me to stop in for a visit.

"Yes, she's fine. She says stop by anytime," Linda said when I called.

I confirmed a three o'clock visit with Charlotte and moved to the next person on my list: Ben Merriweather, who I'd only seen on Sundays now that he was no longer staying in the church fellowship hall. With his job at the grocery store, and with the money he'd made as the site manager for construction of Lizzie's house, he was able to save enough money to rent his own apartment in Bakerstown. He was really adjusting well, and I was anxious to speak to him about his next steps. The phone rang two times before Ben answered: "This is Ben."

"Hey Ben. It's Annie over at Covenant. I was calling to see if I could stop by for a visit this week."

"Oh, sure Annie, I'd love to have you over. How's tomorrow sound? I have some errands to run this morning, and I'm scheduled for a shift at the grocery store later this afternoon. But I'm available tomorrow before four if you're available."

"Sure thing. How about tomorrow at ten a.m.? I don't want to visit too early or too close to your shift."

"Sounds good, Annie. I'll fix us some brunch, so skip breakfast in the morning."

"That sounds delicious, Ben, thank you. See you tomorrow."

I was unable to reach the last two people on my list, Danny O'Reilly and Harry and Earlene Williams, so I pulled out the notes to my sermon draft just as someone knocked on the door. Elizabeth walked in with two coffees, and her step seemed lighter and more jovial than usual.

"Good morning, Elizabeth. You seem to be in an awesome mood this morning," I said.

"I am, Reverend Annie," Elizabeth said. "Everything's just going so well for me right now. The kids are great. Everything has been so smooth with Damien and I since my grandmother's change of heart towards him. His mom Mary really seems to be enjoying keeping Grandmother company and helping out around the house. And yesterday I talked with my advisor, and it looks like I'm on track to graduate in the spring! Staying in school has been so hard with Lacy and Jeremy, and there have been several times when I thought about quitting and picking up an extra job just to help ease things up on my wallet and peace of mind. But I really don't have any technical skills, so without the degree, I'd be stuck in low-paying jobs, and I would never be able to give my kids the life that I want them to have. I don't want them to struggle. So, every time I felt like quitting, I just said a quick prayer, asking God to help me hang in there. And now, I can see the finish line. Five more classes and I'll officially have a bachelor's degree."

"That's so wonderful, Elizabeth." I walked around my desk and gave her a hug.

I'd met Elizabeth just a short time ago when her grandmother and long-time Covenant member Lucille Smith shared with the church how she'd like Elizabeth to be able to be a part of Covenant without being judged that she'd had two children without being married. Elizabeth was a part of a panel we'd invited to Covenant to speak about their feelings toward church in general as imperfect people who had traditionally been rejected or shunned by most churches. I'd offered Elizabeth a job as my assistant on weekdays, answering the phone in the church office and doing other basic secretarial work. Lucille had been concerned when Elizabeth and Mary LeBlanc's son Damien started dating, because of Damien's past and being an ex-con. But Damien was really working hard to keep his job and stay out of trouble since leaving prison, and to Lucille's credit, she'd realized her error in judging Damien and finally gave them her blessing, as well as inviting Mary to live with her to help out around the house.

"I'm so glad I started back coming to church," Elizabeth said. "God has really been moving in my life. It feels good to have positive things happen after struggling for so long. And I know part of that is me choosing to make better decisions also, so I guess I can give myself a little bit of credit too."

"You definitely can, Elizabeth. As the Bible says, faith without works is dead. There are times when God certainly blesses us without us having specifically done anything to receive the blessing, simply because of who He is and how much He loves us. But often times, God waits on us to have faith in Him and take a step, or several steps, and He blesses us as we go."

The phone rang, and Elizabeth said goodbye and took her coffee to her desk, and I said a soft prayer of thanks to God for turning things around for her family. I ate the lunch I'd brought with me from home, then worked on my sermon for the rest of the afternoon until it was finally time to visit Charlotte and Linda. When I arrived at Charlotte's house and walked through the front door, I was shocked to see several brown moving boxes scattered throughout the living room and kitchen. Charlotte sat in the recliner in the middle of the living room, folding a stack of clothes that was lying across the armrest. Her new dog lay at her feet.

"What's going on?" I asked.

"It's time, Annie. I'm going back to Mississippi with Linda."

"Oh, Charlotte. Are you sure?"

Charlotte had been instrumental in all of Covenant's recent initiatives, and she'd expressed to me on Linda's last visit several months ago how she wasn't ready to give up her independence. Charlotte had also been a great friend to me, always checking on me to make sure I was taking care of myself. I quietly hoped that Linda hadn't pressured her to go back with her to Mississippi. But how could I blame her if she had? Linda was Charlotte's only child and caretaker, and Charlotte could have easily died if she'd not been found in her hot car when she was. Maybe this was the best decision after all.

"Yes, I'm sure," Charlotte said, as Linda reappeared from the back of the house. "I could have died on Saturday, Annie. And that really scared me. Thank God I have a daughter and grandkids who *want* me to come live with them, instead of not having anyone and becoming a danger to myself. I wouldn't ever want to go into a nursing home. I'm looking at this as a new life, a fresh start. Don't worry, I'll find a good church once I get down there. But I sure am going to miss Covenant."

I walked over and wrapped my arms around Charlotte as we both shed a few tears. "I'm going to miss you too friend, and I'm sure everyone else at Covenant feels the same. When are you leaving?"

"In two weeks. Linda has taken a leave of absence from her job, and they expect her back after that. So, we've been going through the house trying to decide what makes sense to take. I plan on putting this house on the market, or maybe even renting it out. We haven't decided yet whether I will stay with Linda and her family in their home or get something for myself close by."

I helped Charlotte fold more clothes and pack a few boxes before I left, with Charlotte telling me she'd see me at church on Sunday. She'd already called a few members to tell them the news but wanted to come to Covenant one last time to see everyone in person. As I left, Linda followed me out of the house and closed the door behind her.

"I didn't pressure her, Annie," she said. "My husband and I had been considering leaving Mississippi to come here and be closer to her. It was her choice."

"You don't have to explain anything to me, Linda," I said. "I know you only want the best for your mother and that it's hard to take care of her here with you having a life and family back home. I'm glad she's found peace in her decision to go with you."

"Thank you. And thank you for our conversation we had on my first visit here. I'll be extra mindful to not make her feel like she doesn't have a life anymore and is just waiting around to die. I've already started looking up groups and senior centers in our area where she can go and meet new people and participate in activities that she likes."

"That's excellent, Linda. I'll be praying for you, and if you need anything from Covenant before you leave town, please call and let me know. I know there will be some sad faces Sunday when Charlotte is back in church, but I'm sure they'll understand."

As I drove back to the church, I thanked God for giving Charlotte clarity and peace to make the decision to go with Linda, and I asked God to continue to heal her memory and bless her with many more quality years ahead, filled with family, joy and love.

❀ ❀ ❀

The next morning, I skipped my breakfast as Ben instructed, only having a cup of coffee when I woke up. I showered, watched the morning news, then headed over to Ben's apartment, which was only ten minutes away from the church. My thighs burned as I climbed the stairs to his third-floor apartment, and I made a mental note to find some hills around town to start incorporating into my exercise regimen. My weekly jogs had kept me pretty fit running wise, but with the short distance from the parsonage to the church, I didn't encounter many inclines in my daily routine.

I knocked on the door, then knocked again after Ben didn't answer after a few minutes. This time, I heard steps approaching the door, and there was Ben, a dish towel thrown across his shoulder, the smell of bacon drifting from behind him.

"Come on in, Annie," Ben said. "I'm just about done with brunch if you want to have a seat here at the table."

"Thank you, Ben. It smells delicious." In the small dining room, I sat down at a round black table with three chairs. The apartment was empty except for a couple of large pieces of furniture that looked like they had been donated. A navy-blue polyester sofa with hunter green stripes sat against a large blank wall, with a wood coffee table directly in front of it. On the opposite wall, a late model TV sat on the floor.

"Alright," Ben announced as he emerged from the kitchen, two plates in his hand. He sat them down on the table and returned to the kitchen: fresh salmon croquettes and bacon formed two pyramids on either plate. He returned with a steaming pot of grits, a bowl filled with yellow and fluffy scrambled eggs, and a plate of toast. Then he made one final trip into the kitchen for a pitcher of orange juice, the coffee pot, and strawberry and apricot preserves.

"Wow, Ben, wow" I said, my eyes clearly ready to overeat my stomach. "This is impressive, and all looks and smell so good!"

37

"Thank you, and thanks for coming by. I love to cook," he said. "You're the first person I've had an opportunity to cook for since I left home. I used to cook for my family every Saturday morning."

Ben's voice trailed off with the thought of his wife and kids. I wasn't sure how long it had been since Ben had seen them. "Have you had a chance to speak to them or see them at all?" I asked after Ben asked God to bless the food.

"I've been calling and trying, but Hannah still refuses to talk to me. So, I've been talking with John, and he's helping me out concerning the next steps to take to file for divorce and request visitation rights, now that I have an apartment and a stable job. I'm thinking that being able to see them every other weekend will be a good start. I miss them so much."

It occurred to me that I hadn't seen John since our last date a few weeks ago, and with everything happening with Greg in between, I'd completely forgotten to check in with him. I decided to give him a call that afternoon.

"I'm so sorry, Ben. I'm glad John is helping you. How else can I or Covenant assist you?"

"Mmm," Ben said, nodding and admiring the taste of his salmon croquettes, which indeed were delicious. "Annie, I think you and Covenant have already done so much. I don't know where I'd be right now if you hadn't been so kind as to continue accepting my crazy and sporadic calls when I was on the street. And after the assault at the homeless shelter, I honestly just did not want to be *here* anymore. I've never felt that way before, ever, and I've never been able to relate when I'd read stories about suicide or people trying to end their life. I know life is hard and everyone goes through tough times in their life. The rain falls on the just and the unjust. But to lose everything I had overnight and be left with nothing…well now that I think of it, I supposed that is why Job was in such despair. Not to compare my situation to Job, of course, and I tried not to be judgmental when I was a pastor, but I just could not understand how anyone could get to the point where they didn't want to be here anymore. Now I see. It was so dark and hopeless when I was on the street, and I realize now that I've gone through what I hope is the worst of it. People often don't intend to end up in the situations we find ourselves in. We're all just trying to live and be happy."

"I agree, Ben. I think we're all searching for peace and happiness. Of course, we have that in Jesus, but often times we want something just a little more tangible."

"Right. What's been going on with you? I know what it means to be a pastor. You holding up okay?"

I wanted to cry at the thought of Ben thinking of me, even with everything he had going on. "Sometimes I forget you were in ministry, Ben. I appreciate you asking. I've had a hectic few days, but God is working it all out."

"Well, let me know if you ever need anything. Leading a church is a true labor of love, but I miss it also. I need to take some time to seek God about how I can continue to serve Him and others on this new road I'm on."

"I'm sure He will guide you, Ben, and has something special in store for you. But this moment in your life may just be a time of rediscovery for you. A time to sit still, and get to know God again, this time as the real you."

"The real me. I like that, Annie."

I ate more than I thought I would, possibly because I'd had a very light dinner the night before of chicken salad and crackers, and we finished everything except the croquettes, which Ben said he'd graze off of for the next couple of days.

"Will you pray for me?" Ben asked before I left.

"Absolutely Ben," I said, grabbing his hand as he bowed his head and closed his eyes. "Heavenly Father, thank You for Ben and the sweet fellowship of preparing a meal and sharing it with friends. I'm so thankful to have Ben as a part of the Covenant community. Please forgive us our sins, and guide Ben along the path You would have him take now in this new environment. Please show him how to use the gifts You've given him to bless others and give him discernment on when to serve and when to draw near to Thee. I thank You for his friendship Father, and I ask that You be with his wife Hannah, his two children, and his parents as they all work their way through this difficult time in their lives. Please reconcile them and help us to always be reconciled back to You."

I gave Ben a very tight hug and thanked him again for the wonderful brunch. When I got back to the office, I returned a few phone calls that Elizabeth had taken messages for, then worked on Sunday's sermon. When it was almost five o'clock and I was tired of looking through Bible references, I called it a day and dialed John's number.

"Hey stranger."

"Oh, my goodness, John."

"I'm just messing with you Annie. I'm glad you called. How are you?"

"I'm pretty good actually. I've had some crazy and pretty tiring days lately, and I was visiting Ben this morning and he mentioned you helping him with some legal stuff, which reminded me that it had been a minute since we'd talked."

"Yes, I've been quite busy myself lately at the office, on top of helping Ben. Sad situation he has there. I hope we can help him see his kids again. I couldn't imagine…but enough about that. If you hadn't called me, I would have called you later on. You've been on my mind, and I'll just be frank: I miss seeing you, and I'd like to start seeing you more often. I was going to call and ask you if you'd like to go to the Queen Charlotte Fair with me and the girls."

I couldn't stop the smile that had spread across my face after hearing John express his feelings about me, but I tried my best to bluff and not let my excitement transfer through the phone. "I haven't been to a fair in ages, John. I think that would be fun. When are you thinking?"

"Next Tuesday evening? If you're free. That way maybe we will miss some of the crazy weekend crowd, and I can get the girls in before it's late. I think they even have a promotion where if you bring two canned goods, you will get in free."

"I'm looking forward to it, and it'll be nice to see the girls outside of church. And you, of course."

"Excellent. Well, I'm knee deep in casework. I'll call you before Tuesday to confirm the time. Thank you, Annie. Can't wait to see you."

40

I hung up the phone, gathered my things, and almost skipped across the yard as I let the vision of me at the fair with John and his girls carry me home.

Chapter 8

That Sunday morning, the title of my sermon was "Stay in the Fight." I preached from 2 Corinthians 4:16-17: *Therefore we do not lose heart. Though outwardly we are wasting away, yet inwardly we are being renewed day by day. For our light and momentary troubles are achieving for us an eternal glory that far outweighs them all.* "Paul is tired. He's old," I said. "He's been jailed, shipwrecked, chased, and threatened with death too many times to count. If anybody had a rightful desire to just say 'Hey God. I'm tired. I'm gonna quit preaching Your Word now. Life will be much easier for me. Send someone else to do it,' it is Paul.

"But here he is, in this verse, not only encouraging us, but surely also encouraging himself not to give up on this life and mission that Jesus had personally assigned to him. Can you imagine having a personal encounter with Jesus Christ Himself, walking along a road just minding your business, on the way to slaughter some Christians no doubt, and God's Son Himself stops you dead in your tracks, blinds you for three days, changes your name, and tells you to live the rest of your life spreading the Gospel around the world? Paul knew that his call to Christ was engrained with hardships from the very beginning. Speaking of Paul, Jesus tells Ananias 'I will show him how much he must suffer for My name.' Now, I'm not saying that we all should suffer somehow as Paul and our Lord did, but the walk that we're on, this journey with Christ, is no cakewalk. Life's not easy. Doing the right thing sometimes is not easy. Sometimes doing the right thing causes us to lose some things, things we want or are valuable to us. It takes courage to stand up in the face of wrong when you know what is right. We may lose friends. Jobs. Convenience and comfort. But we must not give up, and we must trust that what was lost will be given back to us, or it was not needed.

"Each and every day, when life hits us, and we feel like giving in, we should ask God to strengthen us, to give us just a little bit more strength, and more patience to wait on Him, more patience with that person in your life who you may not have the best relationship with, more patience with yourself. God is everything we need, and each morning, if we return to Him and look to Him each minute for whatever it is we need, He promises to provide it, to give us whatever it is we need to get through each and every issue."

Alan and Edna walked down the aisle and passed the communion trays down each row. After we'd partaken in the Lord's Supper, I stood at the podium and made one last announcement.

"One of our longtime members, Charlotte Wilburn, is moving to Mississippi this week. She has been a member here at Covenant Baptist Church for thirty years, and some of you may know her if you've ever volunteered for the Fall Bazaar. Charlotte, we just want to say thank you for being a member here and helping to make the church the loving church that we aspire it to be. I want you and everyone else here to know that you have been such a great help and friend to me purposely since I arrived here, and I'll be forever grateful to have known you and served God alongside you. We love you. Everyone, make sure you stop by and say goodbye to Charlotte before you leave today."

Charlotte placed her hand over her heart, smiled, and nodded at me. Linda sat beside her and stuffed a handkerchief into her hand.

I was about to close us out in prayer when Pete Stoudamire stood up and raised his hand. I beckoned him to the pulpit, where he whispered and asked if he could make an announcement. I handed him the microphone.

"Sorry Reverend Annie. I don't mean to interrupt the service, but I just wanted to let you folks know that several of us got together and decided that Charlotte Wilburn needed a proper send off to Mississippi. She has been such a blessing to this church and the people in it, and Charlotte, we just wanted to tell you that we love you and we're gonna miss you. We've prepared a potluck in your honor immediately after service."

"Oh my," Charlotte said, her hands covering her mouth.

"Everyone here is invited, and we have plenty of food," Peter said. "So, don't rush off after Reverend Annie gives the benediction. Save yourself some cooking and come help us celebrate Charlotte and say goodbye."

Pete hugged Charlotte as he made his way back to his seat, and I could see Charlotte and Linda both wipe tears from their eyes. I had no idea anything had been planned, and I felt an overwhelming sense of gratitude to God for placing me in such a loving community.

Most of the members stayed for the dinner, and the fellowship hall was fuller than I'd ever seen it. A long table was full of food: Fried chicken, fried fish, corn on the cob, collard greens, macaroni, candied yams, rolls, sweet tea, coffee, water, milk, and three types of pies. I wondered who on Earth had cooked all the food! Charlotte and Linda were served first, and everyone else snaked down the table, found an empty chair and sat down to eat. Of course, Charlotte's table was very popular, with several people stopping by to hug her and chat. After everyone was served and almost finished with their meal, Charlotte stood up and gestured to Pete.

"HEAR, HEAR," Pete said loudly, his voice booming through the hall. Everyone fell silent.

"I just wanted to say thank you all for this," Charlotte said, looking around the room. "I love you all. Being a member here has been the highlight of my life and I know Covenant will keep doing God's work. I fully expect to be down in Mississippi and one day hear about some crazy church in North Carolina that's doing things that churches have never done before and reaching out to people that churches have traditionally pushed away. I will tell everyone who will listen that that is my church, and I'm so proud to have been a part of it all."

John was right on his hunch that the Queen Charlotte Fair wouldn't be too crowded on Tuesday evening. There were plenty of people there by the time we arrived at six o'clock that evening, but not packed to the rafters like it would have been on the weekend. All the lines for the rides and concession stands were short. John walked over to the booth and asked the woman behind the glass for four wristbands.

"Three," I said.

"What? You're not going to ride anything, Annie?" John asked.

"I get motion sickness very easily, so I'm gonna have to pass. And I'm not too prideful to admit that I'm afraid to ride almost everything here. I will simply take this opportunity to indulge in something very unhealthy, though. I think those deep-fried Oreos over there are calling my name."

"Oooh Oreos!" Emily yelled. "Daddy can we get some, please?"

"Yes, honey, but let's get on a few rides first and maybe get a corndog or something. And then you can have *one* Oreo." John looked at me from the corner of his eyes.

Sorry I mouthed. I had to get used to filtering what I said around the twins.

We walked over to the Caterpillar, a small rollercoaster ride made especially for children. The ride was only ten feet off the ground at its highest height, with the cars painted green and yellow and shaped like the round and wormy body of a caterpillar. There was no line, so Emily and Ella skipped up to the young man working the entrance, showed him their wrist bands, and walked up the ramp and climbed into one of the cars. They sat giddy with excitement as the iron bar lowered over their laps and the caterpillar slowly accelerated and launched them down the track.

John's face mirrored theirs as he watched them loop around and around on the track, their hands raised in the sky with each curve. I wondered if going to the fair was something the family did while his wife Lucinda was still alive. How painful it must be for John and others like him, to find a life partner, your perfect match, and begin to build a life together, then have it all of sudden snatched away, from illness or accidents or any other random thing. This was the part of life that most pastors struggled to explain: why God would take someone away in the prime of their life or allow terrible things to happen to good people.

After riding three more rides, we bought food and sodas and found an empty picnic table to sit down and eat. The sun was beginning to set, and soon the bright lights of the fair would light up the night sky. I decided this would be a good opportunity to make a connection with Emily and Ella. It wasn't lost on me that this was the first time John had invited me to be around them, outside of church. "So how are you guys liking school so far?" I asked them. The girls were now five years old and had just started kindergarten at the local elementary school.

"I made a new friend today," Ella said. "Her name is Whitney. She keeps getting me and Emily mixed up. It's funny because sometimes we trick her, and I'll say I'm Emily, and Em will say she's me."

"I told you girls to stop doing that," John said, shaking his head.

"We're just joking with them, Daddy. Most people can tell us apart."

John shot her a silent glance and let it linger.

"Ookaaaay, we'll stop," Ella said.

"I'd never seen a girl preacher before you, Ms. Annie," Emily said.

"Me either," John said.

"That's because there aren't a lot of us around, Emily. Well, at least not around Bakerstown. That's one of the reasons that I preach, so hopefully little girls like you who might want to be ministers one day can see me and others as an example."

"I want to be a lawyer like Daddy!" Emily said.

"Me too!" Ella shouted.

John looked at his daughters. "You two can be whatever you want, including a preacher. And don't let anyone ever tell you different."

John looked over at me and winked, and I let my smile back to him say thank you. I also quietly thanked God to have a guy interested in me that didn't want me to leave my profession or think I was doing something wrong by being a pastor. If John and I were to ever become more serious romantically, it would be important to have his support. I already had enough to deal with simply leading a church: having a partner who didn't agree with what I did was not an option.

While we were finishing up our food, John left to go buy everyone dessert. He returned with two small trays of deep-friend Oreos. They were coated with powdered sugar on the outside, and warm and gooey on the inside, just like I'd imagined them.

Afterwards, we dipped inside the livestock building so the girls could see the farm animals up close. Emily was especially intrigued by the horses and grew excited when one of the trainers held the horse's bridle so Emily could pet it.

"Can we get a horse, Daddy?" she asked.

"Not now, Em. But maybe one day when you're older."

"Really?" I asked. I hadn't taken John for the animal type.

"Yes, I loved horses when I was a kid. Growing up, my next-door neighbor was a farmer, and I spent a lot of time helping him out on weekends with the animals. Wouldn't mind having a small farm at some point. Nothing major. What do you think about that?"

I shrugged my shoulders. "If having a farm will give you joy, I say go for it."

"Mmm," John responded. "Good to know."

By the time we made it back outside, night had fully fallen, and the lights and sounds gave the fair a different energy. The girls ran ahead of John and I and joined the line for the Ferris Wheel. We caught up and took a seat on an empty iron bench directly across from the ride.

"Mother told me about Greg's father passing away," John said. "I'm sorry to hear about that."

"Thank you, John. That's very considerate of you."

"Are you still seeing him?"

"Um…I guess I am, although I haven't seen him since the funeral last week. Why do you ask?"

"Well." John forced his hands into his pockets and kicked at a torn ticket laying in the dirt. "I wanted to ask you something, Annie. The more and more time you and I spend together, the more I want to be with you. To build something with you."

I felt heat rise from nowhere up to my chest. I hoped I wasn't turning red before John's eyes. If so, maybe the night would cover me.

"So, I guess I'm asking for us to date. Exclusively."

I sat silent for a few seconds unsure of what to say. I'd been meaning to go ahead and choose between John and Greg, but I hadn't expected either of them to ask me to stop seeing the other. I was embarrassed by my naiveté; surely neither of them was going to allow this to go on forever.

"Can you give me a little time to think on it?"

"Sure thing," John said. "No rush. And of course, I'm still wrestling with Lucinda's death and all the feelings that come with that, and even if your answer is yes, that will still take time. But I think I'm finally ready to start moving forward, and I don't want to do it with anyone but you."

I was sure I was red now, and I turned away slightly so John wouldn't see me blush.

"You're very sweet, John. I really like you too. And I know it hasn't been easy knowing that I have continued to go out with Greg, but you weren't ready for anything serious, and neither was I. I promise not to make you wait long for an answer. I just need to make sure I'm making the right decision for me."

"I understand. Take all the time you need. But not too long," John said with a wink, then leaned over and kissed me quickly on the lips, just in time to separate before the ride slowed down enough for the girls to look in our direction.

Chapter 9

The evening of the deacon's meeting finally arrived, and although I was not sure what the outcome would be, I was thankful that the time to decide had come. It had been a long two weeks, but the time was definitely needed so the deacons would not make a decision in haste. I'd had a very productive day and had even talked to John on my lunch break, so I was in good spirits and ready to get the meeting over with.

Edna opened the meeting in prayer, asking God to be with us, guide our hearts, and help us make the decision He would want us to make. After she finished, everyone sat around quietly, avoiding making eye contact with each other. Since Edna had to vote, she sat down in one of the chairs and I stood before the group.

"Everyone, I know it's been a tough two weeks for you. Before you vote, I just want to say thank you for taking the time to seek God about this and giving it your prayerful consideration. No matter what, I'm sure Heather and Dawn will be grateful their request was seriously considered.

"Okay, no need to delay further. Let's get to it," I said. "All in favor of allowing Heather and Dawn to get married at Covenant, raise your hands."

Edward, Jesse, and Edna raised their hands in the air. The other four deacons—Alan, Fred, Danny and Anita—kept their hands lowered.

"That settles it then," I said. "I'll let Heather and Dawn know."

"Annie, may I address the group?" Jesse asked.

"Of course, Jesse."

"I just want everyone here to know that we have drawn a line in the sand today, and it will only be a matter of time before everyone knows about it and calls Covenant out on it. What was the point of seeking out certain members of the community to worship at Covenant, telling them all are welcome here, only to then tell them that it's okay if they come hear a sermon every Sunday, but your union is not ordained by God, so you can't get married here? The outreaches were a sham."

49

"That's not fair," Alan said.

"It's very fair, Alan." Jesse shot back.

"Okay, everyone, let's take a second here to breathe," I said. "I think when we started down this road of reaching out to the community, we all knew that one day we'd have to make difficult decisions like this. Today we made one, and we'll have to live with the consequences of the vote and determine each day what type of church we want to be. Jesse, I understand why you may be upset, especially considering your personal history of being discriminated against. And you have a valid point regarding this vote. I'm not sure how Heather and Dawn, and even Vivian will feel about Covenant after I inform them. Alan, I also can see your point of view, because despite our recent initiatives, the congregation is a mixed group, and we've had several members who have not been on board with them. Again, this is daily work that this group and I will have to do, deciding the future of the church. It has not been easy so far, and I expect that trend to continue."

"Well, I voted no, but I certainly feel bad about it," Fred said. "I'm not sure why. I told my wife how I was voting, and she wasn't happy about it. Will they be able to book another venue?"

"I'm not sure, Fred. I'm sure they have kept all of their options open, considering."

Fred and Edith Miller, like Alan and Faye Emerson, had been one of the couples who were not originally 100% on board with Covenant's Family Day event and its focus on reaching out to all types of members of the community. Edith Miller had even been shunned by her coffee club after the Family Day event, which hurt both her and Fred personally and helped changed Edith's mind about Covenant's mission to accept all people. They had one grown daughter, Belinda, and three grown sons. One of them, Tommy, was comatose, and Fred and Edith cared for him at their home.

We sat for a few more minutes in silence, and there weren't any additional agenda items to discuss. "Well, if there is nothing else, we can dismiss in prayer. Father," I took a deep breath. "We made a tough decision today, one that we hope is Your will for this church. Please continue to guide us and show us exactly where You want Covenant to go, not where we want it to. Help us to

50

always seek You for every decision God, big or small, so that we do not stray away from Your perfect will for our lives and this church. We ask that you be with Heather and Dawn and provide for them a loving and accepting venue to host their wedding. Finally, please mend any hearts broken by tonight's vote, and soften any hardened hearts toward Your people. We love You. Amen."

I walked back to my office and collapsed into my chair. This truly seemed to be a no-win situation. I was certainly disappointed in the vote. How was I going to tell Heather and Dawn that the church had decided that their marriage wasn't approved by God? All the work Covenant had done over the last year and a half could all go down the drain once the word got out. But what would have happened had the deacons voted to approve the wedding? People surely would have protested, and a lesbian wedding would most likely have been the last straw for some members who have been on the fence since my arrival.

Three quick knocks on the door interrupted the pity party going on in my thoughts.

"Come in."

William dipped his head in and held up a bottle of cognac. "Is it time?"

"Yes, William. Definitely time. Please come in."

William closed the door behind him, poured the brandy into two small glasses, handed me one and sat down. "They voted no, didn't they," he asked.

I nodded my head.

"Have mercy. Well, I guess Covenant does have a line that it won't cross, huh?"

"Seems like it. I'm sorry, William."

"No worries, Annie. I am a little bummed about it, but more so for Heather and Dawn. The prime of my life is long gone, and I accepted early on that my path would be a lonely one. I've never been 'out of the closet' per se, so my pain and hurt was of a different kind. I've always felt very restrained, unable to be my full self. But for them, they are free, proud, and doing their best to live their lives, unashamed. I just hate it that this will be another notch

51

of disappointment to add to what I'm sure is already a very long list for them."

"I'm dreading telling them."

"I'm sure you are. I know it sucks, Annie," William said, standing up. "But it's the job. God has prepared and equipped you for it. I'm sure you'll handle it with grace and care."

"Thank you, William. Your confidence in me means a lot."

William left, and I finished my cognac and sat the glass on the table. Ready to get the hard part over with, I picked up the phone and dialed Heather's phone number. Heather answered on the second ring. "Hi, Reverend Annie."

"Hi Heather. I hope I'm not interrupting anything. Is this a good time? I have some news about hosting the wedding."

"Yes, now is fine."

"Unfortunately, the deacons voted to not allow your wedding to be hosted at Covenant. I'm so very sorry, Heather."

"Okay, Annie, we understand, really we do. We'd already pretty much prepared ourselves for it actually and started reaching out to other venues. Thank you for considering it."

"Well thank you for asking," I said. "I know that wasn't easy. I'm not sure what your feelings are toward Covenant now, but please know that we'd be honored to still have you as members of our congregation."

"Thank you. I'm not really sure what this means for us continuing to worship there, but I appreciate the offer."

After we hung up, I stuffed my laptop into my book bag and left the church, a sense of both sadness and relief washing over me. I was not sure what the conflicting feelings meant, and I wished I had another pastor to talk with to help me work through them. My bi-monthly meeting with Brian Stanley wasn't for another three days, and now would be the perfect time to look up the support group for pastors in Charlotte I'd once attended and see when the next meeting was scheduled. A double dose of therapy couldn't hurt.

Chapter 10

The next several days into the weekend were a blur, and before I knew it, another week had begun. The support group for pastors met on Monday nights in Charlotte, so I called my close friends Jane Wilson and Sheila Gray to see if we could get together and meet for lunch beforehand while I was in the city. Jane was getting married in a month, and as her best friends and seminary buddies, Sheila and I were both in the wedding. The preparations this past summer thankfully had given me more opportunities than usual to see them. Jesse Akin had also called me early that morning to tell me that his wife Lorraine had gone into labor the night before and that their son had been born at First Samaritan Hospital, healthy and strong.

"Oh wow, congratulations Jesse. I'm actually going to be in Charlotte today. Do you mind if I stop by to see you guys? Is Lorraine okay?"

"Of course, Annie. Lorraine is doing well. We'd love to see you, and have you meet the new addition to our family!"

Jesse could not contain his excitement, and I was glad to hear him happy again. After the last deacon's meeting, I wasn't sure how he was feeling about Covenant and being a deacon. I'd planned to follow up with him individually to get a sense of his state of mind. Maybe the arrival of his son would take some of the sting off last week's vote.

Sheila wrote in our group text that she was in the mood for pizza, so we all met at Riccio's, a popular pizza spot that had been around for over fifty years. My two friends were already seated when I arrived, and I leaned in and hugged Jane, then slid into the booth beside Sheila on the opposite side.

"We ordered you a black coffee," Sheila said.

"You know me well. Thank you. And thank you ladies for meeting me on your lunch breaks. How's work going for you two?" Both Jane and Sheila worked in ministry but were not pastors.

Jane answered first. "Nothing new on my end. I've been busier with planning the wedding than I have at work. Speaking of, your dress is finally ready, Annie."

"Same here, minus the wedding planning. How are thing's going at Covenant, Annie?"

"Pretty well, I'd say. The deacons recently had a tough decision to make about potentially hosting a lesbian wedding for one of our members. They voted against it, and the group was split four to three, so I'm hoping it's something that won't leave a fracture."

"Oh wow. I don't envy you, Annie," Sheila said. "I know we all went to seminary with hopes of pastoring, but hearing some of your stories makes it all so real. I'm not sure I could handle everything you have dealt with so far since being at Covenant."

"It definitely hasn't been easy Sheila and thank you for acknowledging that. But I'm definitely no wunderkind with special abilities to handle difficult situations. I'm merely depending on God every day to guide me and help me know the right thing to do, something I'm sure you would also do should you ever pastor a church."

"Okay, enough about church," Jane said. "Are you still seeing both Greg and John?"

The waitress arrived with our drinks and to take our order and saved me from an immediate reply to Jane's question. I ordered two slices of five-cheese pizza and took a sip of my coffee.

"Well?" Jane said.

"Technically, yes. But John asked me to be exclusive."

"AND?" my two friends both said at the same time, mouths agape.

"I haven't answered him yet."

"WHY NOT?!?" again, in unison.

"I just wanted a little time to think about it, make sure I was making the right decision."

"Well, what have you decided? This can't go on forever, Annie. If you wait much longer, he may think you're uninterested and move on to someone else. From what you've told us about him, John seems like a great guy. Yes, he already has kids, so that's something you'll have to deal with, but so does Greg. And although you say Greg has been great to you, his wife *did* divorce him for lack of being around. Who's to say he won't fall back into the same habits if ya'll were more serious? John sounds like the winner to me. Don't miss the boat."

"Trust me, Jane, I've considered all the pros and cons for both John and Greg. And I don't intend to keep him waiting any longer. I'm going to accept and tell him and Greg this week."

"Look at you!" Sheila said. "That makes me so happy, Annie. I'm sure getting more serious with John will help balance out the weightiness inherent in your job. But the most important question of all: does he make you happy?"

"You know, he does. He really does."

Our pizza arrived, and we devoured it in no time. Both Sheila and Jane had to get back to their jobs, so I hugged them again and told them I'd see them in three weeks for the wedding.

❀ ❀ ❀

I had to use the GPS system on my phone to find First Samaritan Hospital. I'd heard of it in passing but did not know where it was and had never had a reason to visit. Inside, I followed the signs to the maternity ward, and informed the nurse who I was there to see. After a few minutes, Jesse walked down the hall towards me, a bright and contagious smile on his face. He wrapped me in a warm hug, and I couldn't help but share in his joy.

"Thanks for coming, Reverend," he said as we walked back to Lorraine' room.

Lorraine was propped up in her hospital bed when we entered, nibbling from a plate of food from the cafeteria.

"How are you feeling?" I asked.

"I'm wonderful, Annie. Tired, and relieved, but I'm so grateful God has blessed us with a child at our age. After all we've been though, I never thought a child was in the cards for us. Funny how just when you think you have things figured out and accepted life as it is, God turns around and blows your mind with the unexpected. It's like we have a new lease on life now, a new reason to live."

"And a new reason to not retire," Jesse said, looking at Lorraine, who rolled her eyes.

"I'm only kidding. I was looking ahead to retirement, but we've been pretty good at saving since it's just been us two. Already paid off our house, and we've been investing for a while. We're in a good position financially, and I'll tack on a few more years of working and we should be okay. I'm just excited to finally be able to spend money on kid related stuff, like diapers and formula, and later on school supplies and field trips. I can help chaperone!"

Lorraine reached over and place her hand over Jesse's, and by the way she looked at him, I could tell that even after twenty years of marriage, she was still madly in love with him.

"I have never been to this hospital before," I said. "I've heard about it, but never had a reason to visit. I assumed you guys were over at Main until Jesse told me."

"Yes, Lorraine was adamant that we have the baby here." Jesse looked over at his wife.

"Annie, do you know the history of Main Hospital and African Americans?" Lorraine asked me.

"No, I guess I don't."

"First Samaritan was originally built back at the turn of the 20th century, when African Americans weren't allowed in White hospitals. It stayed that way until the late sixties, when during the height of the civil right movement across the country, Charlotte integrated its hospitals, so Black people finally started going to Main, thinking they'd get better care than at First Samaritan, which was underfunded and lacked a lot of resources. But in the maternity ward at Main, the doctors and nurses were negligent in treating Black mothers-to-be. Twenty-three Black mothers died there before Black people finally stopped going there. Ever since then, most African-American babies in Charlotte are delivered right here at First Samaritan. Almost fifty years later, the distrust for the maternity ward at Main still lingers heavily in our community."

"Wow, that is awful. I had no idea, Lorraine. Thank you for telling me about that. I'm glad your community has somewhere to go that you can trust."

"Yes, as with all other things back then—schools, restaurants, hotels even—when we weren't allowed in White spaces, we created our own."

A nurse gently knocked on the door and wheeled in the hospital crib. The newborn was wrapped tight in a blanket as he lay on his back, quiet but awake. A pale blue beanie covered the top of his tiny head. I stood from my chair to get a better look at the tiny, precious baby boy.

When Lorraine first discovered she was pregnant, she confided in me that she wasn't sure how Jesse would react since they were both well into their forties, and that when they'd first married, they never rushed to have a child for fear of what kind of life he'd have as a mixed-race person. Then they'd changed their minds and tried to conceive but were unsuccessful and had given up on ever having children. Now, the child they feared for and hoped for was here, and I could only pray that the world would be more welcoming to him than it had been to his parents.

"What is his name?" I asked.

"Harris Jesse Akin," Lorraine said. "Named after my father and Jesse."

"May I pick him up?"

"Sure, Annie."

I gently slid my hands under Harris and cradled him in my arms. I'd always wanted my own family, and holding babies always made me want to speed up the process. Here I was pushing thirty, and although I was one "yes" away from being in a serious relationship, I still felt a small sense of being late to the game in my romantic life. John himself had already been married and had twins. I knew comparing myself to other people was a tried and true recipe for mental unhealthiness, but after being around such a loving and committed couple and holding an infant to my chest, it was hard not to wonder if I'd ever have the same in my own life.

"We were thinking about having him dedicated at Covenant. Unless the other deacons thinking dedicating a mixed baby is too radical too," Jesse said with an eye roll.

"Jesse!" Lorraine slapped her husband on the knee. "Don't mind him, Annie," she said. "He's still a little upset over the vote."

"I know, and I understand why. I'd be honored to dedicate little Harris whenever you guys are ready. Jesse, I'm pretty sure dedications don't require votes, but I'm ready to battle with you if need be."

"Thank you, Annie."

I placed Harris back in his crib and left when more family members arrived to visit the Akins. I thanked God for Harris and for rewarding the Akins' lifelong faithfulness to Him and each other, in spite of the years of opposition and hate they had faced when they were younger.

Chapter 11

I arrived at the ministers' therapy group that afternoon an hour early and sat in the parking lot and read my bible until my friend Chad pulled up and parked beside me. I'd called him to ask when the meetings were held and to let him know I'd be attending this week. I climbed out of the car and hugged him, and we stood around catching each other up about family and church happenings until it was time for the session to start. Inside, seven other ministers took their seats in the circle, and Daniel, the priest who led the sessions, greeted me with a smile and a handshake.

"It's nice to see you again," he said. "Please forgive me but I've forgotten your name."

"Annie."

"Ah, that's it. We're glad to have you back again. And you brought this guy with you," he said, ribbing Chad with his elbow.

"Yeah well, I've been long overdue for a session," Chad said. "I felt much better mentally and emotionally when I was attending more regularly. I think Annie's call to tell me she wanted to come was my nudge from above to get back at it."

"Well, let's see if we can relieve some of that stress. Shall we?" Daniel pointed to two empty chairs before us.

One of the other ministers opened the session in prayer, then Daniel spoke to the group.

"Okay everyone. Thank you for coming. As I say every week, this time is all about you. Who would like to start tonight?"

A man whose name badge read "Leonard" raised his hand. "I'll start, just so I can get this off of my chest. I gave my notice to my church's board yesterday. After twenty years, I'm retiring from ministry."

I saw a few eyes shoot up around the room. Leonard looked like he was in his early fifties.

"Okay Leonard. How do you feel about retiring?" Daniel asked.

"Honestly, I feel a little sad and guilty, but I still think it's the right decision for me and my family. After twenty years, I just can't do it anymore. Being responsible for so many people and all of their problems, being on call 24/7, not to mention the personal responsibility to God to shepherd his flock, to know the Bible in and out, be able to interpret what was meant when the authors wrote the words thousands of years ago and communicate it effectively so that your congregation can apply it to their lives. I know they are responsible for studying the Word for themselves also, but what if someone takes my application of a verse and makes the wrong decision in their lives? Or treats people badly? Lord knows we have enough of that going on today, people using the Bible to justify despicable actions towards others.

"Now I know I'm no one's savior and God is not expecting me to solve all the world's problems, or even my own congregation's problems, or even my *own* problems. I know I'm not God. But I've lost my fire for ministry, at least in the leading a church sense. If I'm being honest with myself, I lost it about five years ago, but I figured then it was something I could pray through. I asked God to relight the fire in me, the desire to serve. But that has not happened, and I'm growing more miserable by the day. It's just time. There's a bright young associate minister that has trained under me for several years now, and I've recommended to the board that they hand the reigns to him. He's compassionate and really loves God and God's people. I think he will do a wonderful job as my replacement."

"Thank you for sharing with us, Leonard," Daniel said. "All of us here know personally the seriousness of being a minister. We give up a lot of our lives to answer the call of God. But I don't think God expects all of us to serve in the specific role of leading a church forever."

Lori, a minister I recognized from my last visit, put her hand on Leonard's shoulder. "Leonard, I admire your honesty and your willingness to make a decision to leave the ministry. I've thought about quitting many times, but I've never quite gotten to the point where you are now. Like you, I've also tried to pray my way through it, and I must say, I do feel more peaceful and relieved after I've prayed and handed over to God whatever it is that is bothering me at the time. But trust me, that is a frequent prayer."

"And possibly just how God wants it, Lori," Chad said. "God forbid that we stop needing to come to Him. I guess I look at leaving the ministry a bit more like a job. My wife and I have already discussed it and decided that we will both retire at fifty-five. She is a school teacher, so she feels a sort of calling as well to serve children. We figure by that age, we'll both have about thirty years of service to others, and we shouldn't feel guilty about retiring and being a little more selfish in our later years. Of course, we'll continue to volunteer or serve on boards and mentor, but we'll just do away with the daily grind of being a minister and a teacher. I'm not sure if I'm supposed to feel bad for looking at the ministry that way, but I don't."

Hearing Chad talking about life after ministry was a little shocking to me. It was something I'd never thought about, and it made me wonder what my own plans were after ministry, or if I'd just assumed I'd be pastoring until I was two steps from the grave.

"Well, as you guys may or may not know, priests never really fully retire," Daniel said. "Even if we don't run a parish anymore, we continue to hear confessions, say Mass, and so on. It is essentially a lifelong commitment. But I would be lying to you all if I said I'd never thought about no longer being a priest."

"It's the confessions, isn't it" Leonard said, and the entire group exploded in laughter.

"Actually, no, it's not the confessions, although I've heard some over the years that left me wondering if I ever wanted to hear any more. But every time I think of leaving, it is when I long for another person to share my life with. A wife."

"Oh Daniel," Lori said.

"Don't go having a pity party on me now. I signed up for this, and I knew when I made my vows that it meant giving up any sort of a love life forever. But some of the best times in my life were spent with someone in particular before I felt the call to become a priest. It was a real struggle for me to give up that relationship to answer the call of God. But I did it, thinking that God would deliver me from all desire to be with someone, if I just committed myself to Him, prayed really hard, and dug into my work headfirst and never came up for air. I'm sorry to say that He has not. I do okay with it, but I do get lonely, and no amount of praying has relieved me from it. But again, I don't tell you this for pity. I tell you this to let you know that having thoughts of leaving the ministry is normal, and I, for one, will not judge any of you for making the decision to live a different life."

Everyone sat in silence as Daniel's revelation hung in the air between them. I felt so sorry for him. If he stayed his entire life as a priest, as most of them do, he'd never get to fulfill his God given desire to have a wife. I immediately thought of Paul's advice in 1 Corinthians 7 that it was good for a man not to marry so he could commit himself to God and not have the anxieties that come with having to care and provide for a wife and family, unless he is burning with passion, in which case Paul says it is better to marry. Daniel sure sounded like he was desiring passion to me, and that made my heart ache for him and others like him, even LGBT Christians who felt that they could not act on their sexuality for fear of going to hell, so remained celibate all of their lives. I said a silent prayer for Daniel as we took a ten-minute break for bathrooms and snacks.

"Would anyone else like to share?" Daniel asked when the group re-formed.

I raised my hand. "I'm Annie. I'm not sure if any of you remember me from the one time, I visited about a year ago." Several people nodded at me and smiled.

"What has been bothering me does not seem as serious as Leonard retiring from ministry or Daniel desiring a partner, but I will share anyway. I pastor a Baptist church down near Bakerstown, and being a woman pastor at a Southern Baptist church is a daily toil in and of itself. Although we're Southern Baptist, the church is pretty progressive in our mission to reach out to all of God's children: gay, straight, Black, White, etc. Our deacons recently had to vote on whether to allow two lesbian members to get married at the church. They voted no, by a vote of four to three, and there were some hurt feelings amongst a couple of the deacons. Now I'm concerned about the group going forward, if any of the hard feelings will linger, and if there is something I can do to possibly prevent it. I'm also concerned about something one of the deacons said after the vote to the effect that all of our recent outreach initiatives were really for show since we didn't vote to host the wedding."

"I can see that," a minister named Frank said. "Why seek them out if you're not going to fully accept them?"

"It sounds like even though you guys are progressive by SBC standards, you still have members and deacons in your congregation who aren't ready to fully abandon traditional SBC values," Leonard said.

"That's pretty accurate Leonard. Now I'm concerned that all the progress we've made in reaching out to people will come to a halt. On the other hand, if they *had* approved the wedding, I was having very selfish thoughts about what it would mean for my career, as the local SBC suggested that we'd lose our membership status if we approved."

"And that right there is the type of stuff I am not going to miss, Annie," Leonard said. "We run churches like corporations. I understand the need for structure and procedures, but often times the focus is distracted away from the people and placed on things that I'm sure don't matter to Jesus, like memberships. Sorry, I'm going to shut up now before I convince you all to quit."

After our second round of laughter died down, Chad said, "It sounds like your church has a decision to make, Annie. I'm not sure you can proactively seek out members of the LGBT community to attend your church, and then tell them they can't get married there. Unless you only sought them out to convert them to heterosexuals, and I'm sure that wasn't the case, right?"

"Correct. The members of the church really wanted to welcome people from all walks of life, not just members of the LGBT community, but people who'd served time in prison, or people who'd had children that weren't married, or undocumented immigrants, for example. And despite outside opposition, I thought we were heading in the right direction. Now I'm afraid we may have stalled."

"You're only one person, Annie," Daniel said. "Yes, you are the leader of the church, but you're not God. You won't be able to make it the happiest place on earth, and there is really no need to try. The deacons at your church I'm assuming are grown men who—"

"And women."

"Pardon me. Grown men *and* women who recognize the responsibility of their positions and take it very seriously. Maybe with their vote they are signaling to you that the church is being a little too aggressive for them. And yes, there may be lingering wounds. You will only know with time. Have you already had members leave your church because of some of the outreaches the church has already done?"

"Yes, a few have chosen to leave."

"Okay, so you've had a little experience with that," Daniel continued. "Don't be surprised if there is more. Of course, we never want people to feel hurt by the church, but sometimes it's inevitable simply because people have different opinions and beliefs, and we can't please everyone. This is especially true in your case where you have a church that belongs to a conservative organization but is attempting to do progressive things. There will be growing pains, and it will hurt. You will feel some disappointment. And you may even start to question your place in it all. But unfortunately, it is a part of leading a church, and the only way to get on the other side of it is to go through it."

"Thank you, Daniel. I guess you're right. The only thing I can do is take it one day and one step at a time, and simply continue doing what I've been doing, leading the church where it wants to go."

"And that is all you can do," Daniel said.

After the session, I gave Chad a hug and thanked him for meeting me. Then I hit the road back to Bakerstown with a new resolve to not worry but take things one step at a time and trust God to help me and Covenant cross the bridges when we came to them.

Chapter 12

The next few days were fairly quiet on my end, so I was able to complete my Sunday sermon early in the week and check in with a few church members. But one thing kept nagging on my mind: John and Greg, and I knew I needed to speak with both men and let them know my intentions. I was nervous to speak to Greg, but it had to be done. I reminded myself that I wasn't a teenager anymore, and that Greg was a mature adult and would surely respond like one.

I felt Greg deserved to hear the news in person, so I called him and asked if we could meet for dinner. "Sure thing," he said. "How about 900 South? I think it's halfway between you and me. Seven o'clock sound good?"

"Sounds great, Greg. See you at seven."

I left my church office a little early to make sure I had time to shower and dress before leaving for dinner. After my shower, I opened up the closet and surveyed my wardrobe. I wanted to look nice, but not over the top sexy, especially since the dinner was to inform Greg that we could no longer see each other. I settled on a navy-blue top, blue jeans, and flats, pulled my hair high into a ponytail, grabbed my keys and headed for the car. When I arrived at 900 South, Greg was standing at the front door waiting for me. I walked up to him, and he gave me a "half-hug," totally different from the usual full-and-tight, hug-and-kiss greeting I was used to.

900 South was a newer half-restaurant, half-bar establishment and the inside was filled with what looked to be a mix of local college students and corporate professionals. We waited ten minutes before a hostess seated us in a two-person booth in the middle of the room.

"This place is packed," Greg said. "Let's go ahead and look at the menu and decide what we want so we can be ready when the server comes over. Then we can catch up."

I surveyed the menu and decided on the black bean nachos and a sweet tea. Greg settled on a bison burger with fries and a Coke. After the server left with our order, Greg said, "Annie, I've been meaning to call you and say thank you for being there for me during my father's sickness and passing. It really meant the world to me to have you to talk to about everything and to be there to lean on when he passed away. I've just been busy playing catch up at work from the week I was away, but please know I meant to thank you much sooner than this."

"You don't have to thank me, Greg. I was honored to be there for you. I know you would have done the same for me." This was getting harder by the second, and I didn't think it fair to wait until the end of the meal to share the news and potentially put a damper on the meal. It was now or never.

"Greg, I want to tell you something," I said.

"Sure. What's up?"

I looked Greg in the eye. "The other guy I've been getting to know, John, has asked me to be exclusive, and I've accepted."

"Oh. Okay Annie. It's all good. I understand."

"Wait…that's it?" I said, a little jealous that he wasn't showing not a single ounce of sadness. I wasn't prepared for the punch to my ego.

Greg laughed and reached over the table to grab my hand. "Well, of course I have loved getting to know you, Annie. And I appreciate you dearly, especially after these past few weeks. But the truth is, I've been seeing someone else also, Stacy, the oncology nurse from the hospital."

"Ah." My intuitions about the possibility of Greg and Stacy had been correct. Maybe the fact that I had noticed them, but not worried about Greg losing interest was a sign that I'd made the correct choice in John.

"Yes, sorry about that," Greg said. "Since we met at the hospital, we've really hit it off. And she is also divorced with a young son, so we have a lot in common. Nothing too serious yet, but I'm enjoying getting to know her."

"I'm happy for you, Greg."

"Back at ya. John seemed like a decent guy the one time we met, and I know you wouldn't date someone who was bad for you, Annie. I hope everything works out."

Our dinner came, and we spent the rest of the evening eating and catching each other up about our job and families. And although Greg and I wouldn't be dating anymore, by the end of the evening, I felt like I'd gain a true friend.

The next day was a Friday, and after dinner with Greg the night before had gone so well, I couldn't wait to celebrate the end of the week by calling John and accepting his invitation to date exclusively. Elizabeth arrived for her shift, and even though I felt like an excited school girl with a crush who wanted to tell everyone who would listen, I decided not to share the news about me and John just yet, for two reasons. One, it felt very premature to be telling anyone beside my girlfriends Jane and Sheila; and two, I wasn't sure it was the most professional thing to do. I was Elizabeth's pastor and boss, and I didn't want to blur the lines of our relationship or come across as unprofessional. So, when it was time for me to call John, I closed the door to my office and dialed his number.

"What is it?" John answered.

"Excuse me, John. This is Annie."

"I know who it is. What do you need?"

I pulled the phone away from my ear and looked at it, like a scene in a movie. Surely, he wasn't speaking to me in this manner. "Is something wrong?" I asked.

"Nothing's wrong, Annie. Just in the middle of doing research for a case."

"Oh, I'm sorry. I can call you back when you are less busy, but maybe you should take the edge off of your voice."

"I saw you and Greg holding hands and having dinner last night at 900 South, Annie. I was there with my colleagues from the firm, sitting at the bar. You never saw me, and I left before you and Greg finished your food. The least you could have done is called me and let me know that you'd decided to be with him."

"I couldn't call you and tell you that, because I was too busy meeting with Greg one last time to tell him that I'd decided to be with you."

"Wait, what—"

I hung up the phone. The nerve of John, being rude and acting like a five-year old when he'd incorrectly thought I'd chosen Greg over him! I stood up from my desk to try to relieve some of the anger that had suddenly enveloped me. Is this what our relationship would be like, him resorting to a childish, petty attitude with every misunderstanding? I'd have to make it very clear to him that I would not stand for it, and if that is the way he communicated, our relationship would be over before it began.

I was about to take a walk and blow off some steam when my cell phone rang, and John's number came up on the caller ID. I rejected the call and put the phone on vibrate, tossed it in the drawer, and told Elizabeth I was taking a short walk down the road to get some air. Autumn had arrived, and the chill of the air calmed me as I navigated the fallen leaves on the road. When I returned twenty minutes later, I had five missed calls from John and one unread text message.

I messed up, and I am so sorry.

Later that evening, just as I was getting ready to microwave a TV dinner and settle down on the couch to watch one of my favorite shows, there was a knock at my front door. I wasn't expecting anyone, which made me a little fearful since it was mid-October and now getting dark earlier and earlier in the afternoons. Feeling foolish but cautious, I grabbed the baseball bat from the corner where I kept it, walked to the door and looked out of the peephole.

"It's me, Annie. John."

I sat the bat aside and opened the door. John stood, a remorseful look on his face, in blue jeans and a cardigan, a plastic bag with two white styrofoam takeout containers inside. I didn't move from the center doorway.

"Please," he said.

I let him inside and walked back to the kitchen.

"Isn't it time for your favorite show? Can we eat on the sofa so you can watch it?"

Had I told him about my favorite show? I wasn't sure, but I was dying to see tonight's episode, so I walked into the living room and sat down. I heard John wash his hands in the kitchen, then he walked over to me, handed me one of the takeout dinners, and sat down beside me.

"I don't want to share a meal with you mad at me, Annie. So, let me say again, in person, that I apologize for the way I spoke

68

to you earlier, and for jumping to conclusions about you and Greg. I was a jerk and I'm asking for your forgiveness."

"Is this what being in a relationship with you is going to be like, John? Because I can manage!"

"No Annie, I promise you it won't. I was just upset because...because I really like you. When I saw you and Greg, I just assumed your answer to me was going to be no, and I was a bit hurt. But even if you had chosen Greg and that hurt me, that's no excuse for the way I spoke to you today. I have to do a better job of managing my emotions. Will you give me another chance?"

"Well," I said. "You did bring me dinner and all." A smile started to spread across John's face. "But seriously John, as I called to tell you earlier, yes I want to be with you. But the way you spoke to me earlier was rude and uncalled for. So again, if that is what our relationship will be like—"

"It's not," John said. "It'll be like this."

John leaned in and kissed me, his arm reaching around my waist to pull me closer as my heart raced. The kiss lasted pretty long, and when John finally pulled away, I wasn't so mad with him anymore.

Chapter 13

I had a busy stretch of time ahead of me with Jane's wedding on top of my regular church duties, and I desperately needed to visit my parents before winter arrived. Thanksgiving was coming up in six weeks, but I really didn't want to wait until then. My mother had been diagnosed with diabetes, and I hadn't seen her or my father in several months. Plus my Grandmother was at my parents for one of her month-long visits, so now was the perfect time to hit the road to Columbia, South Carolina where they lived and take a much-needed break. I'd reviewed both the church calendar and my calendar and found a weekend that wasn't loaded with activities to take a few days off to visit them. Then I asked Pete Stoudamire, a former pastor, to preach Sunday service, which he'd happily accepted.

"God has given me several sermon ideas that I haven't had a reason to fully flesh out and deliver since I'm not pastoring anymore," he'd said with delight.

As I packed my small suitcase for the weekend, my thoughts drifted to John. Since the night he'd come over to my apartment, our relationship had been going extremely well. Of course, it was still early, but he'd made it a priority to see me and spend time with me, even with being constantly busy with his job as a lawyer and being a father to his two young girls. He'd also made a point to start inviting me over to his house so that the girls could get used to me. Getting to know them was a very delicate situation for both me and John. Neither of us wanted to rush into anything or force me upon them. They were still dealing with the loss of their mother, and probably would be for a long time, and I would be the first woman they'd seen with their father in a romantic way. I'd found myself praying for guidance about them every night, asking God to guide John and me and help us to always be mindful of the girls and their feelings, and to go at a pace that wasn't too fast for anyone.

The night before, John had invited me over for dinner with the girls and Edna since I was going away on a long weekend and he wouldn't see me for a few days. He'd insisted on picking me up and driving me back home afterwards, just so he could get some alone time with me. It would be the first time that I'd seen Edna outside of my official pastor role with the church and as John's girlfriend. I was a little nervous, even though Edna had been nothing but kind and helpful to me since my arrival at Covenant. She had truly been my go-to person with everything related to the church. When John arrived, he kissed me passionately as he walked through the door, and we continued that way for several minutes before I pulled away.

"We're going to be late," I said. "And I don't want to make a bad impression with Edna."

"My mother already loves you, Annie," John said. "That's not something you're worried about, is it?"

"Well, there is a difference in me being the church pastor and me being her son's girlfriend. We'd better make this work out, because I think I'm more concerned with my relationship with Edna than my relationship with you."

When we arrived at Edna's, the girls ran to the door to greet us. "Hey, Pastor Annie!"

"Why hello, Emily and Ella. I heard you helped Grandma cook dinner for us."

"*I* helped," Ella said, side-eyeing her twin sister. "Emily just played on the tablet."

"Emily," John said. "I thought I said no tablet before dinner."

"It's fine. She was helping me look up a recipe," Edna said. She winked at Emily and walked over and gave me a big, tight hug. "Annie, I'm happy to have you here in a non-church related capacity."

"Thank you, Edna. Dinner smells amazing."

"Well, I hope it is. Trying out a new recipe tonight for chicken and dumplings. I think it turned out alright."

"I'm sure it's fine, Mama, but I volunteer to be the judge of that. Let's eat," John said, ushering everyone to the dining room table.

Ella said grace, and we dug in. The dumplings *were* amazing, and Edna gave all the credit to Paula Deen. After dinner, while John watched TV with the girls in the family room, Edna and I stayed in the kitchen to clean up the dishes.

"I want you to know, Annie, that I'm happy about you and John seeing each other, and I hope this won't create any awkwardness between you and I," Edna said. "I haven't seen John this happy in a long time, and I know that has everything to do with you."

"Thank you, Edna. I must admit I was concerned about our relationship. You've been such a big encouragement to me at Covenant, and I wouldn't want to do anything to jeopardize that."

"Nonsense," Edna said. "I've been around you enough and seen you in enough different types of situations to know your character and what kind of person you are. I know you will be good for my son, and even if it doesn't work out between you two in the long run, you and I will be just fine."

"That means a lot to me, Edna. And thank you for helping Pete out this weekend while I visit my parents."

"Of course! I'm looking forward to hearing him preach again. I used to visit his church sometimes when he was still pastoring. You go check on your mother and grandmother and don't worry about us. We'll see you back on Monday."

John brought the girls in to tell us goodnight, then came back after he'd put them to bed. "Well, Mama, what do you think?" he said, wrapping his arm around me and pulling me into him.

"I think Annie's a wonderful girl, who could probably do a lot better than you, son," Edna said.

I couldn't stifle the laugh that escaped my mouth as John looked at me, feigning shock. "See, she already likes you more than me," he said.

John took me home, and we spent more time on my sofa before settling nicely into each other's arms. "Not that I'm thinking about it or anything, but I don't think I'll ever be able to spend the night with you here, huh?" John said, looking around the parsonage.

"No, I don't think that will reflect favorably on the church once people find out about us," I said.

"I figured. Well, I guess we'll have to figure out a compromise," John said. "When we get to that point."

❀ ❀ ❀

I arrived at my parent's house around noon on Friday, after hitting the road early to avoid the late afternoon heavy traffic. My dad was still at work and my grandmother was asleep in her room, which gave me some precious one-on-one time with my mother. I took a long look at her once I was inside and settled in. She looked slightly thinner than the last time I'd seen her, but other than that, she seemed like her normal self, and that made me happy. Diabetes can be deadly if not properly managed, but my mother seemed to be adjusting well. Even though she seemed okay, I still wanted to get her thoughts on how she was feeling, physically and emotionally, so I asked her how she felt over an afternoon cup of coffee.

"I'm feeling well, Annie. I know your father already told you that we found out I was diabetic." She eyed me suspiciously, and I shrugged and feigned ignorance.

"When you were last here with Tom and Janeen and their families, I'd just learned that my blood sugar was high, and I was doing my best to manage it on my own. Around that time, I'd started growing tired every day, and your dad was doing his best to help me out around the house every chance he got. You know I've always been pretty healthy and active, but with diabetes running in our family, even my healthy lifestyle wasn't enough to keep it at bay. So, after that weekend with you guys, I went back to the doctor, and he prescribed some medicine that I take daily to help keep it in the normal range. Since I started taking it, my blood sugar has been fine, and although I still get tired some, it's a lot better than it was before.

"So, I'm grateful for that. And with Mom coming down periodically now and staying for several weeks, that has made me feel much better emotionally, and spiritually as well. With this change in my health and with Mom in her twilight years, I've grown more aware of life and how precious and fragile it is. Not to spook you, but I'm learning to enjoy every second of this life God has given me with my family. Because we won't all always be here."

73

It was comforting to hear that Mom was feeling good and managing her blood sugar better, but also a little sobering to hear her speak of not being here. I knew the fleeting nature of life, not only from the many Bible verses warning us about it, but also from the people that I'd known but had lost in recent months: Tom and Joy Hearn, Jake Morton, and Greg's father. The old saying "One day you're here, and the next day you're gone," had proven throughout the history of time to be true. Still, I'd never given serious thought to my own family and the fact that, at any given time, any of us could be called Home. It made me deeply appreciative to God that I still had my parents, siblings, and nieces and nephews to love on and share life with.

Just as we were finishing up our afternoon coffee, Grandmother shuffled into the living room, slowly but steadily, and I walked over to her and wrapped my arms around her.

"Hey there, pretty girl," she said, and my heart immediately melted. Grandmother had called me "pretty girl" my entire life, so much so that I couldn't remember a time of her calling me by my actual name. I'd always liked the pet name she had for me but hearing it now as a twenty-nine-year-old adult meant so much more to my self-esteem.

We settled into the living room, so Grandmother could watch her three o'clock talk show, and I made myself comfortable in Dad's recliner near the fireplace and threw a quilt over my legs. How nice it felt to be away from church duties for a weekend and simply spending time with my family.

"What is this I hear about you dating two guys, pretty girl?" Grandmother said when the show went to commercial break.

Mom looked at me with wide eyes and quietly laughed. I was only slightly embarrassed. My grandmother had never been the conventional southern woman, not having married my grandfather until she'd already bore him two children.

"Well Grandmother, yes, I *was* dating two very nice guys, John and Greg, but I'm not any longer."

"Oh?" Mom said. Knowing I was coming to visit this weekend, I hadn't yet shared the news with her or the rest of the family.

"Yes. John asked me to start dating exclusively a few weeks back, and I accepted. He's a very nice guy, a lawyer, widowed with two young girls, and he treats me very well. So, I guess we'll see."

"I guess we will," Grandmother said. "I'm glad you have someone to spend time with dear, but don't feel pressured to settle down, okay? I know what society tells women like you who are about to turn thirty. They did it in my day, and they're still doing it today. It's your life, and you should do every minute of it on your own terms. No one else's. I told your mother the exact same thing when she was your age."

"You sure did, Mom."

"And now I'm telling you. I loved your grandfather, but I didn't agree to move with him to North Carolina and marry him until I was good and ready. I didn't care how it looked or whatever everyone else was doing at the time: no man was going to have his say so over me. My mother told me not to get married until you just can't help yourself."

A deep feeling of pride washed over me while listening to my grandmother, who had been an independent woman before it was trendy. I hoped that I was doing a good job of carrying on her independent spirit in my own life.

"I promise you Grandmother, I won't be making any decisions that are not what I myself want to do wholeheartedly."

"Atta girl," she said.

The next day, my brother Tom, his wife Debbie, and their teenage son Derek drove over to spend the day, and Dad planned to grill one last time before winter came. My sister Janeen and her family had a prior engagement and couldn't make it. As we all sat around that afternoon while my father grilled the meat, I pulled out my parents' chess board and asked Derek to teach me to play. "Okay," he said, with as much excitement as an aunt can muster out of her teenaged nephew. I was just happy he'd said yes. The last time I saw him, Derek had shared with me how Tom didn't approve of anything he did and wanted him to be more involved in sports instead of things like reading and chess. I wondered if their relationship had gotten any better since then.

"So, this is a pawn. You can only move it forward one square at a time, unless it's the first move of the game. Then you can move it two squares. With pawns, even though they can only *move* straight ahead, they can only *capture* other pieces one square diagonally ahead of them."

"Whoa," I said. "So, if another piece is directly in front of one of my pawns, but not diagonal, I can't capture it?"

"Correct. Each piece has its own rules of what you can and can't do with—"

"Put that stupid game away and come toss the football with me," Tom said, standing directly over Derek with a football in his hands.

Derek looked to the ceiling and sighed. "I don't like football, Dad. And it's cold out. *And* I'm teaching Annie how to play."

"Someone needs to teach Annie how to catch a husband."

"Excuse me?" my grandmother said, dropping the Saturday newspaper to her lap before I could respond. I was growing tired of Tom and my dad's jokes about being married. I didn't even care to tell my brother about John, knowing he'd find a way to make a sarcastic remark about us. With Grandmother here to support me, maybe today was the day I finally fought back.

"Awe, I'm just joking with her, Grandma," Tom said.

"Didn't sound like a joke to me, son."

"Me either," Derek said, now fiddling a rook and knight between his fingers.

"Well son, if you had just come outside with me—"

Derek threw the pieces on the board and jumped up. "I DO NOT LIKE FOOTBALL," he yelled. "WHY IS THAT SO HARD FOR YOU TO UNDERSTAND?!?"

"Who are you yelling at?" Tom dropped the football and reached to grab Derek by the arm before Derek snatched it away and stormed off into the room I was sleeping in, shutting the door behind him.

"What is going on in here," Mom said. She and Debbie had heard the commotion and came running into the living room.

"Oh, you know, Tom being Tom." I said. "Picking on me and aggravating his son to death."

"Please Annie. You know nothing about being a parent. Stay out of this." Tom said, glaring at me.

"I will but keep your snide comments about my love life to yourself. You obviously have enough family issues of your own to worry about."

"That's enough!" Mom said. "Tom, go outside and help your father."

Tom glared at me for a few more seconds before shaking his head and walking out of the back-door to the deck where Dad was grilling. Debbie quietly walked over to the closed bedroom door where Derek was and knocked.

"It's me, honey," she said softly, then cracked the door open.

My mother sat down in the chair where Derek had been. "I don't know what's gotten into Tom," she said to no one in particular.

"I know exactly what it is," Grandmother said, lifting the newspaper back to eye level. "He's just like his grandfather."

"I don't remember Daddy every acting like that towards us," my mother said.

"That's because by the time y'all were old enough to start remembering things, he had changed. *After* I threatened to leave him."

"Momma?! You never told me you threatened to leave Daddy!"

Grandmother shrugged. "No need to. You married a good man. I would have told you if I felt you needed to hear it. People think divorce is the end of the world. I always considered it a wonderful option should Richard ever not be the man I married. And when he started criticizing me at every little turn and telling me what I could and could not do as his wife, and being super strict with you kids, I politely informed him that I could change my status as his wife at any time and wouldn't hesitate to take the children and leave if he didn't get his act together. As long as it took me to marry him, he knew I wasn't bluffing." Grandmother looked at me. "Sorry preacher," she said. "I know that's not very Christlike."

"Don't mind me, Grandmother," I said. "I love hearing your opinions on everything and about your life with Grandpa. Hopefully Tom and Debbie never get to that point. I just wish Tom would start considering other people's feelings before he speaks and realize that everyone doesn't have to like the things he likes or live their lives the way he thinks they should. Poor Derek has to live with his constant criticism every day."

"I'm gonna have to ask your father to talk to him before it's too late," Mom said.

Dinner was fairly quiet and awkward, like a powder keg ready to blow with even the slightest disturbance. Derek didn't say a word for the rest of the night, and Tom avoided talking to him and me, which I'm sure suited both of us just fine. When it was time for them to leave, Derek walked over and gave me a hug. "Maybe I can finish teaching you next time."

"I'm looking forward to it, buddy," I said.

Tom hugged my parents and Grandmother but skipped me and walked right out of the door. It hurt my feelings a bit, but I was proud of myself for finally standing up to him. Hopefully he'd get over it and spend some time thinking about the ways he was affecting his relationship with me and his son.

Chapter 14

By Monday morning, I was back in Bakerstown, refreshed and ready to start the week. Jane's wedding was on Saturday in Charlotte, and I needed to be very efficient this week in my tasks and make sure my sermon was prepared by the time I left the church on Friday afternoon. My first call was to Edna to see how Sunday went.

"Hey Annie," she said when she answered the phone. "How was your weekend in Columbia?"

"My weekend was pretty good, Edna. Thanks for asking. And my mother is doing well. She says to tell you hello. How did Pete do yesterday?"

"Oh, Pete was wonderful. He preached from a few verses in Isaiah 43 about God's love and protection for us. The congregation really responded well I thought, and William's selections were beautiful as usual."

"I'm glad to hear that, Edna. I'm going to call Pete to say thank you."

Next, I called Pete. He didn't answer, so I left a voicemail saying thank you for covering for me on Sunday and I'd love to debrief when he had a second to call me back.

By the time Elizabeth arrived, I'd made my morning calls and started on Sunday's sermon. Since the wedding was in Charlotte on Saturday afternoon, I'd planned to drive back late that night to be back and ready to preach on Sunday. There was simply no way I could miss two Sundays in a row, nor did I want to. I loved being the pastor at Covenant, and after my short getaway, I was itching to get back in the pulpit and see all of the members' smiling faces, starting with tomorrow's Tuesday morning prayer service.

I texted John around two o'clock to tell him I was back in town and to ask if he would like to see a movie that night, and he happily accepted. The theater was about fifteen minutes away in the next town over, so we agreed to meet there since John would be coming from his office in Charlotte and I would be coming from the opposite direction. After work, I showered and ate a few bites of some leftovers I'd brought back from my parents, then headed to the theater. I arrived before John, since he was traveling in the middle of rush hour, so I found a parking space toward the back where John could easily find my car, and waited on him to arrive. While I waited, I pulled out my cell phone and found the website for the theater and the movie we'd already agreed to see and bought two tickets for the seven o'clock showing. That way when John arrived, we could skip standing out in the cold for tickets and walk right into the theater and scan the tickets from my phone.

John arrived about ten minutes before show time, and I climbed out of my car and walked around to greet him as he exited his truck. He opened his driver side door and pulled me close to him.

"Hey lady," he said, before locking his lips on to mine.

"Hey," I said when we broke apart. "I missed you."

"I missed you too. Couldn't drive fast enough to get here. Shall we?"

We walked inside, scanned our tickets, and headed straight for our theater, as neither one of us were in the mood for snacks.

"Hi, Reverend Annie. Hey John!"

I turned around and tried to hide the surprise on my face at both John and I being together and recognized by someone out in public. Steve Anglin and Donnie Medlin, a gay couple who had been attending Covenant since the Family Day event, stood before us holding hands, Donnie cradling a big bucket of yellow popcorn against his chest.

"Hi guys," I said, giving both of them a hug. "So, you know John already?"

"Yes, we've met him a couple times at service," Steve said, extending his hand to John. "How are you, sir?"

"Pretty good," John said. "Date night away from the little one?"

"You got it," Donnie said. "Are you two…"

"Yes," John said.

"Well, good for you! You guys are cute!"

I blushed at Donnie's comments, then remembered that William had mentioned that he'd wanted to ask Donnie to sing at one of the services again but hadn't seen him in church recently.

"Thank you, Donnie. But I feel like I haven't seen you guys in a while," I said. "Everything okay?"

"Well, to be completely honest with you, Annie, Heather let us know that the deacons at Covenant had voted to not host her and Dawn's wedding, and we'd be lying to you if we said that hasn't been on our minds. So, we've be trying out a few other churches in the area."

"Ah, I see Donnie, and I totally understand. I…" I was at a loss for words as I stood before the couple shaking my head and lost in space. "I don't know what to say besides I'm sorry. This has been weighing on me ever since the vote, and I'll be frank with you guys, I'm not sure myself where Covenant goes from here. I'm so sorry." John wrapped his arm around me and squeezed.

"Annie, you've done more to welcome me and Donnie than any of the other pastors whose churches we've attended. You have a tough job. We may still pop in here and there, so don't give up on us. You just keep doing what you're doing."

I hugged both of the men, then we parted ways to our different theaters. John stopped and turned to me before opening the theater door. "You okay?" he said.

I took one of the napkins in my hand and wiped the tears that had started welling in my eyes. "I'm okay. It's just all so frustrating!"

"Hey, it's okay," John said, pulling me into his chest now, his chin resting on the top of my head. "You are doing everything you can to lead Covenant in the right direction. And most of the members are there with you, whether you can see it or not. But it won't happen overnight, and you'll have hiccups along the way. Unfortunately, things like this tend to take a very long time, too long. And just thinking about it, Covenant is further along than most churches already. Everything's going to be fine."

"You're right," I said. "I just have to keep going and keep depending on God. Thank you, John." I reached up and gave him a quick kiss.

"Okay, let's get in here," John said, opening the door. "I'm glad you chose a romantic comedy."

The weekend arrived for Jane's wedding, and that Friday, after I'd returned several calls and made sure Edna and the deacons knew I'd be in Charlotte until very late on Saturday night, I grabbed the bag I'd already packed and hit the road to the city.

The rehearsal dinner and wedding would be held at Whitehead Manor, a Victorian era, five thousand square foot house turned event space in Southeast Charlotte. Two wraparound porches overlooked several round tables set up outside in the backyard, where the reception would be held. The ceremony itself would be in a separate outside area, with Jane and Frankie standing directly under a large, oak tree branch that had somehow grown leaning to one side and now ran perfectly parallel to the ground ten feet in the air.

Before dinner was served, the entire party lined up to practice the processional. Frankie was Jane's fiancé, and his brother Eric was my escort. He was very tall and muscular, and I must have looked like a child standing next to him, but Jane never mentioned reassigning the pairings. We ran through the processional several times before Jane was satisfied that everyone had the pacing correct and knew their cue to start walking down the aisle.

There was a taco bar set up for dinner, and I was so full by the time I finished that I didn't have room for dessert. I checked my phone as we sat around mingling before it was time to leave and saw I had a message from John. *Rehearsal dinner go okay?*

Yes, just wrapping up. I responded.

Great. Can't wait to see you tomorrow.

I blushed and caught myself before anyone else saw me. *Back at you. Call you in the morning?* I responded.

Please do.

I sat for a minute with my thoughts about John. Our relationship was still new, but I was already feeling an excitement that I'd never felt with any other man before. And there, across the room, was one of my best friends getting married tomorrow, and the other in a serious relationship also. Our success as women wasn't in whether or not we had a partner or not, but everyone

82

wants someone to share life with, and it did feel good that each of us had someone, at least for the moment.

Back at the hotel, Jane texted both me and Sheila and asked us to come to her suite. When we arrived, we all sat down on the sectional sofa and admired the view of the Charlotte skyline framed perfectly outside of the balcony window. Jane poured each of us some champagne, then went into the bedroom and returned with two small gift bags and handed them to me and Sheila.

"What's this, Jane?" Sheila asked.

"I wanted to give you girls this gift. You two are my very best friends, and I honestly don't know if I would be here without you. I love you both so much, and I got these for you as a token of our friendship. You both mean the world to me, and I feel so blessed to have you in my life."

The tears flowed from my eyes before I could even open the bag. Finally, I was able to pull out the box and open it, and inside was a heavy, white gold, bangle bracelet with the words "BEST FRIEND" engraved on the side. I slipped the bracelet over my hand and admired how it looked on my wrist.

"Do you like it?" Jane asked. "Look, I have one too," she said, holding out her arm for us to see.

"I love it Jane, thank you."

Sheila and I both stood up and wrapped our arms around Jane, forming a tight circle. The three of us had been together since seminary, and now here we were, all on different paths in life, but still together. I realized I needed these two women just as much as I needed my parents, or Edna and William, or even John. Life was just so much better when you had good friends to lean on and support and encourage you along the way.

"Now," Jane said. "Let's enjoy ourselves before the big day tomorrow." She picked up her phone and found a digital radio station of pop hits, and we sat around for the next few hours, finishing the bottle of champagne, reminiscing about bad dates and old boyfriends, and just enjoying each other's company.

The next day was a bundle of nervous energy as Sheila and I stayed by Jane's side, helping her with any last-minute tasks that needed to be executed. The flower girls needed a certain color ribbon for their hair, which required a quick run to the nearest

Walmart. The make-up artist Jane had hired to do all of the bridal party's makeup had car trouble and was over an hour away, so we all banned together and did our own, making sure everyone's face matched as much as possible for the gazillion pictures we'd have to take before the reception.

I was ready to step in as officiant if Jane needed me, but when I peeked my head into the chapel, I saw the minister from Frankie's church, here well ahead of time and walking around mingling with the other guests who'd already arrived. Jane was paranoid that the chapel hadn't been decorated like she's planned it, so I was doing a courtesy check to ease her nerves. She stared at me intently when I returned to her bridal suite.

"Well?" she said.

"Everything looks fine, Jane," I said. "It's almost time. Let's get you in this dress."

The ceremony was beautiful, and Jane was radiant. Frankie was very emotional at the altar, and I thanked God for the love Frankie had for Jane and for the blessing of their union. As I stood beside Sheila and Jane's sister Jill, the matron of honor, I stole a couple of glances at John, who was seated about seven rows back, and on the aisle, in a sharp gray suit.

After the ceremony was over and we'd finished with the photographer, I walked to the backyard where the reception was held. I stayed seated during the first dance, then left the long wedding party table to get in line for food. As I crossed the backyard, the minister who'd officiated the ceremony crossed my path to get my attention.

"Hey," he said. "I wanted to introduce myself. My name is Byron. I'm a minister at Caldwell Baptist where Jane and Frankie attend. Jane told me you were a minister as well, and I wanted to come over and say hi."

"It's nice to meet you, Byron. Yes, I pastor a small church over near Bakerstown. You did a great job today with the service."

"Yeah well, weddings are pretty standard and straight forward, so no real work to put into it besides knowing your cues and reading the text."

"Well, that sounds easy enough," I said. "I've yet to officiate a wedding, but I'll keep that in mind for future reference, so I won't be nervous. Thank you."

"Sure thing. So are you—"

"Hey dear."

John's voice boomed from behind me. I hugged him and turned back to Byron. "John, this is Byron, Jane and Frankie's pastor. Byron, John."

"Nice to meet you John," Byron said. "I'll let you two get dinner. It was great meeting you, Annie."

Later, when the reception was winding down and the DJ invited couples to the dance floor, John took my hand and led me to the floor. I wasn't the best dancer, but the song was slow, so I was confident I could just two-step my way through and not embarrass myself in front of the remaining crowd.

"I think the minister likes you," John said, tossing his head toward Byron.

"What? No, he was just chatting since we're both ministers."

"Eh, I don't know," John said with a smile. "I'm a guy, so I know how guys talk and look when they're interested in someone."

"Well, even if he is, I'm unavailable, aren't I?" I said.

"That you are." John held his hand firm against the small of my back as we slow danced to the music. I laid my head on his chest and followed his lead from side to side. Out of the corner of my eye, I saw Jane sitting at the wedding party's table, looking at me and smiling. I was so happy for my friend, and although I wasn't sure what the future held for John and me, it felt good to be in his arms tonight.

Chapter 15

The service the next morning went great, even though I could have used a couple more hours of sleep after the late night drive back to Bakerstown. John had followed me to town, then veered off when we approached the fork in the road that led to his house. He sent a text asking me to text him when I was safe inside the parsonage, which I did, then crashed on my bed.

The sermon I preached was rooted in Psalm 119:9-11, the New Living Translation version, which states *"How can a young person stay on the path of purity? By living according to your word. I seek you with all my heart; do not let me stray from your commands. I have hidden your word in my heart that I might not sin against you."* I focused on the importance of staying in God's Word, which meant daily taking the time to get alone with God to read the Bible and pray, and how that was the only way to keep ourselves encouraged, filled with faith and joy, and uncorrupted by the world. After the service, I ate the lunch that Faye Emerson had been so kind to bring me and spent the rest of Sunday afternoon recovering in bed from my whirlwind forty-eight hours.

The next morning, I was refreshed and ready to start the week. I fixed myself a bowl of cheese grits and bacon for breakfast and ate it while reading my morning devotional, then I walked over to the church to start my day. I'd been reading a book about being more productive at work, and Elizabeth and I had been working on a daily routine where I had an uninterrupted block of three hours in the morning, followed by lunch. Then there'd be returning calls, having meetings, and going out on visits in the afternoons. I would be flexible when I needed to of course, but so far, it had been working pretty well, and I'd been able to use those three hours to be as productive as possible. Today, I was going over the church's finances for the month when Elizabeth knocked on the door.

"Hey Annie. I'm sorry to bother you, but Edna's on the phone. She said it's an emergency."

"Okay, put her through."

Elizabeth transferred the call. "Edna, what's wrong?"

"Good morning, Annie. I'm sorry to interrupt you, but I'm afraid I have bad news. Faye Emerson just called and said that

86

Tommy, Fred and Edith Miller's comatose son, passed away last night in his sleep."

"Oh no! Not Tommy!"

"I'm sorry, Annie. I'm headed over there now if you want to meet me."

"Yes, I'm on my way," I told Edna and hung up the phone.

I remembered when I'd visited Fred and Edith's home for the first time, and Fred had walked me back to Tommy's room to meet him. Tommy had been comatose ever since he'd had a diving accident three years ago and had since being lying comatose at the Miller's home. Fred had shared that most people they knew had stopped asking about Tommy altogether, but he and Edith and their daughter Belinda had continued to love and provide twenty-four hour care for Tommy, even as others had forgotten about him. Even though Tommy was an adult when he'd had his accident, how horrible it must be for Fred and Edith to lose a child, especially with Thanksgiving coming up in just a few short weeks.

Edna had waited for me in Fred and Edith's driveway, and when I parked the car on the street in front of the house, we walked together to the front door and knocked. Belinda answered the door, her face and eyes red from crying.

"Hey Belinda. Edna and I came as soon as we heard. We're so sorry about Tommy," I said.

She nodded solemnly and opened the door wider to let us inside. Two men that looked to be Belinda's age stood having a quiet conversation in the kitchen.

"My other brothers, Tim and Patrick," Belinda said. "This is Reverend Annie, from the church."

The two men waved and continued talking to each other.

"Mom and Dad are in the family room," Belinda said. As we walked down the hallway, I noticed something that I hadn't seen on my first visit: pictures of the entire Miller family lined the walls; capturing memories of childhood, vacations, and graduations. And I found in all of them, a very vibrant Tommy, life in his eyes and a contagious smile.

Fred stood up and hugged both me and Edna when we entered the family room. There was another couple there also, sitting on a loveseat next to the sofa. Neighbors I presumed.

"Thank you so much for coming, Reverend Annie. We're glad you got to meet Tommy before he left us."

"It was an honor to have met your son, Fred. I know you haven't had time to think about it, but please let us at Covenant know what we can do to assist you at this time."

"Well, you're right, I haven't thought about it, but I know we'll need to have the funeral there in a few days, which is the main thing," Fred said. "But Belinda and the boys will be calling you tomorrow to arrange all of that with the funeral home. Right now I'm just concerned about Edith. She won't come out of Tommy's room. We tried our best to prepare for this day and delay Tommy's leaving as long as we could, but now that that day is here, I see that nothing can prepare you for losing a child. Not a thing in this world feels as bad as this."

"I'm so sorry, Fred. We will do whatever you need to support you. Would Edith mind if Edna and I came in to see her, or does she want to be left alone?"

"I'm not sure. Seeing you may be helpful. Belinda, can you walk Annie and Edna to Tommy's room?"

We followed Belinda back down the hallway to the room where I'd met Tommy just one year earlier. Light flooded into the room now, and Edith sat in the chair beside Tommy's empty bed, staring out of the window.

"Mama," Belinda said. "Reverend Annie and Ms. Edna are here."

Edith nodded and waved at us, her lips pursed as she fought back tears, but didn't stand up. I walked over and wrapped my arms around her, and Edna followed.

"Why, Annie? Please tell me why," Edith said.

I pulled up a chair to sit down next to her and held her as she sobbed. The room had been completely dark when I'd visited before, but now that the curtains were open, I could see all the memories of Tommy across his bedroom. Pictures from when he was a kid and a young adult. Clothes and shoes that I was sure he hadn't worn since the accident. Baseball caps and a signed hockey jersey framed on the wall.

"I don't know, Edith," I said.

The Bible instructs us to mourn with those who mourn. So, I didn't try to encourage her with verses about the hope we have in Christ Jesus or the truth of life after death. I felt the only thing God wanted us to do at that time was to stop and sit with her in her pain.

Chapter 16

The next morning's prayer service was somber, as by that time, the Tuesday morning regulars had heard about Tommy's death. When I asked if anyone had something in particular they would like to talk about or share, no one volunteered or said a word, so we sat some more in silence until the hour had ended. When the service was over, and everyone was leaving, Vivian Artz walked up to the altar where I was standing.

"Reverend Annie, can I talk to you?" she said.

"Of course, Vivian. Let's go to my office."

Once inside, I offered Vivian a seat in the chair in front of my desk. "Vivian, I've been meaning to call you to talk about Heather and Dawn and the wedding. Is that what you want to talk about?"

"Yes, it is. I don't know how I feel about all this, Annie. Heather said her and Dawn were fine with Covenant voting to not allow the wedding, but it really hurt my heart when she told me the deacons' decision. I mean, I know every one of them, and to think that they know me too and chose to deny my daughter the right to get married here really tore me apart. I don't want to leave Covenant, but this really makes me look at everyone here differently."

"I understand how you must feel Vivian, and I am so sorry," I said. "Of course, I can't share who voted what way, but I can tell you that it was only one vote that made the difference, four to three, so not all of the deacons voted to not allow the wedding. Lord knows we don't want to lose you as a member of Covenant, but I'm not sure what else we can do."

"Well, that's good to know, that not all of them were against it. I guess this church is not at progressive as I was hoping it would be. And to make matters worse, the girls are having trouble finding a venue. Apparently, Spring is very popular for weddings in Charlotte, but Heather also wonders if they are being discriminated against. She says that the people she talks to take on a different tone when she tells them their names and they realize it is two women getting married. Of course, we don't know for sure.

It's just sad that in this day and age, people are still discriminated against based on who they love."

I was gutted that Heather and Dawn had not been able to find somewhere else to host the wedding. I had just assumed that they would be able to find another venue that would welcome them. But then again, hasn't the church long been considered the moral guide in our world? If our church had turned them down, did that somehow give permission for other venues to turn them away also? This was such a difficult situation, and the fact that Donnie and Steve were now actively attending other churches because of the deacons' decision didn't sit well with me. I wanted to rid myself of this feeling of helplessness about it. But I had to remind myself that this is life, and that this situation wasn't about me or my uncomfortableness with it, but about Heather and Dawn, and how they must feel being rejected over and over again by people who claim to be tolerant and loving.

"Vivian, I feel horrible that Heather and Dawn have not been able to find another venue. I will share that with the deacons when they meet again in two weeks, just in case, but I'm not making any promises that they will change their minds. But I do think it's something they should know."

"Thank you, Annie. I don't have high hopes either, but I appreciate it."

I walked Vivian out to her car, and then went back inside the sanctuary to sit alone for a bit with my thoughts and prayers. I looked around the church: at the pulpit, and the choir stands, and the empty wooden pews, and wondered what it was all for. To have faith and to believe in a God that we could not see was hard work in itself. "Father, I need Your help," I said. "I don't know what to do about Heather and Dawn, if anything. But this is weighing on my spirit and so many others. Please bless them to be able to find a venue for their wedding, and if the decision we made here at Covenant was not the one You wanted, please give us an opportunity to correct it. Once again, guide our hearts and our minds toward Your will, Father. In Jesus' name I pray, Amen."

Tommy Miller's funeral was on Thursday, and I was glad to see most of the congregation come out to support Fred and Edith in their time of grief. William sang an emotional rendition of "His Eye Is on The Sparrow," and there wasn't a dry eye in the entire church. I did my best to comfort the family and delivered the eulogy from John 14: 1-3: *"Do not let your hearts be troubled. You believe in God; believe also in Me. My Father's house has many rooms; if that were not so, would I have told you that I am going there to prepare a place for you? And if I go and prepare a place for you, I will come back and take you to be with Me that you also may be where I am."*

"Tommy is Home with our Savior," I said to the family and funeral guests. "He is finally free. Free in his body, free in his mind. Free in his spirit. Jesus tells us here to not let our hearts be troubled. Yes, we're going to miss Tommy down here on Earth, but God literally tells us here that He has prepared a place for us. How much better is that home readied for us by the Son of God than anything we could ever have down here in this world? Tommy's suffering is no more. He has a place in heaven and has been welcomed into God's arms. This next few days, weeks, and years will be difficult for you when you think of Tommy. But please try to find comfort in the words of Jesus Christ here, and His promise that, when Tommy left here, Jesus didn't send His angels to come get Tommy. He didn't defer the job. The Lord Himself came down to bring Tommy Home. And He will do the same for us."

Tommy was buried at a small cemetery in town, and the Miller family stood over his grave and said goodbye to their son and brother one last time. The Covenant congregation came together afterwards to make sure there was plenty of food for the Millers to eat for the next several weeks. At the repast, Edith motioned for me to come over and gave me a hug.

"Your words about Tommy made me feel a little better," she said. "He's not stuck in that bed anymore."

"No, he's not," I said. "He's free. *And* alive again. Just gone from your sight."

"Gone from my sight." Edith let the thought settle in her heart. "But I will see him again someday."

"You will."

"Thank you," Edith said, and sat down between Fred and Belinda. I thanked God that the words He'd given me had provided Edith with a modicum of peace.

Chapter 17

My plan of blocking off the first half of my days to be more productive in the office was really paying off. When the three-hour block was up and I came up for air, Elizabeth came in and gave me a list of calls to return that afternoon, including one from Fred Miller. Since it had only been one week since he and Edith had lost their son Tommy, I decided to call him back immediately instead of waiting until my normal time after lunch. I dialed his number, and he picked up on the first ring.

"Fred, this is Annie at Covenant, returning your call," I said.

"Hi Annie. Thanks for calling me back so soon. I was wondering if you had some time this afternoon for me to come in and talk with you."

"Yes, I have a couple of hours free at the end of the day, starting at three o'clock if you want to come in. Is everything okay?"

"Yes, everything's fine, considering. Edith is okay. How about 3:30?"

Fred arrived at 3:30 on the dot, and Elizabeth walked him into my office, then left for the day. He sat down in the chair and watched the snow fall outside of the office window.

"Fred," I finally said after about a minute. "What did you want to discuss?"

"I think God is punishing me," he said, still staring out of the window. "I think God took Tommy away so suddenly because I voted against Covenant hosting Heather and Dawn's wedding."

"Fred," I said with a sigh, heartbroken. "No, He's not."

"How do you know He's not, Annie? God punished people all of the time in the Old Testament for their decisions. And ever since we voted, something just has not been sitting well with me. My wife was upset with the way I voted and said 'Imagine if that was our daughter that was gay and wanted to get married.' Well, I did imagine it, and agreed that it would be hurtful to me for my church to turn away my daughter, and I still voted against it. And ever since, I haven't been able to shake the feeling that I did something wrong. Then Tommy just up and passes away, after two years of lying at home with 24-hour care and no problems? I don't think it's all a coincidence, Annie. It's like the story of Pharaoh. I didn't do what I knew to do, and God took my son away because of it."

"That's not the God we serve, Fred," I said. "Yes, God directly punished people because of their decisions and actions in the Old Testament. And yes, sometimes God does allow things to happen to us when we choose a path other than the one He has said is best for us. But God is merciful and long-suffering, and you weren't enslaving an entire people and willfully ignoring multiple direct commands from God like Pharaoh was. Whatever you think you did wrong, or even *will do* wrong, Jesus has already atoned for. And I don't want to minimize Tommy's passing in any way, but the reality is that people die every day. Unfortunately, it's a part of life, and it's a sure thing. Every single one of us will leave here someday, and every single one of us will lose someone we love, whether we've been perfect little angels or sinned our entire life. I feel confident saying that the way you voted had nothing to do with Tommy passing away. You took the two weeks before the vote to pray and seek God about how to vote, right?"

"Yes, I did," Fred said. "But in the end, I felt like I voted with my mind and not my heart. And I will be honest with you, I was concerned about what Alan and some of the other church members would think of me if I voted yes. I was afraid of them viewing me differently, especially after the Family Day event when my neighbors criticized me, and Edith's coffee club asked her to find another group. So, I took the safe route and figured even if everyone else voted yes and the wedding was approved, at least I could say that I had stood on the 'right side,' whatever that means."

Fred's confession was a revelation of something that I had never considered before: how much people's lives were affected by other people's fears and insecurities. Of course, now that I was thinking about it, it all made sense. This seemed to be the case with almost every major issue that society had ever had, like racism, women's rights, and all forms of discrimination. If Fred had voted with his heart, and not worried about what others thought of him, Covenant would be preparing to host a wedding right now, and

Donnie, Steve, and Vivian Artz would have never felt that maybe Covenant wasn't the church for them.

"Fred, I was planning to share this with all of the deacons at the same time, but Vivian informed me that Heather and Dawn are having trouble finding a venue to host their wedding, believe it or not. I'm not going to ask the deacons to vote again, but I am going to share that bit of news with them, just so you all know."

Fred's eyes lit up a little, something I hadn't seen since before Tommy's passing. "I'm not sure about voting again anyway," he said. "I don't want to open Pandora's box. But what if there was some kind of compromise, if they still need a venue."

"Compromise like what, Fred?"

"I'm not sure, give me 'til next week's meeting to think about it. I think I'll give Ed Anderson a call. He always has ideas."

"Fred," I said. "This is really not necessary. I think we need to focus more on your relationship with God and why you seem to view Him as a deity in the sky just waiting to punish people when they do wrong, or *think* they've done wrong. That's not a healthy view to have. God loves you."

"I know that Annie. I've walked with God long enough to know He's not just sitting around waiting for me to mess up. But losing Tommy so unexpectedly has just hit our family so hard. Edith seems to be becoming a little at peace with it, but I can't get this vote out of my head. I'm not sure why I'm correlating the two. Maybe because I'm just so *hurt*. But if there is an opportunity for us to help Heather and Dawn, I'd like to do that."

"Well, of course I can't stop you from talking with Ed, and we'll need to discuss anything you two think up as a group with the other deacons. But nothing is wrong with wanting to help Heather and Dawn with the wedding, as long as you're not doing it for absolution. Really Fred. Do you mind if I pray for you?"

"I need all the prayer I can get, Annie."

I reached across the desk for Fred's hand. "Father, we know it is never easy when a loved one passes away, and we often wonder why and search for answers and find none. Fred's heart is hurting since You brought Tommy Home, and it is You and You alone who can give him the peace he so desperately needs. Please wrap your arms around Fred, help him to feel Your presence, and most importantly, Your unfailing love for him. We know that healing from Tommy's death may take a long time, Lord. Please help Fred to be patient with himself and with You, and to be assured, without a shadow of a doubt, that You love him, that You only have plans of good for him, and would never take his son away as punishment. In Your Son's name we pray, Amen."

"Thank you, Annie," Fred said.

I gave Fred a hug and walked him out of the church. I was saddened and concerned about his belief that God had punished him, and I thought of all the other people out in the world who held this distorted view of God, and how many of them let guilt and shame stop them from having an intimate personal relationship with Jesus. I determined right then to always make sure that I communicated the love of God and His devotion to His children in each sermon, prayer, and conversation.

Chapter 18

I incorporated my thoughts about God's love for us into that Sunday's sermon, and preached from what was probably the most popular Bible verse of all time, the NIV version of John 3:16: *"For God so loved the world that He gave His one and only Son, that whoever believes in Him shall not perish, but have eternal life."* I felt a little guilty using that verse, which was the equivalent of a basketball layup, but I hadn't yet preached from it before, so I gave myself some leeway and promised to use a more challenging verse next time.

"Can you imagine loving something you created so much, that you give your only child up to die, just to save what you created?" I said to the congregation. "To be able to reconcile them back to you? We can't imagine it because we're not God, and we've never had to do it. *'God so loved the world that He gave His Son.'* This act of sacrifice, by God *and* Jesus, should eliminate any doubts you might have about the degree to which God loves you. Romans 8:39 even goes so far as to say *'neither height nor depth, nor anything else in all creation, will be able to separate us from the love of God that is in Christ Jesus our Lord.'* Nothing in all creation. No person, no sin, no action, no thought. NOTHING in all creation can separate us from God's love. You should find your rest in these words, your assurance that no matter what happens, no matter what you do or think you've done, God's love for you will never cease and will never, ever fail."

After the sermon, Jesse and Lorraine bought baby Harris up to the alter, and I laid my hands on his head and dedicated him back to the Lord. Afterwards, Edna brought up a large gift basket filled with baby supplies that had been donated from the church. I was so proud standing next to Jesse and Lorraine. They were the only interracial couple we had here at Covenant, both were previously divorced, Jesse now a deacon after being denied the opportunity when he first joined the church, and Lorraine a first-time mother. They were the living embodiment of the type of church Covenant was striving to become, and, in some cases, had always been.

❀ ❀ ❀

Wednesday night's deacons meeting arrived sooner than I'd anticipated, and it was the first time we'd all met since last month's vote. I walked over to the fellowship hall early to cover the atmosphere in prayer before anyone else arrived. I prayed for healing amongst the group, guidance, a spirit of cooperation, and for each person's heart to be filled with the love of God toward each other and the church members.

Each deacon filed in one by one, starting with Edna, who greeted me with a hug and a quick kiss on the cheek. Jesse arrived last, fixed himself a cup a coffee and skipped his usual small talk, but shook hands with everyone before taking a seat.

"Well guys, we haven't got much going on right now," Edna said, starting the meeting. "I think the survey visits have slowed down since winter has arrived. Ed, do you want to speak more on that?"

"Sure thing Edna. You're right, we have slowed down with the surveys since the first snowfall we got last week," Ed said. "So, we decided now would be a good time to focus on that resource guide that I mentioned to you all last month. We have Mary Leblanc calling around and compiling and organizing a list of all of the services and activities available in Bakerstown and the surrounding areas. After we get it to some sort of point of completion, we're going to have her daughter Elizabeth put it together for us in a nice booklet layout. Annie, I guess we'll need to discuss if we have the budget for that sort of thing, printing up about two hundred copies. If we don't, maybe we can ask for donations from local businesses or ask a printer to donate the cost of printing them."

"Yes," I said to Ed, "Let's definitely get quotes from a few printers, and Edna and I will review the budget and see what we can do."

After Ed finished telling us about the plans for the directory, Edna turned the floor over to me. "I'd like to revisit a topic from our last deacons meeting, if I may. Full disclosure, Fred and I had a personal meeting last week about a different matter, and I've already informed him of what I'm about to share with

99

you. Vivian Artz shared with me recently that Heather and Dawn have been unable to find a venue to host their wedding. They aren't sure if spring is simply a very popular time in Charlotte for weddings, or if they're being discriminated against. Also, something that I have not already shared with anyone previously is that the decision to not host the wedding has spread among at least a few members of the congregation, members who directly told me that the decision caused them to seek to worship elsewhere."

"Oh my gosh, who?" Edna asked.

"Donnie and Steve. And Vivian has been having her own thoughts about whether Covenant is still the place for her. Deacons, I know your job is a difficult one, especially when it comes to making decisions like this that are not easy nor popular, and I don't share this information with you to ask you to reconsider your vote. But I think it's a sign of a healthy church to gather feedback about how the decisions we make affect—positively or negatively—members of our congregation, so I just thought that this was something you should know."

"Annie, can I speak?" Fred asked.

"Sure Fred."

"I want you all to know that what I shared with Annie last week in our private meeting was that even though I voted to not allow the wedding here at Covenant, I have felt ever since that it was the wrong decision. I was afraid of what others would think of me if I voted yes, but my heart was with Heather and Dawn. I know allowing a lesbian wedding is a step that some people will never be able to accept, and I understand why. Up until recently, I felt that way too. But lately my views and feelings on the matter have softened, and I've tried to put myself in other people shoes to understand how it must feel to be constantly rejected and discriminated against. My wife got to this point well before I did, and I sometimes wonder about us men, we tend to always be the last ones to see things clearly for what they are. Even though I voted against it, in my heart I was sympathetic to Heather and Dawn, and Tommy's death just magnified it even more. And I feel that I made a mistake by not voting my conscious last month."

Everyone was silent as we all processed Fred's words.

"So where does this leave us now, Annie?" Anita Fleming finally said.

"I'm not sure. Again, I don't want to ask you to revote, I don't think Fred does either."

"Annie?" Fred said, raising his hand again to speak. "For the last week, I've been talking with Ed here, and we've been brainstorming about a compromise that we could maybe offer Heather and Dawn if they still don't have a venue and are even willing to deal with us again. And what we've come up with is a garden."

"We don't have a garden here," Anita said.

"Exactly," Ed said, his eyes excited. "We'd have to build one. And if they'd like to, Heather and Dawn could have the wedding there. I'm not sure if they were planning on an outside wedding or not. If not, then, I guess we've done the best that we could. But even if their answer is no, I think building a garden would still be a wonderful next activity for Covenant to take on. It would serve multiple purposes. For starters, it's a garden, where we'd have a section to grow food. You know, small stuff: tomatoes, peppers, greens, potatoes, that type of stuff. We could use the food when we cook here for events, or members could take food home to help feed their families.

"Second, it would also be a memorial garden, and have a section with pretty flowers and plants of all kinds and colors, and we could have a few benches for people to sit down and reflect while being surrounded by nature. Third, we'd build—or buy—a gazebo and place it in a third section that's just flat open area, and that could be used for weddings and parties and such. And lastly, growing and maintaining the food and plants will give some members something to do around here. Make them feel like they have a special assignment here that is their responsibility at church. We have lots of gardeners in our congregation. I know because I'm one of them. All of this would be developed on that half acre of flat land on the west side of the church."

"Wow, Ed. You've really thought this through," I said.

"Well Annie, you know how I am with these things. I have all the time in the world, so when Fred called me, I was all too excited to get my wheels turning."

"How do the rest of you feel about the garden, and the idea to invite Heather and Dawn to have their wedding in it?" I asked.

"I'm all for it," Jesse said. Edna nodded along with him.

"I don't see the difference in having it inside this building or outside next to the building," Danny O'Reilly said. "It's still at the church. But I suppose if Fred has flipped his vote, then it doesn't really matter, does it?"

"Every opinion matters, Danny," I said. "Just like Jesse's mattered last month even when he was on the side whose vote did not pass. For what it's worth, I agree with you: having it outside or inside is still having it here at Covenant and splitting hairs, but oddly enough, it may put some people at ease who can't support having a same-sex wedding inside the church. And if we offered Heather and Dawn to have it in the garden and they accepted, we will probably still be at risk of getting voted out of the local association and, therefore, the Southern Baptist Convention."

"I'll just say that I have honestly never cared to keep our membership in the SBC," Edna said, throwing her hand up in exasperation. "Covenant Baptist Church has been pushing the envelope on SBC protocol and the way they do things for forty-some odd years now. I'm not sure what difference it would make to not be officially apart of the organization anymore. And when I think about it, I find myself asking what matters to Jesus more, that we reach out to all people to spread the love of God or maintain the status quo so we can continue to be included in what is basically a male fraternity."

I was pleasantly surprised at Edna's thoughts toward the SBC, and I struggled to stop a smile from spreading across my face. Of course, Covenant had hired me as their pastor knowing that female preachers were not encouraged in the Southern Baptist Convention, but I'd never heard any of the deacons or long-time members express unhappiness with the Convention outright. At the same time, I was a little heartbroken: all of us here had grown up Southern Baptist, and there were a lot of things about it that I absolutely loved. It was a shame that the more time passed, the more I felt I and Covenant would eventually have to choose between staying or leaving.

There were a couple more minutes of quiet before I noticed that Alan, the most vocal deacon against the wedding last month, hadn't yet said anything. "Alan, we haven't heard from you," I said. "What are your thoughts on this?"

Alan shifted in his seat. "The garden sounds like a nice project idea for the church. As far as the wedding, I still don't agree with having it here, but that is my single opinion based on what I believe. I have seen the writing on the wall regarding Covenant ever since the Family Day event, and even though I voted against that also, I still felt welcomed here afterward, and have enjoyed seeing people unlike myself find solace at this church. We will not always all agree with each other. As a matter a fact, it's probably rare to get every single person on the same side of any issue. But if this group wants to build a garden and offer Heather and Dawn to host their wedding in it, and they accept, I will be there on the first day with my hammer and nails."

Jesse's mood changed instantly. "Well I'll be," he said.

Alan looked at Jesse directly. "Jesse, I know you and I were on opposite sides last month, and I guess I have my convictions. I can see that the world is changing around us, and I'm one of those people who believe that the church doesn't change when the world does, that we stay constant and true to God's Word, no matter what is going on around us. But I want you to know that I'm not a man who finds joy in discriminating against other people who aren't like me. I recognize that what you and your wife have gone through was just flat out wrong. But in situations like this with Heather and Dawn, and gay marriage and whatnot, what I do know is that even if I don't agree with something or how someone lives their lives, the best decision I could ever make is letting God be the judge and not me. I'm sure there are several things that you and I may never fall on the same side about, but I'd like to hope that we could still be friends regardless of that, if you'll start giving me a little more credit."

"I will, Alan," Jesse said, then stood up and shook Alan's hand again.

"I appreciate you both being willing to hear and consider the other person's perspective," I said. "That is important for us to be able to lead the church in an effective and cordial way. Okay then, does this group want me to call Heather and Dawn with the offer to host their wedding in the newly built garden?"

Jesse, Edna and Fred answered with a vocal "yes," while Ed and Anita Fleming nodded their heads. Danny and Alan sat still and silent.

"Okay then," I said. "I'll set up a visit with them, and call each of you as soon as I have an answer. Thank you for listening to my feedback and agreeing to revisit this issue again, and also for agreeing to serve on this board. I know these types of decisions are never easy, and I applaud you for working your way through it and your feelings about it."

Edna prayed us out, and afterward I noticed Fred, Alan, and Jesse all standing in a circle and talking to one another. These three men had all brought their various experiences and feelings to the vote, worked through them, and were now putting their differences aside and coming together to work toward a common goal. I was proud of them and the entire group. The example they were setting was an important one for the future of Covenant Baptist Church. I left the church with joy in my heart and looking forward to a potential visit with Heather and Dawn.

The next morning, I called Heather to schedule a last-minute visit to their home to talk with them about the deacons' change of heart. Thankfully, the snow from last week's storm had mostly melted away, and the sun was doing it best to warm things up a few degrees. I continued with my regular daily routine, then drove to Heather and Dawn's house for a six p.m. visit. Normally I wouldn't schedule a visit so late, but that was the only time that both of them would be home. Dawn greeted me at the door, and offered me a seat in the living room and a glass of water, which I accepted.

"Thank you ladies for allowing me to stop by," I said as they both sat down on the sofa across from the chair I was sitting in.

"No problem," Heather said. "What can we do you for?"

"Well, your mom shared with me a couple of weeks back that you hadn't been able to find a venue for the wedding. Do you mind if I ask if that's still true?"

"Yes, it is," Dawn said. "We still haven't found a place yet. And we're getting so frustrated with the process that we are considering eloping or just going to the courthouse. We really wanted to have a ceremony, so our families could come and be a part of our union, but it's getting too aggravating, calling place after place and getting turned away."

"Why do you ask?" Heather said.

"I ask because, as I think I mentioned to you before, the vote was very close, and one deacon in particular has had a change of heart regarding the way he voted. Long story short, it looks like the church will be building a large garden on the west side of the church as our next big project, and the deacons want to ask if you'd like to christen the garden by having your wedding there."

"Wow," Dawn said, looking at Heather, then back at me. "Who was the deacon that changed his mind?"

"Fred Miller."

"Tommy's dad?" Heather said.

"Yes," I said. "Did you know him?"

"I went to high school with him and Belinda. He was a nice guy. After the accident, we all just kinda stopped talking about him, and I feel bad about that now that he's gone."

"Well, Fred feels bad about not having voted to allow your wedding the first time around."

"I hate to be flippant, Annie," Dawn said, "but are they going to change their minds again next week? Because we could really do without the drama. It's totally fine that the deacons originally said no. We're aware of the way people still view being gay, especially older people and older Christians. But the last thing we need is to be the center point of a back and forth with the deacons. We don't want to be the cause of any fractures in the church."

"I understand Dawn, and I appreciate you thinking of Covenant and its members, but you two and Vivian are a part of Covenant too, and I really don't think the deacons are going to change their minds again. They are a determined group, no matter what they choose, and they are aware of the potential consequences or backlash that could come along with hosting your wedding. And they want to move forward with you anyway, if you are willing to accept their apology for the inconvenience. *Our* apology."

Heather looked at Dawn, who shrugged and leaned back on the sofa, then said, "We were considering an outside wedding anyway, love. May need to push it back 'til May to give them time to build it and give it time to warm up."

Heather tossed her head to the side—as if she couldn't believe what she was hearing—and smiled. "I guess we accept, Annie."

"Excellent," I said. "I'll let them know. And again, we truly apologize for the inconvenience."

I hugged both her and Dawn, gathered my coat, and stepped back out into the cold.

"Oh, and Annie?" Heather called after me. "Tell Fred we said thank you."

Chapter 19

The next morning, I delayed my usual three hour block of uninterrupted time and called each of the deacons to tell them that Heather and Dawn had accepted the offer to have their wedding in the garden. Edward responded that he'd get with Fred and start sketching out a blueprint and making a list of everything that needed to be done. When I called Fred, Edward had already beat me to the punch.

"Heather wanted me to tell you thank you," I said to Fred. "And said she knew Tommy and went to school with him, and that he was a nice man."

"Hmm…now that I think about it, I guess they were in school at the same time, although I don't think they were in the same grade. Well, that makes me even happier, Annie. Wait 'til I tell Edith. Ed and I are on it and we'll have something ready to present to the church soon."

After I had informed all the deacons, I sat silent for a while and marveled at how God had completely turned this situation around, simply by changing one person's heart and giving him the courage to speak out, even when he was afraid it would cost him acceptance amongst his peers. And even though I didn't agree with Fred that God was punishing him, Tommy's death did seem to be the catalyst for where we at Covenant now found ourselves, helping plan a wedding for a LGBT couple.

After lunch, Elizabeth bought me messages to return. There was only one, from Vivian Artz.

"Hi Vivian," I said when I called her back. "I'm guessing Heather has told you the news."

"Oh yes, she has Annie, and I just wanted to call and tell you thank you so much. My heart is just full knowing my daughter will be able to get married at Covenant and they don't have to look for a venue anymore. And I've already called Fred Miller also to say thank you. He apologized to me, but I told him there was no need. I can't imagine what he and Edith are going through losing Tommy."

"Well, thank you for calling Vivian, but this was all because of Fred and the other deacons, not me. I'm happy we will be able to help Heather and Dawn. And we'll be looking forward to your help with the garden. I know that is something you enjoy doing."

"Oh yes, I'll have to gather up some of my seeds to donate. I'm already itching for this snow to melt and winter to go away so that we can get started. As a matter of fact, I think I'll go look in my catalog and pick out some plants. Thanks again, Annie."

That afternoon was my mentor meeting with Brian Stanley, and it also happened to be his birthday, so I stopped at a local bakery on the way to his office and picked up a half-dozen cupcakes for us to celebrate.

"Oh wow," he said when I entered his office with the assorted treats in my hand. "What a surprise. Thank you, Annie."

"You're welcome. And Happy Birthday. I thought you were going to cancel our meeting this week and be off somewhere enjoying your special day. Why are you at work?" I asked.

"You know, I thought about it, but my wife still had to work today, and I didn't want to sit at the house all day by myself. It's too cold to go out fishing, which is what I'd *really* would have liked to have done today. So, I just decided to come on in. Debra and I are going out for a nice dinner later at a steakhouse."

"Good. I'm glad you're doing something to celebrate. So, I have an update on the wedding that we were considering hosting at Covenant?"

"Oh?"

"Yes. I know the last time we discussed it; the deacons had decided not to host the wedding. Well, they've had a change of heart, spearheaded by one deacon in particular, and now we'll be hosting the wedding in a newly built garden next spring. I wanted you to hear it from me first."

Brian sat back in his chair but didn't take his eyes from mine. "And you and the deacons know what this means regarding membership in the local association here and thus, the SBC?"

"We do."

"Alrighty then," he said. "You guys sound like you're confident in your decision. I will let the necessary people know. Just so you are aware of the process, once I inform the local association members, there will most likely be a motion drafted at

108

one of the upcoming meetings, basically stating that any church who 'believes, supports, or participates' in any marriage not solely between a man and a woman cannot be a member of the association. That motion would then go before a vote, and if passed, would end Covenant's membership in the association. Covenant would be welcome to attend the meeting to present your case, but quite honestly, I'm pessimistic on what good it would do for you. And your deacons seem to have already accepted no longer being a member of the SBC."

"Thank you for clarifying the process for me, Brian. I too, think it may be pointless to attend the meeting at this point. Also, I'm not sure if getting thrown out of the SBC will mean the end of you mentoring me, but if so, I want you to know that I appreciate everything you have done to help me navigate being a new pastor. I know it must not have been easy among your peers being connected to me and all."

"Yes, some of my fellow pastors have definitely had their opinions, but I am my own man Annie, and I make my own decisions. Mentoring you has been a blessing to me, believe it or not. Through you, God has shown me so many things that I never would have been exposed to before. You and Covenant have really opened my eyes to what the Kingdom of God should really look like and feel like, and I appreciate you and thank God for that. And I'll continue to try to help you as long as you would like me to."

Tears welled in my eyes as I listened to Brian share his thoughts with me. It wasn't that long ago that I was walking into his office for the first time, where he told me it wasn't within the guidelines of the Southern Baptist Convention to have female pastors. But he'd graciously met with me anyway and later volunteered to mentor me, and our friendship had come such a long way since. I knew that when I became overwhelmed with my pastoral duties or just needed another minister to talk or vent to, I could call him, and he would help me.

"I should have known the tears were coming," he said and passed me a tissue.

"I just really appreciate what you've done for me. I'll never forget it."

"Well, just do me a favor and pay it forward," Brian said. "You never know, in a few years' time, you may have another young female minister knock on your door needing advice. Should that ever happen, I know you will help her."

I stood up, gave Brian a hug, and prepared to head back out into the cold.

"Oh, one other thing that I don't think I ever updated you about," I said. "Greg and I are no longer seeing each other, just in case you happen to speak to him. But it was amicable and there are no hard feelings. I'm seeing John exclusively now, and I think Greg is seeing a nurse from the hospital."

"Is that so?" Fred said, smiling. "Well, it sounds like both of you made out okay in the end. Are you happy with John?"

"I am. Having him in my life has been great so far. He's very understanding of my job as a pastor and everything that it requires of me. He's also a widower and a father, so while we are exclusive, we aren't rushing things. Just enjoying being with each other."

"I'm glad to hear that, Annie. Having a partner that's not involved in ministry has been a life saver for me personally. When I'm with my wife, I don't have to be a pastor or be a Bible scholar or a gateway to God. She only wants me to be myself, and it helps balance things out. I hope John can be that for you, and I'm sure you'll be good for him also."

I drove back home after our meeting feeling a little better about everything that had happened with the deacons and the wedding. I'd accepted that whatever happened with the SBC, it was what Covenant wanted, and it would not be the end of the world.

Chapter 20

The Wednesday night before Thanksgiving, Covenant Baptist Church held a special worship service to give members the opportunity to come and express their gratitude and thanks to God. I sat in my office with the door closed as members slowly but steadily streamed in for the hour-long service. We'd scheduled it at seven o'clock p.m. to give members time to arrive from work, especially if they were coming from Charlotte.

The alone time before preaching was a special designated time for me to pray, ask God to speak through me and give me the words He wanted me to share, and visualize myself speaking in front of the congregation. Even though I'd been a pastor for over two years now, I still got a little nervous tingle when I had to stand up in front of people and preach. I was constantly concerned about whether I've chosen the right topic, if I was clearly communicating what I believed God wanted me to say, and whether the congregation was receiving the message.

At about ten minutes before seven, there was a strange knock on my office door. It sounded like multiple knocks at the same time, like someone had used both their hands. I slowly announced, "Come in," and the office door cracked open.

Emily and Ella burst into the room, followed by a laughing John. The girls ran around the desk and gave me a hug, then turned their attention to the different trinkets around my office. Emily picked up a snow globe from the bookcase and shook it, and Ella peered at a picture of me, my brother Tom, and my sister Janeen standing behind my seated parents at Disney World.

"Is this your family?" Ella asked.

"Yes Ella, those are my parents, and my sister and brother."

"Oh," she said, with what I thought was a hint of sadness. I looked over at John to see what I missed. He shrugged, clueless.

"The girls just wanted to come by before the sermon to see you. For some reason it couldn't wait 'til afterwards," John said.

"Why, thank you girls. I'm sure you two will give me good luck."

"Is this the room where God tells you what to say?" Emily asked.

"Well, yes, but God talks to me everywhere I go, and He can talk to you at anytime and anyplace."

"Is Mommy with God?"

"Emily, baby," John said, kneeling down to eye level with his daughter. "We've talked about this. Yes, Mommy is with God."

"Can we see her?"

"No, we can't see her sweetheart. But one day we will."

"Okay Daddy," she said. John hugged her tight and reached for Ella, who walked over and dug her face into John's shoulder. I stood silently, feeling like an intruder in a very intimate moment between John and his girls, and also feeling awkward since I was John's girlfriend. But I knew this would not be the last time the girls' mother would come up, and I needed to be comfortable giving them the space to talk about her, remember her, and express their feelings about her being gone.

"Sorry about that," John said to me as he stood up, each girl's hand in both of his. "I hope we didn't throw you off mentally."

"No worries, John," I said. "I'll see you guys after the service."

John leaned over to kiss me goodbye, which was our custom, but paused after he'd taken the first step and remembered what had just happened with the girls. "I'm sorry," he said.

"It's fine. Go."

When they closed the door, I took two more minutes alone to refocus, then walked out of the office and into the sanctuary. William was at the organ, playing and singing a beautiful rendition of "Come Thou Fount of Every Blessing." I sat in the pulpit and looked out over everyone who was in attendance: John and the girls with Edna, Jesse, Lorraine, and baby Harris, Ed and Mia Anderson, Vivian Artz, Fred, Edith and Belinda Miller, Ben Merriweather, Julio and Carlita Alvarez and their four children, Mary LeBlanc and her son Damien, Elizabeth and her two children, Harry and Earlene Williams and Pete Stoudamire. All of these people had played such an important part in my journey here at Covenant for the past two years, and I whispered a thank you to God for bringing them into my life.

The verses I'd chosen to preach from for this special service were 1 Thessalonians 5:16-18: *"Rejoice always, pray continually, give thanks in all circumstances; for this is God's will for you in Christ Jesus."* The message was fairly straight forward: I encouraged the congregation to always keep a thankful spirit as the verses command us to, even when times are hard, and it seems like there isn't much to be thankful for.

After I finished, Julio and William came to the front and sang "I Thank My Savior For It All," and as several people stood up to worship, I couldn't help but notice Donnie Medlin's absence, as he'd occasionally sung with Julio and William as a trio. But I trusted God to make things right with Donnie and Steve, and to lead them to a church where they felt His love for them, whether that be at Covenant or somewhere else.

The service ended quickly, and we all gathered in the fellowship hall to share a pre-Thanksgiving meal. There was turkey and gravy, stuffing, macaroni, green bean casserole, cranberry sauce, a special fruit punch that Ben had made, along with sweet potato, buttermilk, and pecan pies. Pete blessed the meal, and we all made our plates and dug in. Tomorrow I'd be with my parents and my siblings, my blood family, but tonight, I was grateful to God for giving me another family to love and be loved by.

The next morning, John called at five a.m. and insisted on driving over to meet me before I hit the road for the two-hour drive to my parents. I'd planned to leave as early at seven a.m. so that I could get to Columbia early to help my parents with the cooking and have most of Thanksgiving Day with them. Daylight had just broken by the time John arrived at 6:15, with two to-go plates from Waffle House in his hands. I blushed and wrapped my arms around his neck, thankful to be with someone who was so thoughtful and caring towards me, and this time, I was the one to pull him close to me into a long, passionate kiss.

"I should get Waffle House more often," he said when we broke apart.

I was already showered and packed to go, so the only thing left to do was to sit down and share a Thanksgiving breakfast of grits, bacon, toast, and waffles with my boyfriend. And how grateful to God I was: to be living and working in my dream job of pastoring his people, and to have family to share holidays with and a guy in my life who liked me and treated me well.

"I'm sorry again about last night," John said randomly, looking up from his food.

"No worries, dear. I think it's something I will need to get used to anyway. The girls need to be able to remember their mother, and I know it's hard for you also."

"It is and thank you for being so understanding. It was a long time before I was able to even think about dating someone, so I'm not sure how much time it will take for the girls to truly process that Lucinda is gone and not coming back. Thankfully, they are young enough to where I suspect they will be in a good place soon and can be okay with seeing me with someone else. Their happiness is my top priority. And yours."

"Thank you, John. We can go at whatever pace you want to. Just let me know."

After we finished eating, John wrapped me in one last hug and kiss and walked me to the car, throwing my bag in the back seat. "Let me know when you make it," he said. "And Happy Thanksgiving."

"Back at you," I said, and pulled away, and I spent the next two hours daydreaming about him and where our relationship could possibly go.

Chapter 21

Thanksgiving at my parents was wonderful, filled with good food and a great time with my family. Tom and Debbie, and Janeen and Joey were there with their families, and there were no disagreements and arguments as we sat around and enjoyed each other's company. I spent Thursday and Friday with them, then came back to Bakerstown on Saturday refreshed and ready for Sunday's service. I carried my Wednesday night Thanksgiving theme into my Sunday sermon, as the Bible has no shortage of verses about being thankful, and it was a message that I felt we could never hear enough. I preached from Philippians 4:6-7: *Do not be anxious about anything, but in every situation, by prayer and petition, with thanksgiving, present your requests to God. And the peace of God, which transcends all understanding, will guard your hearts and your minds in Christ Jesus.*

The week after Thanksgiving went by without fanfare. I made my weekly calls and visits to Covenant members and worked on a sermon series titled "The Gift" that I planned to preach every Sunday in December, focusing on Jesus, His birth, and His gift to us. It was the first series I'd attempted, and I was excited to dig into the Bible and other references to find verses, themes, and stories that complimented each other and wove a thread throughout the Old and New Testament, that I could then use for four different, yet related sermons, with a common theme running throughout.

It was two weeks before Christmas, and I'd delivered the first two of the four sermons already. They'd been well received by the congregation, and I was already thinking about the next series I would put together, maybe for Easter. William had just left my office discussing special musical selections for the Covenant Christmas program when Elizabeth knocked on my door.

"Come in," I yelled, knowing it was her by her signature soft, two-knock cadence.

Elizabeth stuck her head in. "Pastor Annie, I have Brian Stanley on the phone asking to speak with you."

My senses were certainly on alert. I hadn't heard anything from Brian since I'd shared with him that Covenant would indeed be hosting Heather and Dawn's wedding. "Put him on," I said. "This is Annie."

"Hi Annie, It's Brian. How are you?"

"Hi Brian, I'm well. It's good to hear from you. How are you?"

"I'm doing pretty well myself. I was hoping to schedule a time to come over to Bakerstown and meet with you about Covenant."

"Sure thing, Brian, but this sounds pretty formal. Is it about the local association's vote about Covenant hosting Heather and Dawn's wedding?"

"Yes, I'm afraid it is, Annie."

"Okay. When do you want to come by? Looks like I have a two-hour block of time open tomorrow afternoon around 1 p.m."

"Do I have anything from 12:30 to 2 p.m. tomorrow?" I heard Brian ask his assistant Evelyn. "One p.m. sounds good, Annie. I'll see you tomorrow."

I hung up the phone nervous, but also with a sense of relief. In a way, because of the deacons' decision, this situation had already worked itself out to an inevitable conclusion of Covenant no longer being a member of the Convention. The only thing left to do was to meet with Brian, who would undoubtedly make it final. My heart did break for what this could mean for the Covenant members who are tried and true SBC folks and would want to find another SBC church to attend. I never wanted to lose any members who had made their home at Covenant.

The next afternoon, Brian arrived promptly at 1 p.m. and sat down across from my desk. "Well Annie," he said, "No need for formalities. I just wanted to officially give you this." Brian handed me a white envelope with the local Southern Baptist's association's logo in the top left corner. "I'll let you read it, but to summarize, at the last association meeting, the motion I mentioned to you was officially drafted, *and* voted on. I think they were in a hurry to make this official before your wedding, so that Covenant could not be officially associated with the Southern Baptist brand while hosting a same-sex wedding. So unfortunately, Covenant Baptist Church has officially been disfellowshipped from the SBC."

I scanned the letter, which explained that "The Southern Baptist Convention constitution outlaws churches that act to affirm, approve or endorse homosexual behavior..." then I folded it to read in detail later. "Thank you. I appreciate you bringing this by personally. I'll share it with the deacons and the church."

"You're certainly welcome. And I want you to know that even though Covenant is no longer a member of the SBC, I'd love to keep chatting with you about ministry things, if you'd like. You might say I've helped you over these last couple of years, but I imagine there are a lot of things I could learn from you and the good people here at Covenant. Sitting here, I just realized this is my first visit to Covenant, and I've never heard you preach."

"Well, to be fair, I've never heard you preach, either."

"Let's remedy that sometime in the near future," Brian said.

Brian had another afternoon meeting back at his office, so couldn't stay long. I hugged him before he left and read the letter in full afterwards. Covenant was officially no longer a member of the Southern Baptist Convention, and I was no longer a Southern Baptist minister, something I'd wanted to be my entire life. I was a little heartbroken, but I was confident that I was exactly where God wanted me to be, and that this had been His doing. As I sat in my office with the letter in my hand, the only thing I could do was pray that one day the denomination that I had grown up in and fell in love with would grow and minister to the needs of *all* people, and not just a few.

Chapter 22

Before I knew it, it was a few days before Christmas and the end of one year and the beginning of a new one was upon us. I'd let my parents know that I'd be spending Christmas Day in Bakerstown with John and his family, and although they were slightly sad that I wouldn't be joining them, they were delighted that I was spending it with John, with side remarks about how nice it would be if I brought him to Columbia soon to meet them. I promised them that day would come but didn't make any concrete plans to speak with John about it. Both of us were busy people, and our relationship was humming along quite nicely, and I didn't want to come off as the eager girlfriend rushing a man down the aisle. Meeting a woman's parents wasn't the step immediately before marriage, but it was still a big deal to most men. And even though I'd long ago met John's mother and worked with her every week at Covenant, I didn't want to do anything to cause a wrinkle in what John and I had going.

John and I had agreed to exchange gifts, and I also wanted to get something for Edna and the girls, so I made a special trip to Charlotte to walk around Southland Mall to shop. I'd invited my two best friends Jane and Sheila to join me, but both of them had prior arrangements, so I took the opportunity to enjoy the time alone. The mall was filled with people all doing their last-minute holiday shopping. Teenagers out of school for Christmas break walked the mall in groups and hung out in the food court area. Oversized decorations hung from the mall's glass ceilings, large, golden bells and red velvet bows suspended in midair. A tall Christmas tree stood in the middle of the mall's center, its height spanning the three floors of the mall. A Santa Claus picture booth was set up at the tree's base, with a long line of parents and their kids waiting to snap a photo with him.

I took my time—more so *forced* to take my time due to the massive crowds—as I went from store to store looking for anything that I thought John would like. I'd already purchased a nice navy blue Ralph Lauren cardigan from Macy's: John wore a lot of cardigans I'd noticed since we'd been dating, so I was sure he would like it, but I hoped that he didn't have this particular sweater already. It was nice gift on its own, but I wanted one more item to go with it. John had shared Ella and Emily's Christmas lists with me, and I'd chosen a diary for Ella, one that had a lock and could only be opened if it recognized the voice of its owner, and an artist kit for Emily, with over one hundred different colored markers, pencils, and crayons, and a notebook of blank white pages to draw on. For Edna, I'd bought a cast iron pot with a lid, something that John had also shared with me that she wanted. But he'd given me no hints as to what was on his list, so I was on my own.

I walked into Brookstone and looked around at the different gifts and gadgets on display, but nothing jumped out at me as something John might like. Next to the store was Raymond's, a jewelry store occupying a corner space across from the giant Christmas tree. There were two couples inside, along with several single men leaning over the display cases and pointing as the jewelry store employees unlocked the cases and retrieved the valuable pieces for closer inspection. Hopefully there would be some unsuspecting ladies who would be getting a nice surprise from their significant others this Christmas.

"Can I help you, ma'am?" A man's voice said from behind the counter and close to the door.

I walked over to him. "I'm not sure actually. I guess I'm just looking, but I'm trying to find a gift for my boyfriend. Nothing too serious, though."

"Nothing too serious, huh?" The man said. He was middle-aged, slim man and was dressed in a dark suit and tie. "What does he do for a living?"

"He's a lawyer."

"Hmm…okay. How about a nice watch? We have those priced as low as $50, and that could be a nice, but not-too-serious gift for him. Something with a leather band, maybe."

"That actually does sound like a good gift. Can I see what you have?"

I followed the man—Prescott his gold name badge said—as he snaked behind the U-shaped counter, to the display in the front corner of the store. I meandered my way through the customers until I was opposite Prescott and staring down at the different watches in the case. There was everything from very simple watches with silver faces to gold Rolexes with thousand-dollar price tags. One watch in particular caught my eye, a classic looking piece with a square face, black background with gold clock hands, and a mahogany leather band. I asked Prescott if he could remove it from the case, so I could see it up close.

"Of course," he said, as he found the key to the case, unlocked it, and slid open the door.

When he placed the watch on top of the case in front of me, I removed it from the plastic molding and held it in my hands. The band was wide and thick, and it felt like something that John would wear with his business attire he wore daily to his law office. The price was reasonable, so I told Prescott I'd take it.

"Good choice," he said.

Chapter 23

Christmas Day arrived and fell on a Thursday, and John called me early that morning and woke me up. "I wanted to be the first person to tell you Merry Christmas," he said.

"Well, you succeeded," I said. "And Merry Christmas to you too. What time do you want me to come over?"

"I'm going to come get you in a few hours around eleven if that's okay."

"You don't have to come and get me, John. I'm fully capable of driving the fifteen minutes to Edna's house."

"I know," John said. "I just like having the alone time with you. I have to take advantage of any opportunity that I can have alone with you, with me having the girls and all, even if it is only a few minutes. Dating was a lot easier the first time I did it."

"Well, in that case, thank you for wanting to spend time alone with me and going out of your way to do so, and eleven o'clock is perfectly fine with me. I'll be waiting. Is there anything I can bring? I asked Edna yesterday when I saw her here at the church, but of course she said she had it all taken care of."

"And she does, so just bring yourself. See you at eleven my love."

I hung up with John and set my phone alarm to go off in an hour. I'd already wrapped the presents I'd bought for them, so getting one more hour of sleep should still leave me a couple hours to shower and get ready before John arrived. I nestled back under my heavy blanket, and had just started to drift back to sleep when the phone rang again. It was Charlotte Wilburn.

"Merry Christmas, Reverend Annie," she said when I answered the phone.

"Charlotte, it's so good to hear from you," I said, sitting up in the bed now. "Merry Christmas to you, too. How have you been?"

"Oh, I've been just wonderful, Annie. Moving to Mississippi wasn't anywhere near as bad as I was imagining it. And being around my grandkids every day has been just the fountain of youth I needed. I was afraid moving away would be my death bell, but it's been quite the opposite. You know it never

121

really gets too cold and never snows down here, so I've been very active despite it being the middle of winter."

I remembered my own upbringing in Mississippi and watching Christmas movies set in cities like New York and Chicago where there was always snow on Christmas Day. North Carolina was still technically considered the South, but it got more snow in one year than Mississippi got in twenty.

"I'm glad to hear you're enjoying it, Charlotte. That has truly made my Christmas knowing that you're okay. And please forgive me: I've been meaning to call and check in on you, and just hadn't quite gotten around to it." The truth was I'd had several opportunities to call Charlotte, but every time I thought about it, I was immediately flooded with worry that somehow my calling would be a negative thing if Charlotte was indeed unhappy in Mississippi. So, instead of risking a setback, I'd let the worry paralyze me and stop me from calling.

"No worries, Annie," Charlotte said. I could hear kids playing in the background. "Everything's all good. I don't want to keep you long. I have a long list of people there in town I want to call and give my greetings to before the day gets too busy. But do keep in touch. I'm planning a trip back in the Spring or Summer once it's warmer up there. I must say Mississippi has spoiled me weather-wise. Merry Christmas again, Annie."

"Merry Christmas, Charlotte. I'll certainly keep in touch. Take care and give my greetings to Linda and the rest of your family."

I didn't bother attempting to fall back to sleep after that, so I climbed out of bed, showered, and slipped on my favorite pair of jeans and a red Christmas sweater with Mrs. Claus on the front. Edna had mentioned something about a Christmas lunch when I talked with her yesterday, so I ate a small bowl of cereal and had one cup of coffee as I waited for John to pick me up. He arrived at 10:55, and when I opened the door to greet him, he pulled a mistletoe from his coat pocket and held it high over my head, a guilty smile on his face.

"John Allen, you know you do not need a mistletoe to kiss me," I said.

"I was hoping it would help me get an extra-long, extra wet kiss this fine Christmas morning."

"Well, there's only one way to find out."

John slid the mistletoe back into his pocket, put his hands on my waist and hoisted me into the air. My legs instinctively wrapped around his waist, and my scream was cut off by that passionate, wet kiss John was angling for. We stayed like that for several minutes, wrapped around each other as we kissed, and I realized John was stronger than his frame let on, since he was able to hold me in the air for several minutes without assistance. Finally, I pulled away and looked John in the eyes. He looked drunk, and I felt how he looked.

"I'm glad you stopped us," he said. "Because I certainly wasn't going to."

"I know. And as much as I'd like to keep going, we have to get going to your mother's. I'm sure the girls are waiting to open their presents."

"They are, but a few more minutes won't hurt."

John came in for another kiss, and I obliged him before pulling away again and jumping out of his arms. I locked the parish door as John loaded the presents into the car, and after I'd sat down in the car and John had gotten into the driver's seat, a terrible thought suddenly crossed my mind. "Oh no!" I said, suddenly horrified.

"What is it?" John said.

"Ben! I didn't check with him to see if he had someone to spend Christmas with! I'm sure he's not with his family. It must be killing him."

"Oh gosh, me either." John said. "Let's call him now. I'm sure Mom won't mind if we invite him."

I pulled out my cell phone, dialed Ben's number, and activated the speakerphone so that John could hear. "Ben," I said when he answered. "It's Annie over at Covenant. I apologize for the early morning call, but I wanted to see what you were doing for Christmas. John and I were worried and didn't want you to spend it alone."

"Thanks for checking on me, Annie," Ben said. "I tried to call Hannah again to see if I could come by and see the boys today, but no go, so I signed up to volunteer at the homeless shelter in Charlotte where I stayed when I left home. I felt like it was important for me to go back there as part of my healing and forgiving process after being attacked. I'm actually getting ready to walk out of the door now. I'm volunteering for lunch and dinner, so I'll be there all day."

"That sounds good, Ben. But I'm sorry you weren't able to spend it with your family today." John slowly shook his head as he listened and looked through the windshield.

"Me too, Annie. It's tough, really tough." Ben's voice started to break on the other end. "But I know it won't be like this always. I'm trusting God that it won't, anyways."

"You're absolutely right, Ben. Just hang in there. And if anything changes today with your schedule at the shelter, we'll be at Edna's all day if you want to stop by."

"I appreciate it, Annie. Tell John and Edna I said Merry Christmas. Thanks for thinking of me."

"Boy," John said after I'd hung up, reaching over and grabbing my hand as it rested on my thigh. "I know the pain he's feeling all too well. Different kind of pain, but pain, nonetheless. My first Christmas after Lucinda died was some of the worst days I've ever had. I'm going to do everything in my power to make sure he gets to see his kids again. My colleague Mark thinks Ben's situation should be an open and shut case. I sure hope so." John pulled out onto the road.

"I hope so too. I know you'll do all you can to help him." John's demeanor was totally different now than it had been inside with me before we left. "You okay?" I asked.

John shook his head again, faster this time, as if to snap himself out of a trance. "Yeah," he said. "Just thinking about life. Just when you're comfortable, settled in and think you have it all figured out, everything and everyone you care about can be taken away from you in the blink of an eye. I never thought that would happen to me until it did. Just wish Ben wasn't going through this. I guess the bright side to his situation is that his loved ones aren't gone for good."

I reached over and wrapped my hands around John's arm, and he leaned over and kissed me. "Sorry," he said. "Didn't mean to get all sad on Christmas Day."

"Don't apologize," I said. "Your sad feelings about Lucinda and the holidays and Ben and his situation are just as valid as someone's happy feelings about Christmas. I never want you to suppress or not talk about what you're feeling, unless you don't want to talk about it."

"That's why I love you."

I leaned away from John and then stopped myself, trying not to show how caught off guard I was about John's comment, but I think I failed miserably.

"Uh oh," John said. "Too soon huh?"

"No, John. I'm sorry. Not too soon. I just wasn't expecting it."

"You don't have to say it back. I've just always done what feels natural to me. I've never been a fan of those silly dating rules, even when I was younger. They all seem so dumb, especially now that I've lived, loved, and lost. If you care for someone, you should tell them before it's too late."

"I agree," I said. "And I do love you too. And I'm not just saying it because you did."

John smiled. "Good," he said. "Good."

Edna's house was decorated outside in the yard—with a full Santa sleigh complete with nine reindeer, Rudolph and his bright red nose included—and inside in every room, with a beautiful tree with white, blinking lights in the living room across from the fireplace. Several expertly wrapped gifts sat under the tree, and I added my bunch to the group.

"Look Ella, more presents!" Emily yelled.

"We'll open them after lunch girls," John said.

As usual, Edna had completely prepared a delicious lunch by the time we arrived. Seafood was the theme, and she'd fried catfish, shrimp, and hushpuppies, along with collard greens, macaroni and cheese, and a key-lime pie.

"Edna," I said, "how on earth did you cook all of this by yourself?"

"I've been cooking all of my life," Edna said. "It's like second nature to me by this point. The more you cook, the more you learn about it, and you know what can be prepared in advance and what needs to be cooked fresh. I made the pie a few days ago, put the collard greens on last night, so all that was left to do today was throw the macaroni in the oven and fry the seafood and the hushpuppies. Wasn't bad at all."

"I don't know if I could ever get to your level, Edna."

"I'm sure you could if you wanted to, Annie. I admit I have a lot more time on my hands then you do."

"Mom has always been a good cook," John said. "Dad used to always joke that that's why he married her."

"He was only half-joking," Edna said. "His dad loved to eat. He found out I could cook four months after we'd started dating and damn near pushed me down the aisle."

"I hope I can get to your level one-day Edna, although not for the purpose of being pushed down the aisle."

We sat around the dining room table and enjoyed the meal that Edna had prepared. It had been along time since I'd had good quality seafood, and I loved fried shrimp. We all ate until we were stuffed, then moved to the living room to open the presents.

"Daddy, daddy! Look what Ms. Annie got me!" Ella yelled as she jumped up and down in front of John after unwrapping her gift from me. "It's the diary I wanted!"

"That's awesome, sweetie. Go tell her thank you."

Ella ran over and threw her arms around my neck, something I was not quite prepared for. "Thank you!" She yelled as she hugged me.

"You're certainly welcome, Ella."

Emily was more subdued after unwrapping her art kit, but still seemed to appreciate it, as she immediately thanked me for it, then opened it and laid on her stomach on the floor with it spread before her as she ran her fingers over the colored pencils, then chose a brown one and began to draw in the notepad.

"Your turn," I said, handing John his gift bag. He pulled out the rectangle box first and opened it.

"You know me so well," John said, holding up the sweater with both hands in front of him. "I love cardigans."

126

"We noticed," Edna said, a slight smirk on her face. "That boy has been wearing sweaters all winter since elementary school. A sweater every day in the winter for what, twenty-five years now John?"

"I like what I like, Mother," John said, smiling at me. "They're warm and fashionable. And usually match any pants I put on. I don't have to think about what to wear much with a nice, solid-colored sweater."

"Oh yes, Annie. Only solid colors. Please remember that," Edna said, waving her eggnog in my direction.

"Duly noted," I said.

"You two," John said, then noticed the small box at the bottom of the gift bag for the first time. "What's this?"

"The rest of your gift."

John made an inquiring face at me, then quickly tore open the wrapping, revealing the black Reynold's Jewelry box underneath. He made another funny face at me as he removed the lid and peered inside.

"Well look at that," he said, wrestling the watch from its tight fit in the box. He slid the piece off of the tiny pillow, undid the clasp and placed it on his left wrist. "I love it, Annie," he said, holding his wrist out as he admired how the watch looked on his arm. "Thank you."

John walked over from his chair, bent over and kissed me on the lips, then pulled a large green box from under the tree and sat it in my lap. "Merry Christmas."

The box had some weight too it, and I had no idea what could be inside. I hadn't shared a wish list with John either, as we'd opted to trust and surprise each other. Sheila thought it was a terrible idea when I told her, but I trusted John, and honestly would be grateful for whatever gift he chose for me, big or small. I carefully unwrapped the green paper and unveiled a white box embossed with the Dillard's logo, then slid my finger under the tape that held it close and lifted the top off. The gift was wrapped in tissue paper, with a single piece of tape holding the paper closed in the middle. I lifted the tape, opened the tissue paper and peeked inside. A toffee-colored, square, leather purse lay inside, the same purse that I'd picked up and admired once while out walking through the mall with John. We'd gone to the Cheesecake Factory to eat, then decided to walk through the mall to work off a few of the pounds and settle our stomachs. We'd wandered into Dillard's, and as John went off to the men's section, I'd hung out around the makeup and perfume area, where the handbag section was close by. I'd seen the purse and really liked it. I'd picked it up and inspected it inside and out, talked with a Dillard's attendant about it, and held it down at arm's length to see how it would look by my side. But the price was a little high, and while I don't mind buying myself nice things or splurging on myself every once in a while, I knew I'd be spending money in December on gifts, so I sat the purse back on the shelf, thanked the attendant, and filed it away to get later, possibly for my birthday. John must have been watching me the entire time.

"Look inside," he said.

I unzipped the purse: inside was the matching wallet, perfectly set in between the inner tan walls and pockets of the purse. I pulled it out and admired the two pieces together. The cool of the leather felt good in my hands, and I was already ready to ditch my current purse and transfer all of its contents to the new bag.

"Do you like it," John said, a tinge of worry in his voice. I realized that I hadn't said a word since opening the gift.

"I love it, John. I wasn't expecting it. You saw me in the store?" John nodded. "Thank you so much." I stood, sat the purse and the wallet on the chair cushion I'd just abandoned and wrapped my arms around John's neck and kissed him.

"Eww," Ella said behind me.

"That's a nice gift son," Edna said. "And you have good taste, Annie. That's a beautiful bag."

"Wait," I said to John. "Where's my gift for Edna?"

John walked over to the tree and grabbed the box, pretending like it weighed hundreds of pounds and that he couldn't lift it off the floor.

"Daddy," Emily whined, then pushed her dad out of the way, picked up the box, and took it over to Edna.

"I told you, that you were stronger than him baby girl," Edna said, unwrapping the paper. "Well look at that," she said, admiring the cast iron pot. "I think I'll use this bad boy tomorrow and make some chili."

"Make sure you bring me a bowl," I said to John.

We spent the rest of the afternoon and evening watching a variety of Christmas movies on television, from *It's a Wonderful Life* to *Home Alone* to *Elf*. As I sat under John's arm as he dozed off on the sofa, I settled myself into him and allowed myself to revel in and enjoy the feelings of love and gratitude that had washed over me.

Chapter 24

True to Covenant's southern setting and roots, we held a New Year's Eve Watch Night Service to ring in the new year together as a church family and with the Lord. I got the idea for the service from the Reverend John Nelson, an African American pastor that I'd met once at the pastor counseling group in Charlotte. Watch Night services were a tradition in Black churches, and originally began with Black people coming to church on New Year's Eve night to celebrate the Emancipation Proclamation. But in current times, the gathering had evolved into an opportunity for people to bring in the new year in "the Lord's House." Per my usual custom, I stood at the door of the sanctuary and greeted members as they arrived. I was delighted to see several new faces that I didn't recognize, and some I just plain old hadn't seen in a while including Elinor Bigsby, who stopped at the door and gave me a hug.

"Thought I'd come see you in your element," she said. "Happy New Year."

I wasn't one to get too nervous anymore while preaching, but now my stomach was doing a little dance with the appearance of Ms. Bigsby. She was a tough and stern woman, who had wanted to be a preacher herself when she was my age but wasn't allowed to here at home in the States. Instead, she'd served in Liberia as a missionary, and fulfilled her calling as a pastor in a different way.

I finished greeting the members as they arrived, and as I looked around the sanctuary as I approached the alter to begin the service, I noticed just how full it was, about double the amount of people who regularly attended each Sunday. The arrival of a new year has that effect on people, second only to Easter Sunday. Whether people came once or twice a year, or each and every Sunday, I was grateful to have the opportunity to share a Word from God with them tonight.

"I welcome everyone to this New Year's Eve service," I began. "I know you all might be wondering why we started it at eleven p.m., as opposed to ten or even nine. And the answer is that I don't believe in sitting here in church just for the heck of it." Laughter sounded from the pews in front of me, as people leaned over to comment to each other. "So, we will be in here until at least midnight, so we can truly welcome in a new year here in the Lord's house. I promised you, we'll be wrapped up a few minutes after that and get you ladies and gentlemen on your way home. Now, William has a special selection that he will sing, and then I'll be back with the message."

William sat at the piano and beautifully sang a stripped down version of "At The Cross," and as I listened to him sing, I realized that although I knew a lot about William's life from what he'd confided in me, I had never visited his home. I try to make a point to visit my church members regularly, and somehow— maybe because I saw him so often at church throughout the week—I'd neglected to ever set up an in-home visit with him. As he finished the last verse of the song, I put a reminder in phone to make sure I set up a visit with him the next time I was in the office.

The sermon I'd prepared was titled "First Things First" and rooted in Matthew 6:33: *But seek first His kingdom and His righteousness, and all these things will be given to you as well.*

"Tonight, as we go into the new year, I chose this single Bible verse to focus on because I think it perfectly captures what the new year is all about for us as people. Humans are natural goal setters, and every year, we set goals for ourselves that we hope to achieve. Maybe we want to lose a few pounds and make healthier eating choices. Maybe we want to save more money, or land a new job, or finish school. Maybe we're hoping God will send us the perfect husband or wife, someone to love or share life with. Or possibly, you already have a spouse, and you're praying that God will make some sort of change in them in the new year.

"We set these goals, and then we go about trying to achieve them, often in our own might instead of God's. We take a few steps toward the goal, and we try, try, try. We try to go to the gym every day. Or try to be patient with the kids. We say we're going to go out on more dates this year, and that will increase our chances of meeting the perfect person. But in the middle of all of our toil and planning, we forget to include God. And when our goals don't materialize in the ways or the timeframe that we planned for in our head, we often times get frustrated with ourselves, others, or

131

maybe even with the goal itself. Before long, often before January is even over, we've given up on that dream, that desire.

"We do this year after year after year, without stopping to analyze where we may be failing. If you are a Christian, I believe that most times when we fail, it is because we never invite God to be a part of the goal in the first place. Or, as this verse implies and warns us against, we focus more on the desired thing itself, as opposed to focusing solely on God. God is the Giver of all things. The Bible says that success and promotion come from above. If God is the Giver of all things, created all things, owns all things, and knows us better than we know ourselves, how silly of us is it to not seek Him in our planning, or not seek Him in our desires, wants, and needs. This verse is here to show us the way, and it clearly and succinctly explains how to achieve our goals. Seek Ye first the Kingdom of God and all His righteousness. There it is, plain and clear. Seek Ye First.

"And the latter part: and all these things will be given to you. God says don't worry about what you're going to eat. What you're going to drink or wear. He says just keep your eyes stayed on Me, and I will make sure you have everything that you need. There is no need to worry nor fret. So, I want to encourage you as we step over into this new year, whatever your goals for the year are, whatever your desires, yes, plan them and work toward them. God certainly helps those who help themselves. But make sure that every day, in everything that you do, that you talk to God, involve God, and keep Him first. In every decision, in every intent, every morning when you rise out of bed, seek Him and His righteousness. Seek to know Him, to love Him, to listen to Him, to serve Him and be available for Him. Put God first, before your plans, before your family's plans—let me clarify that last part.

"Do not neglect your family. I've heard stories of people who gave their entire lives to the church, but their kids barely knew them and never had them around. That's not healthy and not of God to not take care of your family. There's a balance. The point of this message is it's okay to have goals and desires and to work to achieve them, but don't let them get in the way of your first priority: to know and love and serve God. And if you put first

132

things first, I think you'll find that everything else just falls into place."

I finished my sermon five minutes after midnight. As I wished the Covenant members a Happy New Year, gave the benediction and prayed for their safe return home, I hoped the message I'd delivered was timely and relevant and would hopefully settle into the hearts and minds of us all as we began this new chapter in our lives.

Chapter 25

The New Year brought the first Wednesday of the month back around on the calendar, which meant the deacons and I would be meeting tonight at Covenant. So far, I'd had a pretty good day today, returning Happy New Year emails and calls, when the alarm went off on my phone. I checked it: *Call William and schedule an in-home visit* it read. Before I got distracted by another email or call, I picked up the phone and dialed William's number.

"William, it's Annie," I said when he answered.

"Hey Annie. Something wrong?"

"No, nothing's wrong, William. I just wanted to give you a call. A thought occurred to me the other night while I was listening to you play at our Watch Night service. I realized that I'd never visited your home, and I'd like to remedy that if it's okay with you."

"Oh Annie," William said, chuckling on the other end. "You ain't missing nothing."

"I think I am. Visiting members is my way of reaching out to check on everyone and let members know that I'm available should they need me or the church for anything. I know you and I have had plenty of fireside chats here in the office, but if it's okay with you, it would mean a lot to me if I could swing by one day at your convenience."

"It's totally fine with me," William said. "I'd love to have you over. I live about ten minutes away from the church. Address is 739 Whistler Street."

"739 Whistler," I said, scribbling the address down on my desktop calendar until I could transfer it to something more permanent. "When do you think would be a good time for me to come visit?"

"How about Saturday? I know that's not during your working week, but I think it's supposed to be a sunny day and a little warmer. If that's too soon, we can schedule your visit for some other time in the next few weeks."

"Actually, Saturday is pretty good. I don't have anything planned. Is the afternoon a good time?"

"Yes," William said. "How about two p.m.? That should give it time to warm up a little. Maybe we'll be able to sneak a walk in."

"Two is perfect, William. I'm already looking forward to it. If I don't see you here tomorrow when you come in to practice, I'll see you on Saturday."

I hung up the phone and programmed William's address into my phone. After Elizabeth left for the day and I'd wrapped up my last calls and tasks, I went home to grab a bite to eat before the deacons' meeting. John had come over the night before, and we'd ordered pizza and watched a movie together before John left to go home. There were three slices left in the refrigerator. I warmed them up in the microwave and ate them with a glass of water, then showered and relaxed a little before walking back over to the church for the meeting. It was dark outside already, and I usually hated how fast it got dark in the winter time, but the new year almost always injected me with a healthy dose of anticipation. I knew that in just a few months, winter would be over, and Springtime would provide warmer temperatures and more hours of daylight.

Edna, Jesse, and Alan had already arrived and were chatting with each other as they help themselves to the hot chocolate that Elizabeth had prepared for the deacons before she left for the day.

"Nice touch, Annie," Alan said. "If it gets any colder outside we're all going to freeze to death."

"Thank Elizabeth next time you see here. It was her idea," I said. "And William said it may warm up some this weekend?"

"Yes," Edna said. "I saw on the five o'clock news just now that this cold front is supposed to loosen its hold on us starting on tomorrow, and move on out into the Atlantic, taking the cloud cover with it. I hope they're right. I could use a little sunshine. I feel like it's been cloudy for weeks."

Edward, Fred, and Danny hustled in from outside and rounded out the group. Anita Fleming had sent word that she wasn't going to be able to make it because she had to sit with her sick mother. I promised to stop by her house tomorrow to fill her in on the meeting and to pray for her mother's healing.

Edna stood by the whiteboard easel set up before the group and opened the group in prayer. "Father, thank You for bringing us all here together once again on another Wednesday night, to manage the activities and happenings of this Covenant community. And thank You for being with us and giving us ideas and solutions for every task that presents itself. We first pray for Anita's mother, for her healing, and we ask that You strengthen Anita in body and spirit as she cares for her mother. Please bless each member here and their families also. Finally, we ask that You be with us here tonight as we discuss the garden construction plans for Heather and Dawn's wedding, and any other items that are on the agenda tonight. Help us to always keep You first and have Your heart and eyes as we shepherd Your people. And a special prayer for Annie, the shepherd of this house and community, please strengthen her and provide for her whatever she may need. In Jesus name, Amen."

"Amen," everyone said in unison. I mouthed a quick *Thank you* to Edna, who nodded with a smile.

"Before we get started on the plans for the garden, I want to let you all know that Brian Stanley visited me recently and brought the official letter of disfellowship from the local association." I took the letter out of my folder and passed it to Edna. "We are no longer members of the SBC."

"Well I guess that does it then," Fred said. "When are we going to tell the church?"

"I think as soon as possible would be best," I said. "I'll announce it after my sermon on this Sunday, and we can also tell them about the garden and Heather and Dawn's wedding. I don't want anyone to be blindsided by that if possible. I don't expect everyone to be over the moon about it, but we'll manage the blowback as it comes."

"We support you, Annie," Edward said.

"I know you do, Edward. And I'm grateful for this group."

"Anything else before we move on to the garden?" Edna said. Everyone shook their heads. "Alright men, what do we got?"

"Edna, I have a drawing here that Fred, Alan and I have kinda sketched out. I made copies," Edward said, and passed the stack of papers around the group. "But if you don't mind, I'd like to transfer the sketch to the whiteboard. Won't take but a minute, as you can see that this is truly a rough sketch, and my drawing is not all that great. I wanted to discuss it with this group first and get approval before we talk about possibly getting a more polished rendering from an artist or an architect."

"Don't mind at all," Edna said, holding the black marker out to Edward as he rose from his seat. Edward removed the cap from marker, somehow managed to slide his copy of the sketch under the top gray border of the whiteboard, then proceeded to copy the sketch directly to the whiteboard, starting with the main road out front and the church building, which was a simple, 3D black square with a triangle prism on top. That alone was more than what I could sketch, I thought. To the right of the church, he drew a much larger square, and within it, another smaller square, a vertical rectangle beside it, another square on the other side of the rectangle, and a final odd-looking shape in the middle back. He finished the drawing by drawing what I could only assume were trees in the area at the top of the whiteboard.

"Okay everyone," Edward said, replacing the cap on the marker. "I know the drawing is terrible but try your best to visualize this with us. This is the church building," he said, pointing to the 3D square with the prism on top, "and as you can see, the main road is here out front. So, this sketch is from the vantage point of us standing at the road and looking toward the church."

"Got it," Edna said.

"Here is the area immediately to our right, right now." Edward pointed to the shapes on the board with one hand and held his other arm toward the hallway to the sanctuary. "Inside this large square area is the space that will house both gardens, the gazebo, and the open narrow strip area leading to the gazebo. This first square closest to the church will be the garden where we grow plants and vegetables and such. We think that space will get more sunlight that the other space here closer to the trees," he said, pointing to the square furthest away from the church. "So, this square area, closest to the woods here, will be the memorial garden. Hadn't settled on a good name suggestion for that one yet. We're thinking only plants here, annuals maybe, and few small trees. Something colorful and lively for people to look at while they sit at the benches placed throughout. Alan had the idea for maybe adding some type of water effect, a small pond or waterfall as the centerpiece for that area, but we're still thinking over what affordable options are out there and whether they would fit. Fred, do you want to talk about the gazebo area?"

"Sure," Fred said, standing up opposite Edward at the whiteboard. "Well, it's simple. The middle area between the two gardens will be a somewhat narrow rectangular strip of land that leads to an octagon wooden gazebo, which will be placed at the back of the area close to the woods. We tried different renditions of it being in the middle of everything somehow, but it always broke up the open land, and we need the strip of land leading to it to place chairs for the wedding guests. Of course, we could show this to a real land designer and he or she would probably tell us we're idiots and center it perfectly."

"I think it's a good plan," Danny said, beating me to it. "Probably would help to run it by a professional before we go too deep down the road though, so we don't encounter any surprises and waste time and resources."

"I agree," I said. "Because as great as this is, I'm already wondering about the costs that the church is going to incur. I'm guessing we don't have an estimate on that yet because we don't know the costs of materials and labor and such at this early stage, correct?"

"Correct," Edward said. "But I am working on it. I've been on the internet making a list of things we may need. You can buy those gazebos already built with the wood treated, but the starting costs of even a small ten foot one is several thousand dollars and go up the larger the gazebo gets. So, Annie, I'm thinking you and Edna might want to look at the budget and tell us deacons what the church can afford to put towards the project. We then can discuss it and see if there is any shortfall, and if so, ask for donations from the community businesses on plants, lumber, and any other materials. I'm hoping the members here can donate a lot of the labor, under supervision of course. We may need to ask Ben to oversee another project. He was a great supervisor when we built that house for Lizzie."

"That sounds like a plan, Edward. Edna and I will schedule some time before the next meeting to review the budget and get back with you all. I'll also run the idea by Ben and see what he thinks. With his supervisor experience, he may also know some companies who are willing to donate materials. So, keep working on that list. Better yet, maybe we should go ahead and bring him into this planning phase for this. I know he's not a deacon, but we need all the expertise and assistance we can get if we're going to take this on. He's also a former pastor and can give me a little guidance on the budget and raising funds if necessary. I'll give him a call in the morning if it's okay with this group."

Everyone nodded silently and continued to look at the board. "Alan, Jesse?" I said. "You two have been awful quiet."

"After almost being at each other's throats the last go around, huh?" Jesse said, then looked at Alan and smiled.

Alan returned the gesture. "Actually Annie, I've been sitting here racking my brain while you guys talked. I could have sworn we had an architect here as a member at Covenant. I remember talking with someone at the Family Day event who told me they were an architect. I've been trying to think of who it was, but the memory is escaping me."

"Hmm," Edna said. "That sounds familiar to me also."

"Well, you guys keep thinking on it. And maybe Ben knows someone since he has construction experience," I said. "Is there anything else about the garden that we need to discuss as a group at this point?"

"I don't think so, Annie," Edward said. "I think we need a little more information before we can start making some concrete decisions, but we definitely need to have all of our ducks in a row by the end of the month, because once the winter is over, we'll have a very short window to get the garden built for a late spring wedding. But now that I say that, I guess if push comes to shove on the garden part, we can maybe get the gazebo in place first so that area will be usable. But I imagine Heather and Dawn will want to come out with their wedding planner to finalize the layout for chairs and the reception and such."

"Absolutely, so let's all jump on our tasks and move as fast as possible. I'll call Ben first thing tomorrow and pass his number on to you if he agrees to help out.

"Anything else?" Edna said, reclaiming her space beside the whiteboard and flipping it over.

"Yes, I have something small just to remind you guys about." I said. "If you remember last year, we held a singles dinner at Antonio's on Valentine's Day for the members who were interested and didn't have someone special to celebrate the day with. That day can be very tough for singles, especially ones whose loved ones have passed on. Pete Stoudamire put it together, and it was such a hit with everyone who attended that he wants to do it again and possibly making it an annual tradition. So, like last year, he'll be making an announcement in one of the upcoming Sunday services for people to sign up."

Last year, I'd come up with the idea for the Valentine's Day dinner after Pete had confided in me about feeling sad about his late wife Belle. Valentine's Day had been a special holiday for them that they'd always celebrated. I'd also somewhat cowardly used the dinner as a reason to not have to choose between whether I would be seeing John or Greg that night. This year, I did not have that problem, and I was not single. Valentine's day fell on a Friday, and John had already asked me to block off both Friday and Saturday on my calendar. I wasn't sure what he was planning, but I was excited to have someone to spend the special day with.

Edna prayed us out of the meeting, and I went home thankful for the group's dedication to building the garden and making sure it was complete for Heather and Dawn's wedding.

Chapter 26

The next morning, the first call I made when I made it to the office was to Ben Merriweather to ask if he would volunteer to lead the garden construction project.

"Now, unfortunately Ben, unlike Lizzie's Habitat house, this is an unpaid project," I said. "I haven't quiet reviewed the budget for the project yet, but we think the total costs may be a bit expensive, so we're planning to ask some of the local companies for donations and materials, and we'll be asking members to kick in to help cover the labor, so we can keep the number as low as possible. I just wanted to tell you that before you said yes."

"That's fine, Annie," Ben said. "I'll do it without pay. I know how things can go sometimes with church finances, and you guys have given me so much already, it's high time I start paying it back."

"Well, we certainly didn't help you in expectation of any payback, Ben. You know that is not God's way. But we think you're the perfect person to supervise this project, so we would be very grateful for your service on this project. "

"Count me in," Ben said. "Besides, I'd love to somehow contribute to Heather and Dawn's wedding. They give me hope for my own future."

"Excellent. Thank you, Ben. If you don't mind, I'm going to give Deacon Edward Anderson your phone number. He's kind of our idea man and project planner around here, so expect a call from him soon so he can fill you in on the details. Knowing Ed, he may call you as soon as I give him your number."

"Okay Annie. I'll wait here by the phone for the next few minutes just in case. Thanks for thinking of me. I'm happy to help out."

After hanging up with Ben, I dialed Edward's cell phone and when he answered, passed on the news that Ben was on board, and gave him Ben's phone number.

"I'll call him right now," Edward said, just as I'd predicted.

Next, I made a few more follow up calls to other members, then set out for Anita Fleming's house. Since she'd missed the deacons' meeting last night, I'd asked if I could stop by briefly just to check on them and pray for her mother. Anita had agreed, and I'd put together a small care package for her mother. I didn't actually know what *kind* of sick she was, so I included some tried and true staples that I hoped they could use to help her feel better: four cans of Campbell's Chicken Noodle Soup, two packages of Halls cough drops, a bag of peppermints, and a cooking magazine.

I'd been to the Fleming's home before when the church had voted on the Family Day event, and Wayne and Anita had voted against it, along with a few more couples. I'd made it a point to visit each couple afterwards to let them know that Covenant cared about their opinions and values even though the Family Day event has been approved by the other members. Much to my delight, the Flemings had informed me that even though they didn't necessarily agree with Covenant hosting the event, they had no intentions of leaving the church. Since then, Anita had been a great member of the deacons.

When I arrived at her home, Anita opened the door and invited me in. "Please sit down, Pastor," she said. "And thanks for stopping by. Wayne's out right now, he'll be sad that he missed you."

"Of course," I said. "And tell Wayne I'll see him on Sunday. How is your mom feeling?"

"I think she's feeling better today. She has the flu, so she hadn't been out of the bed since we came home from the doctor's office two days ago. My mother is eighty, so I'm trying to keep a good watch on her. The flu can be deadly to people her age this time of year. We always have her get the flu shot, but apparently, she contracted a different strain than the strain the shot protects against. I've also been cracking windows and disinfecting every chance I get so I don't catch it myself," Anita said with a chuckle. "But since she hasn't been out of her room, I think I'm okay. And the doctor prescribed me and Wayne some Tamiflu as a preventive measure."

"Good then. I'm sure you'll be fine, Anita," I said. "I didn't know what exactly was wrong with her, but I brought her a small care package of things I hope help her."

142

"Oh, thank you! I'm sure we can use all of these, especially the cough drops and the soup. She's been weaker than normal, but not weak enough to miss her daily soap operas."

"Sounds like my grandmother," I said.

Anita and I sat in her living room and chatted like two schoolgirls, which was quite refreshing. Beside her mother Wanda being sick, she didn't have any urgent issues going on in her life, and it was nice to visit a church member and be able to just sit and talk about random, non-important things and let the time pass, like visiting an old friend. I'd appreciated that Anita and Wayne hadn't left Covenant when they had good reason to, and they'd stuck by me and the church and continued to contribute to the non-judgmental, welcoming environment we were trying to create. We needed members like them: members who didn't agree with every initiative and event we planned but were mature enough to see others' viewpoints and still be active.

Before long, an hour had passed, and I needed to get back to the office. "I was going to ask to see your mother and pray for her while I laid hands on her," I said, "but if she has the flu, I guess I better stay away. My flu shot might miss this strain too. And the Centurion had faith enough in Jesus to ask Him to just speak a word instead of visiting his sick servant, so I reckon I can have that same faith in Him also and pray from out here."

Anita reared back in laughter. "Yes, Pastor Annie, I think so too. I wouldn't want you getting sick and having the entire church saying we gave you the flu!"

Now both of us were laughing, and after we'd settled down, I grabbed Anita's hand and bowed my head. "God, we ask that you heal Ms. Wanda. She isn't feeling well, but we know that you are the Ultimate Healer, and that with a single word from Your lips, she will be healed. So, we ask for that from You, and also ask that You cover Anita and Wayne as they care for her. Please spare them from getting sick too. I thank you for this entire family Father, and especially for Anita and her contributions to the deacons and to Covenant in general."

Anita gave me a hug, and I left feeling better now that I had stopped by to check on her and her family.

Just as William, Edna, and the weathermen had predicted, it was indeed warmer when Saturday afternoon arrived, if you can call the temps in the upper 40s *warm*. The sun had come out and helped melt most of the two inches of snow that remained on the ground from last week's snowstorm, which was now somewhere over the Atlantic.

As I drove to William's home—which took me down a long dirt road that I'd never been on before—I couldn't help but take a minute to appreciate the small, country nook that was Bakerstown, North Carolina. It wasn't unlike my rural upbringing in Mississippi. And although I'd loved living the city life in Charlotte, I'd always been able to appreciate the slow and simple life of the country. Tall, multi-million dollars office buildings and apartment complexes on every corner were replaced by well-kept, single family homes and barns, some of which had probably been around for over a hundred years. The cattle casually grazing in the fields, unbothered by cars passing by just a few feet away. Small mom-and-pop restaurants and stores lined the street every few miles, owned by locals who depended on the continuous support of people right there in their own neighborhoods to survive.

I arrived at 739 Whistler, which was marked by a mailbox encased in brick, a stark contrast from the red dirt and woods around it. A white, wooden treble clef was glue to its side. The road had been anchored by towering pine trees on both sides, and when I turned right onto the driveway by the mailbox, the driveway turned from dirty to gray stone, and I had to stop the car to take in what I saw. The beautiful, stone driveway led to a single, one story brick home that sat about one hundred feet back from the dirt road, in the middle of what seemed like acres and acres of grass. Even though the home was one level, it looked massive, like a family of five could live there and still have plenty of space. It looked like the kind of house you'd see in the wealthy suburbs of Charlotte or in one of those *HOMES* magazines. For a minute, I wondered if I'd pulled into the wrong driveway, until William strolled from the side of the house and waved, beckoning me to come on up the driveway.

144

"William," I said after I'd parked and got out of the car. "I'm not sure what I was expecting but it surely wasn't all this. What a beautiful place."

"Thank you, Annie," William said with a wide grin. "I don't get many visitors out here, but when I do, I just love seeing their reactions. Welcome to Adagio."

"Wait: I'm not a musician like you William, but I do remember a little bit from school. Is that a musical term?"

"It is, and good catch. It means 'slow,' or 'leisurely.' 'At ease.'"

Now that I was up further into the property, I could see a glimpse into the back yard: more stretches of green land and what looked to be the beginning of a walking trail that delved into the woods. "You have this all to yourself?" I asked.

"Yeah, probably too much house and land for just me alone," he said. "But I built it hoping that one day, just maybe there would be someone else here with me to enjoy it. So far, that hasn't happened, and as I shared with you before, it truly sucks being "in the closet" about my sexuality. Still, I can't say I haven't enjoyed this sanctuary I built for myself out here. I decided long ago that if I couldn't have a lifelong partner and if I was going to be alone, I was going to make my home a place that I truly loved to come to at the end of the day. I bought this piece of land for a great deal during an economic downturn about twenty-two years ago, and since the home construction industry was in the tanks at that time as well, I was able to build this house and add some nifty little features to it that I otherwise wouldn't have been able to afford probably. I have thoroughly enjoyed living here."

"I'll bet you have. Well, William, I don't want to sound like a crazy stalker person, or like I'm glorifying materials things, but will you show me the inside please? I'm dying to see it!"

"Follow me!" William said.

The inside was just as beautiful as the outside, and I discovered that William had great taste. Every piece of furniture felt like it was perfectly placed, with plenty of open space throughout the house. An L-shaped sectional sofa and matching chaise centered the family room, directly opposite a large flat screen tv that hung over the fireplace. Bar stools sat under a countertop that formed a half wall into the open kitchen, complete with stainless steel appliances and ambient mood lightning that ran throughout the house. Modern art clothed the walls, and the mahogany-colored hardwood floor glistened like it had never been walked on.

"Even though the house looks big from the outside, it's actually quite cozy." William noted, "Only three bedrooms—albeit very large bedrooms—three and a half baths, the family room here, kitchen, and I asked the builder to forgo a traditional dining room for a special custom room instead."

William beckoned for me to follow him down the hallway and stopped in front of a closed door where the same treble clef from the mailbox hung on the door. He opened the door and held it open for me to step inside. The room was bathe in a blue light, and what must have been thousands of records and CDs completely filled one of the walls. Six guitars stood on their various stands throughout the room, along with a piano, a keyboard, four box speakers in each corner, and several pieces of equipment that I didn't recognize. Posters and pictures of famous musicians hung on the wall, everyone from Johnny Cash to The Oak Ridge Boys to Prince.

"This is where I sing, listen to, and practice all of my music. It's acoustically sound and my favorite room in the entire house," William said.

"William, this is amazing. I knew you loved music by your devotion every week to practicing the song selections and your long career of teaching music, but this is a treat to see. I'm so happy you were able to carve you out a spot in the house to devote to your craft that you love so much."

William played a couple songs for me, so I could experience the sound quality in the room, and it was amazing. Afterwards, we ate sandwiches at the kitchen bar and talked about our lives. William had already told me so much about his that I felt I really knew him and most of his story. I knew that I could trust William, so I decided to be transparent with him when he asked me how things were going with John.

"Actually," I said, "everything has been going very well. He wants me, he desires me, and he treats me so well. That's all a person really wants out of a relationship, right? It's almost as if everything is going too well."

"Whoa. Don't go doing that, Annie Adams. John seems like a good man. You don't have to question a good thing just because it's good."

"William, you're absolutely right. Thank you for not allowing that seed of doubt to grow in me. As long as John is being everything that I've always dreamed of, I'm not going to worry or doubt."

"There you go. Annie, now that were finished with our food, if you don't have anywhere to be, there is one more thing I want to show you before the sun starts to leave us and the temp starts to drop."

We walked the entire length of the backyard—which looked to be about the size of a football field—and picked up a trail once we got to the tree line. The trail was worn and narrow—like it had been walked thousands of times by one person—so I fell into step behind William as we snaked through the woods. Although the sun *was* still out as William had mentioned, the trees were now blocking it, and I shivered a few times as my body reacted to the drop in temperature.

"Almost there," William said.

Finally, after a few more minutes of walking, the trail emptied into a clearing, and William stepped aside. A sparkling pond lay in front of me, the sun's rays bouncing shards of white off of its surface. The pond was neither big nor small, with eight iron benches circling its edge at various points.

"I walk out here often," William said. "To just sit and look and talk with God."

"What a blessing this is, William."

I wanted to say more, but nothing quite felt right. William took a seat on one of the benches, and I sat down on another, and we both stayed that way, being still, looking at the water and the sky above it until the sun started to dip and William led me back home.

Chapter 27

The weather the next day was the same as Saturday, warmer than usual and sunny. I hoped the clear skies was an omen from God that the meeting after the service would go okay. I'd been nervous about it for a few days now, fearful about how people would react when I informed them of Covenant's Spring plans. The night before, after I'd returned from William's and John had come over to watch a movie, I'd asked him to make sure he came to church today because I needed all the friendly faces in the pews that I could get.

"Of course, I'll be there," he'd said. "But try not to worry about it. This is natural. The church has to grow, or it will die. And as you know, oftentimes growth means pruning. Not to be mean about it, but sometimes losing people is necessary."

I'd also called Elinor Bigsby and asked her to attend. "Elinor, I'm making a major announcement at church tomorrow, and I was calling to ask if you could come visit us again? I think seeing your intimidating face in the crowd will somehow give me strength to properly manage whatever else might happen."

"Ha!" Elinor said. "I'll be there. Thank you for asking me, dear."

Now the time was here, and there was nothing left to do and no one else to ask to show up for support. As I sat through the first part of the service, my constant prayer was that God's will would be done, and that I'd remain gracious in the face of any disagreement, or even worse hatred or bigotry.

"We'll have a special announcement after the service about some changes at the church and a special upcoming project and event if everyone can stick around for a few minutes," I said before William's musical selection.

I delivered the sermon I'd prepared, a message on faith from Mark 5:21-24, which told the story of the woman with the issue of blood whose faith was so strong that she fought through a crowd just to touch Jesus's clothes, and was immediately healed of her sickness. After I'd finished, the deacons passed out a prepared statement we'd typed up just in case members wanted something concrete to take home with them after the service. I'd warned

Heather and Dawn that I would be sharing the news about their wedding at church today, and they'd decided to stay home, to spare themselves from any negativity that may come from the announcement. Vivian Artz *was* in attendance, and she kept her eyes forward as I began the meeting.

"I have three important pieces of information to share with the Covenant family today, all three of which are somewhat related and point to the future of this church. The first thing I'd like to share with you is that two of our members, Heather Artz and Dawn Fisk, will be getting married in the Spring right here at Covenant Baptist Church."

I saw several eyebrows shoot up, but no one said a word as I paused for just a moment, enough time to mark the significance of what I'd just said, but not enough time to overemphasize it or make it dramatic. "The second thing I'd like to share with you today is that, because we have decided to host Heather and Dawn's wedding, the local association of the Southern Baptist Convention has voted to remove Covenant Baptist Church from their membership."

Now people adjusted themselves in their seats and looked down at the statement and around the sanctuary with bewilderment. The deacons were all sitting up front close to me, and I instinctively looked to Jesse and Fred for assurance as whispers started to rise from the congregation. Jesse gave me a firm nod and a thumbs up. John, sitting behind him, silently mouthed "You got this."

"And lastly, to host this wedding, and future weddings, our next big project will be building a garden on the west side of the church. The garden will be part food garden, part memorial garden, with a designated middle area for weddings and other types of events. More details are on the second page of your handout, and we'll need all the help we can get from anyone who's interested in building, planting and growing food and flowers. We want the garden to be a place members can call their own, take care of, and be a place for peace and reflection."

"Does anyone have any questions about anything Reverend Annie shared?" Edna asked.

"Who approved this?" One member said. "I don't remember voting on having a gay wedding here."

I cleared my throat. "The deacons voted on this request a couple of months ago. It was not unanimous. We understand that all members will not agree with the decision. That is your right. As you know, we have been working over the past two years to be very intentional about welcoming all types of people here to Covenant. This is just the next step."

The man who asked the question, which I'm not sure I knew, picked up his bible from where it lay beside him and left the sanctuary. Another couple seated in the back followed him out. I immediately wanted to cry, but I forced myself to hold it in and keep my face stoic until I could be somewhere alone. I wanted to look down at John, but I realized the entire congregation was staring at me, so I looked at Elinor instead. She sat up straight, held her head high and made a stern face at me, as if to say *Don't break, not here.* It was just the motivational rebuke that I needed, so I reached back to my days in public speaking class and briefly looked down at my notes, then back up again at the crowd and started scanning the room and making eye contact.

The sanctuary was awkwardly quiet now. "Does anyone else have anything they'd like to share?" Edna asked.

"I'm glad we're free from the SBC business," someone yelled from the back, and the comment broke the tension in the air and brought laughter and looseness back into the sanctuary.

"Amen!" someone else said loudly.

I smiled, grateful that the worse seemed to be over and that there were people here who truly wanted to welcome Heather and Dawn into the Covenant family all the way, not just in words, but in deeds.

"If there's nothing else," Edward stood up and said, "we're truly gonna need all hands on deck when the weather warms up and we start to build the garden. You'll see a layout on page two of your handout here. Ben here is going to supervise us, but we're gonna need donations of plants, crops, materials, and labor. Whatever you can give. This will be a fun project, and one that all of us can enjoy anytime we want. There will be a list posted in the coming weeks for you to sign up to volunteer. And we'll figure out a way to manage donations. Thank you everyone."

Chapter 28

The rest of January was pretty uneventful, as winter really set in and people used the month to hibernate and recover from the busyness of the holiday season. Now, it was already the second week in February, and since the month was so short and always had a tendency to fly by, we were making our final plans for the garden construction. I'd met with Edna to look over the church's finances, and with Ben's advice, we'd decided that five thousand dollars was all we could responsibly put towards the building of the garden.

"We can work with that," Ed had said when I'd called to tell him. "We already have people bringing in donations of seeds and other odds and ends to the church. I suspect we'll be fine on labor also. So maybe we can do as much as we can with the donations and use that money for some of the big things like the gazebo."

"Thank you, Edward. And thank you for always planning our events and maintaining such a positive attitude all the time. It really makes my job easier."

"I love what we're doing here, Annie. We are making the world a better place. Soon as this weather breaks, we'll be ready to go."

We'd set aside March 14 as a soft kickoff day that was subject to change due to any last-minute snowstorms that might blow through. I was confident that no matter when we started, the group at Covenant would be ready to dive in and pull off the project.

Friday was Valentine's Day, and I was going somewhere with John, so I met Pete Stoudamire for lunch on Tuesday just to check in and make sure everything was prepared for the single's Valentine's Day outing on Friday night. "I'm sorry again that I can't join you this year for the dinner," I said to Pete as we shared a sausage pizza at a diner not far from the church. "I feel like we had such a good time last year, and now I'm abandoning you."

"No worries, Annie," Pete said. "I'm glad you and John both have each other this year. Besides, I wouldn't wish that feeling of being alone on anyone, although I'm sure there are lots of people who are fine with it. We decided on Antonio's again this year, and I'm wondering if this is going to turn into a little tradition for us. I'm looking forward to it. We have twenty people signed up this year, and I've already called the restaurant and reserved the party room. We're gonna have an awesome time. You and John go enjoy each other and don't worry about us."

"Thank you, Pete. I know the group is in good hands with you leading the way."

My alarm went off at 5:30 a.m. on Friday morning, and even though it was really early, I woke up excited and in a wonderful mood. John still hadn't told me what we were doing, but it didn't really matter. The important thing was I'd be with him and we'd be spending Valentine's Day weekend together. I turned on the bedside lamp, then sat still on the side of the bed and took a minute to really feel the positive emotions that were welling up inside of me. I was happy: with John, with Covenant, and with my life in general. I was living in my calling as a pastor and dating a wonderful guy. My family was healthy and still with me, and I still had my entire life ahead of me. I was truly blessed. "Thank you, God," I said aloud. "For the good and the bad. For everything, I give thanks."

It had been a long time since I'd felt the excitement that comes with the anticipation of taking a trip. I knew that John was planning to take me somewhere, because the only instructions he'd given me was to pack a bag for two days and to be ready by seven a.m. Of course, he didn't tell me what *type* of outfits to wear, and I didn't know if I needed casual or formal or somewhere in between. In the end, I decided that we couldn't do all that much in two days' time, or travel all that far, especially since I was preaching on Sunday and he'd promised that we'd be back on Saturday night. So, I put on some blue jeans and a green sweater for the day, threw two more pair of both into a duffle bag, along with a black dress, a pair of heels, and underwear and sleepwear.

John was never late, and he did the usual routine of getting out of the car and coming in to greet me with a kiss and to collect my bags. I could see the sun rising behind him through the open doorway. "Good morning, beautiful," he said, and gave me a quick kiss. "Happy Valentine's Day. Ready for a quick adventure?"

153

"I am, even though you still haven't told me what we're doing or where we're going."

"It's a surprise. Nothing major, just wanted to kidnap you for a day or two without the kids. Let's hit the road."

After we were loaded into the car and settled, John programmed the GPS for the quickest route to Interstate 77. Once we'd reached the interstate, he turned the GPS off and settled into his seat, as if he were going to be there a while. We were headed south toward Columbia, South Carolina, where my parents and family lived. I eyed him suspiciously. "John Allen, where are we going?"

"On a drive."

"Duh. To where?"

"Lady," John reached over and placed his hand on my thigh. "Stop asking me so many questions and just trust me. Capisce?"

I really wanted to know where we were going, but I also didn't want to nag him. Besides, there were a lot of people who'd love to have a significant other plan something for them like this.

"Capisce," I said, relenting.

"Thank you. Tell me about your week."

I told John about the plans for the garden, my lunch with Pete, and the sermon I was preparing for Sunday. He told me about the latest cases he was working on at the firm. Then, the monotony of riding in a car and the couple of hours of sleep I'd missed that morning caught up with me, and I dozed off. When I woke up two hours later, a quick peek at John's phone showed we'd passed through Columbia, and Charleston too apparently, and had exited the interstate but were still headed south. Live oaks dotted the two-lane road we were traveling on, their tops leaning over the road and connecting to each other to provide a shaded, relaxing ride through town.

"Hey sleepyhead," John said.

"COMPLETE THE ROUNDABOUT TO TURN LEFT ONTO KIAWAH ISLAND PARKWAY," the female GPS voice said.

Ah, I thought. I'd recognized the name from the Charleston travel brochures my dad always thumbed through after we moved

154

to Columbia. The narrow road we were on and the Spanish moss made sense now: we were close to the Atlantic. I let down my window to see if I could catch a whiff of the saltwater smell that you can only get when you're close to the beach. John looked at me like he expected me to say something, but I kept quiet, entertaining his surprise until we slowed to a crawl on the red brick entrance to The Sanctuary at Kiawah Island Golf Resort ten minutes later.

"The Sanctuary huh," I said before the valet opened my passenger door.

"Yes," John said, looking around. "I thought it was fitting for the both of us."

I quickly discovered that the resort was dreamier than my dad could ever get a feel for from a brochure. I'd never stayed in a place so luxurious. The moment we stepped out of the car, we were greeted, helped, and waited on with every step. I sat down in the lobby while John checked in and was immediately offered a glass of champagne, which I happily accepted and also asked for one for John. Since I knew we'd be back in Bakerstown by Saturday night, that meant we were only spending one night here, and I fought the urge to feel sad at not getting to stay longer. I remembered William's advice to me and decided to be grateful for the brief moment I did have here with John and for the quick but wonderful escape he'd planned for us. Even if we did nothing more than go sit on the balcony and watch the ocean or take a long walk on the beach, I was thankful.

We took the elevator up to the seventh floor. It was a long and winding walk to our room, and when John swiped the key in front of the electronic pad and opened the door, I knew why. It was a suite with an unobstructed view of the Atlantic Ocean. Smooth jazz played on the clock radio by the king size bed, and the curtains to the balcony were open. John set our bags down, chugged his champagne, then collapsed onto the bed. I wanted to join him, but the sight of the water was too much to resist. I opened the balcony door and stepped out into the beachside air. I was shocked at just how much warmer it was here than in Bakerstown: it's amazing the difference traveling just a couple hundred miles south can make.

"Come join me on the balcony," I yelled back inside to John.

"Come join me on the bed."

"Hmm..how about a compromise," I said, stepping back inside but leaving the sliding door open. "I'm starving. Let's go find food."

"That's a great idea, and also works with my next surprise for you: we both have spa appointments at 1:45."

"Oh my gosh, John. We just got here and I'm already just...thank you is all I know to say."

John sat up and reached for me, pulling my hand until I was sitting on his lap. "Happy Valentine's Day. Thank you for choosing me. You mean the world to me and I'm so grateful to God to have you in my life." He lifted his chin and closed his eyes, and I rewarded him with a long kiss.

"Now," he said afterwards. "Let's go eat."

We found lunch at an onsite restaurant called Jasmine Porch. We'd wanted to eat at one of the lighter, poolside dining options, since John had also made dinner reservations for seven p.m., but the outdoor eating sites were closed for the season.

"We'll come back when it's warm," John said.

Jasmine Porch was definitely a worthy alternative. I had the signature shrimp and grits, and John had the Blackened Mahi sandwich.

Afterwards, we walked around to the spa, where I stood behind John again as he checked us in at the front desk.

"So, this is two individual massages, and not a couple's massage," the lady behind the counter asked, looking at her computer screen.

"Correct," John said, then leaned over to me. "I didn't want to assume."

"Thank you, John. I appreciate you thinking of that."

We separated as two attendants came from the back of the spa to show us to the dressing rooms and the other amenities that we had access to for the day.

"Enjoy love," John said. "See you afterwards."

I waved goodbye to him, undressed and waited in the women's lounge with another glass of champagne until my massage therapist came to get me. The massage was amazing, and just the thing I needed to destress and clear my head. I lay on the table as the therapist worked my muscles and I wondered to myself if this was all real. This relationship with John seemed to be blossoming into something serious. Bringing me to Kiawah was obviously a sign that this wasn't just a causal relationship to him. Since we'd been exclusive, he had done nothing but show me that he wanted a committed relationship with me. Was he thinking about marriage?

The therapist softly whispered in my ear and asked me to turn over on my back. I decided then to stop overthinking about our relationship and just enjoy the moment.

John and I took a long nap after our massages—deciding that we'd get up early tomorrow to watch the sunrise over the ocean and to go visit the beach before checkout—then dressed and went downstairs for our dinner reservations at The Ocean Room, another onsite steakhouse. I was glad I packed my black dress and heels, as the place was elegant and probably the fanciest restaurant I'd ever been in. The walls were dark, and the lighting was low, creating a romantic mood, perfect for Valentine's night. Each table held a clear vase with a single red rose rising from it and a candle. Couples—mostly older than John and I—dotted the restaurant, having conversations over drinks, steaks, and the finest seafood from the Atlantic.

"Are you enjoying yourself," John leaned over and asked me after our food arrived and we'd both dug in.

"I am, baby. Thank you again for bringing me here," I said. "The entire day has been amazing."

"You're welcome. I'm glad you had a good time today. I have one last gift for you."

"John—"

"Last one, I promise."

John reached behind him and retrieved a long, red box from his coat pocket, then placed it on the table in front of me. "Open it," he said.

I eyed him suspiciously, then wiped my hands and carefully removed the silver bow from the box and opened the lid. A diamond tennis bracelet lay inside.

"Oh my goodness, John. It's beautiful. I can't—"

"Yes, you can," John said. "It's just a bracelet. Here, put it on."

John unsnapped the clasp, slide it under my wrist, then close the clasp again. I admired the bracelet on my arm, and it looked so nice on my wrist. The diamonds glistened under the candlelight, and I immediately felt the urge to cry. I didn't know if I'd ever felt this loved and appreciated by a man before. Sure, I'd had a few good relationships over the years that ended amicably, but this felt different.

"Thank you for choosing me," John looked me in the eye and said for the second time today. "You could be with anyone. You could be with Greg. I want you to know that I want you, I love you, and I want to continue building this relationship that we have."

"You're going make me cry, John. I love you too. And I want to keep building our relationship also. You keep saying I chose you, but you chose me also. Thank you for trusting me with your heart after everything you've been through. I promise to do my best to always take good care of it. And thank you so much for today. It's been the best Valentine's Day I've ever had."

"What a difference a year, makes huh?" John said. "This time last year we were both single and eating at Antonio's with the Covenant gang."

"Yes, we were. I hope they're having just as good of a time as we are. But that reminds me. Did you purposely sign up to go to the dinner last year just because I was going?"

"I sure did."

John lowered his head and took a sip of his drink and ducked when I threw my napkin across the table at him. "John Allen!"

"What was I supposed to do? I knew you were just avoiding choosing between me and Greg. I could not let you get off that easy. Figured I'd make it hard on ya," John said with a wink.

"Well, you did. I spent the night wondering whether you and Belinda Miller had something going on."

John chocked on his drink. "What? No—I mean, Belinda's great and all, but I've never tried to date her."

"Well now I feel stupid. I hate that we women do that: make up entire scenarios in our head to convince ourselves that someone doesn't like us."

"Men do it too," John said. "I guess it's just human nature."

"Did you two save room for dessert?"

The waiter hovered for a second while John and I quickly skimmed the menu and decided that we would pass.

Afterwards, we strolled through the property hand in hand, enjoying the ambiance and the atmosphere under the soft yellow light that now gave the resort a lazy, yet sophisticated vibe. Couples sat at the main bar, nursing cocktails and watching a basketball game on the TV that hung behind the bartender. We approached the bar and ordered more drinks but took them upstairs to our room. It was still a little warm out for winter's standards, so John grabbed the beige throw blanket from the bed and led me out to the balcony, where we sat under the blanket, chairs side-by-side and holding hands as we watched the moon rise and enjoyed our drinks.

"Did you have a good day today?" John asked.

"I had a *great* day today, John. I'll never forget this. Thank you again."

"You're welcome. Thank you for coming. We'll stay longer next time." He took another sip of his whiskey and I felt him lean over toward me. "Hey…"

"Yes," I answered.

John looked nervous, like he was unsure what to say. "I know this is our first time spending the night together," he said nervously. "I don't want you to feel nervous or awkward. We don't have to—"

"I'm not nervous nor awkward, John, and I know what I don't have to do if I don't want to."

"Okay," John said, quickly turning his eyes back to the dark ocean. I had been thinking about it too and was *way* ahead of him. I had already made up my mind.

"Good thing I *do* want to."

John turned and met my eyes. I gave him a quick kiss, then held on to his hand as I stood up and downed the last of my cocktail. John did the same and didn't object when I led him into the room and closed the glass sliding door behind us.

Chapter 29

I sat in my office at the church and attempted to focus on my sermon for the upcoming Sunday service. It had been a little over a week since we returned from Kiawah Island, and I was still daydreaming about the place daily. I'd video-called Sheila and Jane the Sunday night after we'd returned and told them all about my trip. I couldn't wait for all of our schedules to line up for some free time to meet in Charlotte for lunch as usual.

"Oh my gosh," Sheila had said after I'd finished detailing the entire trip. "So, do you think you're in love?"

I could see my friends' faces on my phone, and my own face in the top right corner of the phone screen as I thought about Sheila's question. "You know what, I think I am!"

We giggled like schoolgirls, and Sheila and Jane both caught me up on their own relationships with their significant others. "I'm married now, ladies," Jane had said. "Not much more excitement to report on around these parts. Maybe when I'm pregnant."

"Are you guys already trying?" I asked.

"Not yet. Frankie wants to save more money first. Maybe in a couple of years."

My friends were the only people I'd told about my weekend with John. I hadn't told my parents where I would be that weekend, partly because I didn't know where I'd be since it was a surprise, and also because I knew Edna knew where I would be and could get in contact with me for them if necessary. I just didn't want to go telling the world like I was sixteen and it was my first crush. But mainly, I didn't want to deal with the inevitable questions about my dating while being a pastor. I didn't think there was anything in Covenant's handbook listing rules for the pastor's dating life, and the deacons already knew about my relationship with John. However, people had their own preconceived notions about what a pastor of a church should or should not be doing, especially a female one. Covenant had enough going on at the moment without me being the cause of more controversy for the church.

I'd just collected my thoughts and asked God to help me focus when the office door shook on its hinges as someone banged on it from the other side. The door sounded like it was going to explode.

"Annie!" a man's voice yelled. "Annie!"

My heart jumped in my chest: I sprang up from my desk and ran to the door. I didn't immediately recognize the voice, but the pounding on my door and the desperation *within* the voice let me know that it was an emergency or that something terrible had happened. I grabbed the doorknob and yanked open the door. Ben Merriweather was distraught, pacing back and forth with a white sheet of paper crumbled in his hand and his face wet from tears.

"Ben! What's going on?" I said.

"She's trying to take my kids away from me, Annie," he said.

"Who is?"

"My wife!" Ben shook the wrinkled papers in the air between us. "She's asking a judge for full custody with no visitation! She can't stop me from seeing my kids, Annie. She can't do that!"

"Come inside, Ben." I grabbed Ben by the elbow and led him into my office. He sat down in the chair and dropped his head into his hands.

"How can she do this to me?" Ben said.

"I'm so sorry, Ben. Do you mind if I read the papers?"

Ben handed me the papers—which I now saw included divorce papers—and I quickly scanned them and tried to get an understanding of what Ben's wife Hannah was asking for. I was no lawyer of course, but it looked like Hannah was requesting full and permanent custody with no visitation rights for Ben on the grounds of "emotional abuse." and "religious differences." I'd only known Ben for a short while and had no firsthand insight into his marriage with Hannah, but based on my own experiences with him, it was hard to picture Ben being emotionally abusive to anyone. I surely didn't want to discredit Hannah and her own experiences being married to him—which is entirely different than being his pastor— but my mind couldn't help but wonder if this was Hannah's way of getting back at Ben for coming out as gay.

162

"Ben, haven't you been working with John?" I said. "I think you should show these to him and let him give you his expert legal advice. I don't want to give you false hope, as I'm not a lawyer and am unsure about how these things works, but I think Hannah will have to prove to the court what she is claiming here, that you are emotionally abusive—"

"That's bullshit," Ben said, then looked around, remembering where he was and looked to the ceiling. "I'm sorry, Lord," he said. "I never abused Hannah or the kids in any way, shape, or form. Our marriage wasn't perfect, but it was pretty darn good before I told her I was gay. Well, as good as can be when your husband is secretly in the closet. And 'religious differences?' I'm a former pastor for Christ's sake." Ben looked to the sky again and sighed, as if God was right there in physical form listening to him swear.

"I'm so sorry this is happening, Ben. How can I help?" I said.

Ben leaned back in the chair and tried to compose himself, wiping his face with his hands and then on his pant leg. "I don't know right now, Annie. I think you're right; I definitely need to call John. Maybe he can make some sense of this. I always figured Hannah and I would divorce, but I had no idea she'd try to permanently stop me from seeing my kids. No idea." Ben shook his head and stared into space. "Maybe if I need it, you can be a character witness or something for me? Tell the judge about your experiences with me here at Covenant and since we met? I'm not sure if that's something I'll need, but I don't think anyone from my past life would still be willing to vouch for me, since my parents and former church don't want anything to do with me. God, I was so blind. You never realize how it feels to be discriminated against until it happens to you."

"I'll definitely tell the judge about my experiences with you if you need it, Ben. Let's pray about it before you call John. Get things moving in the spiritual realm, shall we?" I stood up from my chair and walked over to Ben.

"Thank you, Annie. Can you pray for Hannah too? Despite the hurt and disgust I'm feeling towards her right now, I know she is hurting too, and is probably embarrassed by all this. I know this

163

isn't the real Hannah and it's going to take a lot of time with God for her to heal of the pain I've caused her and my family. And pray for my boys too, Jacob and Riley."

My heart swelled at Ben's discernment that even though he was hurt by Hannah's actions, she and his boys were hurt too by his own actions, right or wrong, and by not having him in their life. It's a sure mark of a seasoned Christian when a person can pray for and forgive the person who caused them pain.

"Father," I started, "Ben needs You right now. He needs to know that You are always present with him, no matter what trials and difficulties he may be facing. You are still right here with him in the midst of it. He needs to feel Your love and Your assurance that You are working everything out for his good, and for the good of his family. I ask that You not only be with Ben, but with Hannah also. Please be with Jacob and Riley, and with Ben's parents also. Please heal their broken hearts with forgiveness and reconcile this family back to one another, whatever that looks like, God. Help Ben to be able to see his sons and move forward with his life with You by his side. Help him to trust in You, even when circumstances urge him to worry and abandon his faith. We love You and we know that You are moving on his behalf. In the name of Jesus, Amen."

I wrapped Ben in a long hug before he excused himself to call John. Then I said another private prayer that John would be able to make sense of the custody order and come up with a sound strategy to convince a judge to allow Ben to see his sons again.

"I met with Ben today about his custody case."

It was Friday night, and three days after Ben had come to the church in hysterics about the divorce and custody papers he'd received. John and I hadn't seen each other all week, as we were both busy at our respective jobs. John had called me early that morning before our workdays had gotten started and told me that he was coming to my place for dinner and a movie.

"Oh," I said, laying my head on John's chest as we lay on the sofa. "Do you think you'll be able to help him?"

"I hope so," John said. "An old law school friend of mine named Mark is a custody lawyer, and he agreed to take on the case with me and act as lead. But I'm not sure what grounds his wife has to be granted sole custody. I don't see that happening just because Ben is gay, but then again, this is the South, and Mark doesn't know if there is any previous case that we can use for precedent or can be used against us. We're still digging." John pulled me tighter to him and adjusted the blanket, so it was completely covering me. "Thanks for volunteering to be a character witness for him. Not sure if we'll need you yet, but we could definitely use all of the that special pastor prayer power that you have. I'm not sure I could deal with what he's going through now, not having my girls."

"I have been praying, and of course I will continue to. I'm glad he has you to help him."

We stayed snuggled that way for a while, before John kissed me goodnight and left for Edna's. We still hadn't figured out the answer to the question of if it was appropriate for him to spend the night in the parish, and we both would rather be safe than sorry.

Chapter 30

March had arrived. Spring had not. But I did not let that put a damper on my anticipation for the pleasant weather that would soon be making its way to North Carolina. I felt like I'd been cooped up in the parish and the church for weeks, and I was anxious to get out and about to do what was probably one of my favorite pastoral duties: visiting Covenant members.

I first scheduled a call with Heather Artz and Dawn Fisk to see if I could stop by to update them on the plans for the garden.

"Sure thing," Dawn had said when I called. Heather and I will be home on Tuesday if you want to come then."

Next, I called the number for Harry and Earlene Williams. I'd tried to set up a visit with the Williams' several months ago, but was unable to, so I was happy when Earlene answered the phone and said she and Harry would love for me to visit.

On Tuesday, I attended the early morning prayer meeting as usual. I continued to say a special prayer for Ben regarding his upcoming custody hearing, and I added Heather and Dawn and the Williams' to my petitions to God that morning. I asked that all would be well with them when I arrived and to reveal to me any special word for them from Him or anyway in which I could help them.

Not only were Dawn and Heather home when I arrived at their place, but their children were also. Codi sat at the kitchen table eating a bowl of cereal, and Kami ran into the room, whispered something into Dawn's ear, then giggled and ran back down the hallway. It was a school day, so I asked if everything was okay with the kids.

"Yes, thank you for asking," Heather said as the adults all settled down in the living room. "Sometimes we allow them to take a mental health day if they're having a rough time or acting out. Not too many, because each day of school is important. Only when we think it will help them refocus and help their wellbeing. Even though they both see a therapist, we really have no idea what either of them may be feeling inside when it comes to their biological parents, so when the therapist suggested this to us, we thought we'd give it a shot. I'd say it's helped quite a bit. We also have a rule that they can't take more than one per month: we don't want them taking advantage of it. Cody's been pretty good with it. Most times if they take a day, we stay home and let them sleep, read, or rest their minds, but sometimes we may go out and ride up to Charlotte and see a movie or do something else fun."

"I love that. I've heard of mental health days for adults, but not for kids. That's great that you two are trying out things to help them keep a healthy state of mind."

Heather went to the kitchen to get everyone some coffee and returned with three mugs and the entire pot.

"I just wanted to meet with you ladies as we are set to begin construction on the garden in two weeks. Here are the renderings we had drawn up of what it will look like." I passed Dawn the updated layouts Edward had commissioned from an architect. "I know it would be more helpful for you to see it in person, but of course, it doesn't exist yet. I was hoping this rendering might be helpful to you and your wedding planners as you finalize the details of the wedding."

"Yes, this is helpful, thank you. But we are the wedding planners," Dawn smiled and looked at Heather. "We're trying to save money, and we figured between two women we could do a pretty good job if we planned everything ourselves. Besides, neither of us ever wanted an expensive, well-to-do ceremony. Just something simple with our loved ones present to enjoy and share the moment with us."

"I'm sure you two will do an excellent job and will make it the wedding you always dreamed of."

"We did have one other question, Annie. We wanted to ask Ben if he would marry us. No offense against you of course because you're just as great. We just thought that it would be pretty cool if the lesbian couple was married by a gay former minister. Maybe it would also help him feel he could pastor again in the future if he really wanted to. You know, show him that there is a place for him in the Kingdom, just how he is."

"Wow. What an idea. I'm mad that I didn't think of it before," I said. "I think that would make Ben very happy, but let's sit on it for a bit while I gauge when might be the proper time to ask him. Ben's going through a lot right now personally with his wife and kids, and I want him to be able to focus on that and give your request the proper perspective without letting the other situations in his life cast a cloud over it. But if I know Ben, like I think I do; he'd be honored to serve as officiant. Thank you for thinking of him."

"Sounds good. And if all else fails and for some reason he can't or doesn't want to, you're our backup," Heather said.

"I'll surely be ready to jump in if needed."

I said goodbye to Heather and Dawn and headed over to my next appointment with Harry and Earlene Williams. Like Alan, Harry was one of the members who was not so quick to accept it when Covenant started welcoming and inviting different members of the community to come to church. His wife Earlene had been much more open to it, and she was the main reason that Harry probably hadn't given up and completely found a new church all together. They were in attendance the Sunday I announced Heather and Dawn's wedding to the congregation, and I had glanced their way after the announcement to gauge their reaction. Harry had sat with no recognizable expression on his face at all, and Earlene had been smiling and looking around at other people's reaction. I wasn't quite sure what I'd be walking into today, but I needed to check in with them to see how they were feeling and to see if there was anything, I could do for them.

"Hey there, troublemaker," Harry said when he opened the front door for me, and I was immediately glad that he was in a joking mood. "Come on in."

I'd been to the Williams' house before, so I took a seat in the same spot that I had the first time. Earlene came in, and we spent a few minutes talking about some happenings in Charlotte before I asked them their thoughts on Covenant hosting the wedding.

"Well I'm just over the moon about it," Earlene said. "And trying to wrangle an invitation out of Vivian."

"Oh my gosh!" I said, laughing. "Believe it or not, I actually just left Heather and Dawn's, and I know they are planning the wedding themselves, but I have no idea about the guest list. What about you Harry? What do you think? I know accepting gay people at Covenant have been tough for you."

"Yes, it has, and I appreciate you recognizing that. But you know what? My buddy Fred Miller's son died last year, and I'm not going to spend another minute waffling over who deserves to be accepted into God's Kingdom or not. It's simply not my job, and life is too short. I'm gonna get on board. So, I'll be there in two weeks with my toolset ready to work." Earlene patted him on the knee.

"Oh Harry, that's so great to hear. But just remember, I'm not interested in making Covenant a church full of robots or clones who all think alike, talk alike, and agree on everything. It's our diversity that makes us strong, so please don't feel pressured to go along just to get along. We need your true and honest opinions, always."

"I appreciate that, Annie. Knowing that's the kind of church we're aiming to be is why I want to stay around."

I prayed for Earlene and Harry before leaving, and when I got to the car, I thanked God again for giving Harry a heart toward his people.

Chapter 31

I started the following morning with a light jog around Bakerstown. It was starting to warm up, and I'd been neglecting my exercise routine for far too long. Running had always been a good way to clear my head and keep me in touch with God in a different way as I marveled at his beautiful, natural creation as I ran. But what really motivated me to get back out there was being with John. We were starting to become more and more physically intimate, and although I knew John loved my body as it was right now, I wanted to make sure I kept everything as tight as I reasonably could.

It was fifty degrees out and cloudy when I set out at 7:30 a.m., and I struggled to finish the three miles I was used to completing when my jogging was more routine. I ended up walking back to the parish after two miles, but still enjoying the morning outing and being out in the fresh air.

I showered and walked over to the church to start my day. It was Wednesday, the first one in March, so there was a deacon's meeting tonight. I also had to work on Sunday's sermon and return a few calls that Elizabeth had left messages for from the day before.

By early afternoon, I'd finished the first draft of my sermon, ate lunch, returned all the messages and had just settled down in my chair with a cup of coffee when my cell phone rang in my purse. I rummaged for it and found it. It was my mother, and it was odd for her to call early on a weekday morning. Our routine was to talk on Saturdays.

"Annie?" she said when I answered.

"What wrong, Mom?" I could hear the panic in my mother's voice.

"Derek has run away. He wasn't in his room this morning when Debbie and Tom got up, and Carson said he saw Derek leave with his backpack."

"Oh my God. Have they called the police?" I asked.

"Yes, but you know the routine. He hasn't been gone long enough for them to file a missing person's report, and the officer they talked to seems to think that this is common among teenagers, and Derek would probably show up back at home soon. Of course, Tom is angry, and Debbie is a wreck. They've been trying to call Derek's phone, but it's only ringing once and going to voicemail."

I knew what that meant from a previous experience that my friend Jane had had with a boyfriend back in college: Derek had his parents blocked.

"Did something happen at home to make him leave?" I asked Mom.

"Well, Debbie did say that he and Tom got into a heated discussion last night about him not going to a dance or something. I'm just worried sick that something has happened to him."

"Okay Mom. I'm on my way down. Try not to worry."

I hung up the phone and immediately called Edna.

"Hey Edna," I said when she answered. I could hear the girls in the background. "My teenage nephew is missing in Columbia. My family doesn't know where he is or if he's okay. So, I'm going to run down there and see if I can help, which means I'm going to miss the deacons' meeting tonight. Was there anything that the group specifically wanted to talk with me about tonight?"

"No, not at all, you go on down and be with your family. We'll be fine, and we'll say a special prayer for your nephew tonight. Please call me if you need anything," Edna said.

"Thanks Edna. I should be back tomorrow. I just want to go and see what I can do."

"Okay dear. Be safe."

My next call was to John. "Hey you," he said.

"Hey John. Quickly! I'm rushing out the door. My nephew Derek is missing. Or, run away we think. I'm gonna run down to Columbia for the night."

"Oh no, Annie. Do you want me to go with you? I'm sure I could reschedule my—"

"That's okay, John. But thank you. I don't want you to do that. Hopefully Derek will turn up soon and everything will be over. I'll check in with you when I get there."

Before I left the office, I pulled out my cell and called Derek's phone, which I realized I'd never done before. I'd programmed his number into my phone from a list that my parents kept on the refrigerator, but I'd never had a reason to call it. It rang seven times before finally going to voicemail.

"Hey bud," I said. "It's your Aunt Annie. I was just calling to see if you're okay, everyone is worried about you. I love you and please call to let us know you're okay." I ended the call, went back to the parsonage and threw a few outfits in an overnight bag, then hit the road to Columbia.

I'd gotten on the interstate just before the madness of rush hour traffic began out of Charlotte and made it to my parents faster than normal. Dad was sitting in the living room making calls, and Mom was in the kitchen, distracting herself with the task of fixing dinner. Her eyes were red and puffy as she seasoned chicken portions in a Pyrex baking sheet, preparing them to go in the oven. I gave her a hug and asked if I could help.

"No sweetie," she said. "I'm okay. Just trying to keep myself busy, and not think about where Derek is and what could be happening to him out there."

"I'm sure he's okay, Mom. If there is a bright side to it, thankfully he left on his own, and wasn't robbed or carjacked or something." I wasn't even sure if Derek was driving yet, but that was all I could think of to try to make Mom feel better. "He'll come home soon I bet."

I was worried about Derek and wanted him to come home, but not as worried as I would have been had he been a girl. I wasn't sure if that was sexist or not, but there are dangers out in the world that women face that men usually don't. When I'd gone off to college, Dad had bought me a can of mace that attached to my keychain, and a stun gun, and taught me how to use both in case of danger. Mom had insisted that I call at least once a week just to check in and let her know that nothing bad had happened to me. And being alone and away from family for the first time, I was certainly more aware of my surroundings if I was out at night. I always tried never to be alone after dark. When Tom had left home a few years before me, my parents had sent him off with a pat on the back and a smile, and it would be weeks sometimes before he called home to check in.

Debbie and Tom arrived an hour after I did, and I don't know if I ever remember seeing Debbie look so out of it. I could

172

tell she had been crying as well, and I immediately went over to her to give her a hug. "It's gonna be okay," I said to her as I held her. "He'll be back."

She sobbed a little bit into my shoulder, then pulled away and wiped away her tears. Ten-year-old Carson and little Maddie sat down on the sofa, quiet and sad as they watched their mother try to pull it together.

Tom was on the phone when he and Debbie first arrived and had stayed outside and finished his conversation before walking inside the house. He looked at me sitting beside Debbie, then back down at his phone. "What are you doing here," he said.

"Tom, I came here to help," I said.

"We don't need your help, Annie. Especially after your little stunt the last time we were all here. He probably got the idea to run away from you."

"*Stunt* Tom? So, it's crime now to take up for myself from your constant bullying? And trust me, Derek didn't need my influence to decide to run away from you. You did a good job of pushing him away all on your own."

"That's enough," Dad said to both of us from the front doorway.

I hadn't come down to Columbia to start a fight, and immediately felt guilty for responding to Tom in such a defensive way. This wasn't the right time with Derek being missing. But I wouldn't let him use Derek's running away as an excuse to beat up on me either. I began to think that maybe I'd should have stayed in Bakerstown.

Tom took a step in my direction, more so to intimidate me then a threat of physical assault. "You've got some nerve," he said, "coming here pretending like you care— "

"STOP!" Debbie stood up from the sofa and pointed her finger at Tom. Carson and Maddie jumped at the sharp sound of their mother's voice. "Stop it right now!"

"Honey— "

"Don't," Debbie said, her face contorting from sadness to anger. "It's your fault he ran away, and no one else's. No matter what Derek does, it's NEVER good enough for you— "

"Oh please, Debbie," Tom said. "I'm the bad guy for wanting my son to be interested in things other than books and chess?"

"What's wrong with chess?" Debbie shrugged with her hands palms up in the air. "Derek doesn't like sports. What's the big frigging deal? That may be your interests, but it's not Derek's, and that's perfectly okay. And I've sat quiet too long, watching you pressure him, trying to live vicariously through him when I should have been defending my son."

Debbie walked up to Tom and brought her wet face to his. Tom flinched in return, and I guessed that he'd never seen this side of his wife before.

"But this is the last straw," Debbie said, searching Tom's eyes, their noses mere inches apart. "And I will NOT choose you over my son anymore. So, before we find him, you need to get your act together or you're gonna lose all of us."

You could hear a pin drop in the room as Debbie pushed past Tom and into the kitchen, my mother following close behind. Tom stood motionless, like he was in a state of shock, before Dad finally beckoned for him to step out on the back deck. This time there was no accusatory or dismissive look towards me as he'd done the last time. Debbie had just turned his entire world upside down with just a few words. It felt good to see someone else finally stand up to him. I think the entire family had finally had enough of Tom and his constant judgement.

I retreated to the guest room, closed the door, and sank down to my knees. "God, we need You. Derek needs You. Tom and Debbie need You. I need You. Wherever Derek is, good or bad, I know You are with him. Please disperse Your angels around him to keep him safe from all hurt, harm and danger, and bring him back to us Father. Be with Debbie and Tom and in the center of their marriage. And please heal my relationship with my brother. Before Tom, show me if there is anything within me that I need to change for us to be better toward each other. Amen."

Tom, Debbie and the kids left after dinner, wanting to be home in case Derek showed up, and I spent the night with my parents, then left for Bakerstown the next afternoon. My mother was teary eyed and hugged me longer than normal. Derek being missing was taking a toll on her. I prayed for Derek and my family the entire drive home.

Chapter 32

Thursday, I sat in my office and edited the week's sermon, but my heart was sad as Derek still hadn't shown up or called. I was in continual prayer to God for his safety, and also in a constant battle with my mind for control over negative thoughts. I kept finding myself daydreaming about all the possible horrible scenarios that could be happening to Derek out there. I repented for the negative thoughts and tried to envision positive things, like Derek all of a sudden showing up at Tom and Debbie's doorstep, safe and unharmed. When John called to ask to come over on Friday night, I really wanted to say no, but figured that maybe seeing him would take my mind off of things.

"That will be fine, John," I'd said when he asked. "But I have to warn you that I'm not in the best mood with everything going on with my nephew."

"I understand," he said. "We can just sit if you want."

Friday was more of the same, although I did a better job of controlling my thoughts. According to Mom, Tom and Debbie had filed a police report, but the police still didn't think anything bad had happened to Derek. I didn't know whether my doing a better job controlling my mind was actually a good thing, or if I'd already started becoming apathetic toward my nephew being gone. I decided I'd talk to John about it when he came over tonight and was at home checking to see what I had in the fridge when my cell phone rang. It was a 704 number that I didn't recognized. "Hello?" I answered.

"Aunt Annie?"

"Derek! Oh my God, are you okay? Where are you?"

"I'm at the Greyhound station in Charlotte. Can you come get me?"

"Yes, I'm on my way," I said, happiness and relief suddenly rushing through my body. I needed to get to Derek quickly. "Stay put. Are you safe?"

"Yes, there are plenty of people here. But don't tell my parents where I am please."

"Derek, you know I— "

"Please Aunt Annie. I just need some time away from my dad."

My heart broke a little at Derek's words. Parenting was a hard job, a job that I had zero experience in. I hoped I never made my child feel like they needed to run away to get some space away from me.

"Okay Derek. I won't call them now, but we'll talk about it once I get there. I'll be there in thirty minutes. Stay put."

I hung up and called John. "Hey there. I'm really sorry about this, but I'm going to have to cancel our date. Derek just called me to come get him from the bus station in Charlotte."

"Okay, that's fine sweetheart. Is he okay? Do you want me to come with you?"

"He sounds okay. And I appreciate the offer and would love to have the time with you, but I think it may be better for Derek if I showed up on my own. Might make him feel more comfortable to open up and talk to me."

"Yes, probably so. Text me when you get there and let me know you got him and that he's okay."

My entire drive to Charlotte was a mixture of driving too fast, thanking God that my nephew was seemingly fine, and worrying whether I was doing the right thing by not immediately calling Tom and Debbie. I knew they were both worried sick. But I had made a promise to Derek, and he didn't need another adult that he couldn't trust, so I decided that God could handle the next thirty minutes that it was going to take for me to get to Derek and that some sort of tragedy wouldn't happen to him in that short time frame.

I arrived at the station, parked on the street in front and ran inside. I must have stood out, or looked like a crazy woman, because a security guard immediately yelled a loud "Ma'am, can I help you?" in my direction.

"Yes," I said, walking over to her. "I'm looking for my nephew Derek. Skinny kid, tall, long brown hair—"

"Here I am, Aunt Annie."

I turned at Derek's voice, who stood behind me with a backpack slung over his shoulder and his coat in his hand. He had on a black knit hat pulled down over his ears, and his jeans were very wrinkled, but other than that, he looked perfectly fine. I ran over to him and wrapped him in my arms.

"I'm fine, Aunt Annie," he said. "I know I scared you guys. I just needed to get away."

"Well, I'm just glad you're okay. Have you eaten?"

"I ate at the last stop, but I could eat again. Can we get pancakes?"

"Pancakes it is."

I thanked the security guard and walked with Derek back to car, then sat a few minutes as I pulled up directions to the closest IHOP on my phone. Once we arrived, we settled down in a booth and immediately placed our order: two full stacks of old-fashioned pancakes. The place was virtually empty except for one couple and a family of four, and I was grateful to have the alone time with Derek.

"Do you want to talk about what happened?" I asked him after the waiter left with our order.

"You know, my dad just being my dad," he said, toying with the cream and sugar packets that were left on the table for coffee drinkers. "This time he was mad because I didn't want to go to the winter formal."

"I'm so sorry, Derek. I know it must suck to be constantly pressured to do things you are not interested in. I was at Mom and Dad's a few days ago when your parents discovered you were missing, and your mom was not very happy with your dad. I'm praying that when you go home you will see a change in him."

"I've been praying that prayer for a while now Aunt Annie, and nothing has changed much."

I didn't know what to say to Derek. His admission was common among people who had given their lives to Christ, and were daily trusting Him to either deliver them from something, or *someone*, or heal them from some sickness or disease, or pay a bill that was past due. People could literally pray to God for years for a thing and never receive any sort of answer, at least from their perspective. How frustrating that must be to desperately need or desire something from what is supposed to be a loving and providing God, and seemingly not receive the answer to your prayers, and not know why.

"I know that is frustrating, Derek, and please forgive me because I'm totally going to give you a typical pastor response here, but God is always working in the background, even when He seems quiet and it feels like He doesn't hear our prayers. I promise you that He does, and even when it seems like He has said 'no' or is refusing to answer our prayers, in actuality, He is always moving things around to deliver us from our situations. He's always stirring people's hearts to help us. We just have to give it some time, have faith in the waiting, and remain patient. And often, the answer to our prayers never quite looks like we envisioned it. And if all else fails, just remember, you're fifteen. You have only three more years until you'll be away at college somewhere and on your own. Try to hang in there until then. I don't want to make my brother out to be a monster that you desperately need to get away from, but often when kids grow up and leave their parents' home, the relationship with them gets a whole lot better. The leash gets a lot looser, then suddenly one day disappears."

"Well, if God doesn't change my dad soon, I'm not sure how much more I can take of him. I don't understand why he can't just let me be myself."

"I think your dad has unfulfilled expectations of his own life that he is trying to create through you," I said. "And no, it's not right nor fair. You are your own person. Hopefully he'll take your mother's words to heart and things will be better for everyone."

Derek's eyes shot up. "What did Mom say to him?"

I wasn't sure whether it was smart of me to rehash what had happened at my parents'. At the same time, I thought it would be good for Derek to know that Debbie was in his corner. "She sort of vaguely threatened to leave him if he didn't change."

"Oh," Derek said, his eyes dropping back to the sugar packets sprawled before him.

The waiter arrived and sat two stacks of fluffy and hot pancakes before us, and we both drowned them with old-fashioned syrup and dug in. Derek was a skinny, yet growing fifteen-year-old boy, and his appetite proved it, as he scarfed down his stack before I could even make it halfway through my own. After a few more bites, my belly told me to stop before it made trouble, and I pushed the rest over to Derek, who happily and easily finished them off without pausing to breathe.

We each ordered a cup of coffee afterwards and sat a little more as a few more people came in for dinner. "So, what now?" I asked. "At some point very soon, I have to let your parents know that you're okay. They are worried sick."

"I know," Derek said, slouching and staring into his black coffee. "I was hoping I could stay with you for the weekend, and then go home."

"Hmm…that's perfectly fine with me. There is a guest room in the parsonage. But we do need to still let your parents know, and tell them you'd like to stay with me, then maybe they can come get you on Sunday? How does that sound?"

"That sounds good, Aunt Annie. Thank you. And that will give me a chance to hear you preach on Sunday!"

"Awee Derek." My heart warmed at Derek's desire to hear me preach a sermon. "I'm certainly nothing to write home about."

"I'm sure you're great. I've been asking Dad to come visit, but of course he makes up a million excuses why we can't. Did you guys get along as children?"

"Yes, for the most part. Tom was your typical big brother, Janeen your typical younger sister. I don't know, people change when they get older, usually for the better. But your dad has his unsolicited opinions about what everyone else in the family should be doing with their lives, and I'm not sure why. I guess me going into ministry instead of settling down and being someone's housewife gets a lot of people riled up inside, including your dad. Thankfully, I don't care about what he thinks of my decisions, and I hope that as your father, you never have to feel that way about him as I do."

We finished our coffee, I paid the bill, and we hit the road back to Bakerstown. When we arrived, I texted John to tell him that I had Derek and we'd made it safely back home.

Good, he texted back.

Then Derek and I sat down in the living room, and I asked if he was ready to call his parents. "I guess," he said. We had no idea what Debbie and Tom would say to Derek's request to stay with me for a few days, but all we could do was ask. I dialed

Tom's number and put the phone on speaker. "Tom, it's me," I said when he answered, holding the bottom of the phone close to my mouth. "I have Derek with me."

"What? Where? Put him on the phone."

"I'm about to," I said. "We're in Bakerstown at my place. He caught the greyhound to Charlotte and called me to come get him."

"He's at Annie's," Tom said to Debbie. "We're on our way—"

"No, Tom, don't come tonight. He doesn't want to come home just yet."

"I don't care what he wants—"

There was a ruffle on the other end and muted voices, then silence. "Annie? This is Debbie. Derek is with you?"

"Yes Debbie, I'll give him the phone now."

Derek took the phone off speaker and held it to his ear. "Hi Mom."

I stepped across the room to give him more privacy. Tom didn't sound like he'd considered anything that Debbie said at my parents' house, and I was a little taken aback that he was still being his rude self. Not that I'd expect a person to change overnight, but you'd think having your wife threaten to divorce you would be more than enough to take the edge off.

"I'm sorry, Mom. It wasn't about you."

I began to pray silently under my breath as I stood in the kitchen, far enough away to not seem like I was actively listening, but close enough to still hear Derek as he talked to his parents. I prayed for healing, for change, for perspective and understanding, not just for Tom, but for all of my family.

"I just want to stay here for a few more days and clear my head, and maybe you guys can come to Annie's service on Sunday and we can go home afterwards," I heard Derek say. "I want to hear her preach while I'm here."

After a few seconds, Derek looked at me and smiled and gave me a thumbs up from across the room. "Thanks Mom," he said. "I love you too. Hold on." Derek held the phone out for me. "Mom wants to talk to you."

I went to the phone. "Hey Debbie."

"Annie, thank you so much for going to get him from Charlotte. We really appreciate it. He says he wants to stay with you a few days. Is that okay with you? I don't want him to be a burden with you having to run a church and all."

"You're welcome, and Derek's no burden at all. He's welcome to stay. He may be a little bored here tomorrow, but something tells me he has a good, thick book in his book bag to keep him occupied until Sunday." Derek nodded his head beside me. "But I'll make sure he's well fed and safe until you guys get here on Sunday."

"Okay, thank you again, Annie. We'll be there bright and early on Sunday, and I too am looking forward to hearing your sermon. I think we all can use a good encouraging word at the end of a very stressful week. Love you."

"Love you too Debbie. I'll be glad to have you and Tom here."

"I think I'm going to go take a shower," Derek said after I'd hung up, picking up his bag. "Thanks for letting me hang out Aunt Annie."

"Anytime kid. Everything you need should be in the room. It has a walk-in bathroom. And feel free to help yourself to anything in the kitchen. If you text me a few of your favorite things to eat, I'll run by the grocery store in the morning and get them for you. And oh yeah, unblock your parents on your phone."

Derek sighed at the thought of being accessible to his parents again. "Tomorrow. I will unblock them tomorrow," he said. "Give me one more night of peace."

"Sounds like a deal."

I took the opportunity to shower also and told Derek goodnight before I looped my hair into a small bun on the top of my head and collapsed onto my bed. It had been a long day, and with the unexpected drive to Charlotte, I was exhausted, and looking forward to the first night of restful sleep since Derek ran away. I turned onto my side to get comfortable when my phone beeped on my nightstand: I had one unread text message from Tom.

Thank you sis, it said.

Chapter 33

Mom called me the next morning to check on Derek while I was at the grocery store picking up a few of his favorites. "I wanted to call last night, but it was late when Tom called to tell us the good news, and I figured you and Derek might be sleeping by then. How is he?"

"You figured right, Mom. We both crashed soon after. And physically, he's totally fine. I think he just rode the greyhound for a few days from stop to stop. Mentally, I'm not sure. He seems very exhausted with Tom's daily expectations of him. So, I'm not sure that he won't just leave again if he goes home and Tom is still his same old self."

"Well let's do some praying that he isn't. I had Dad give him a good talking too, so maybe he listened. It doesn't make sense to pester a child over something so unnecessary."

I had never heard my mother speak of Tom in this manner. I guess everyone had finally had enough. Derek's running away was the last straw.

"We're gonna come down too on Sunday, if you don't mind," she continued. "Janeen and Joey also."

"Whoa," I said. "Bringing the calvary, huh?" I'd have to make sure my sermon was extra good this week. I also quickly realized that it would be a good time for the family to meet John, since they'd all be here. It would save us at least one trip to Columbia now that we were seriously dating.

Mom read my mind. "Yes, we are, to support Derek *and* you. And it would be nice to meet your friend also."

I hung up with Mom, then finished grabbing the items for Derek: one box of Frosted Flakes cereal with milk, frozen hamburgers with buns, sliced cheese, apples and bananas, a big family-sized bag of Cool Ranch Doritos, and a gallon of unsweet tea. I knew he wouldn't be able to eat it all in just one day, but I wanted him to have a variety of choices to choose from.

Later that afternoon, as I sat in the church office adding some last-minute tweaks to Sunday's sermon, John stopped by with lunch since I had to cancel our date the night before.

"It seems that my entire family is coming to town to collect Derek tomorrow," I said. "And my mom mentioned wanting to finally meet you."

"Mm," John said between bites of his pimento cheese sandwich. "Yes, it's about time, huh. I'm looking forward to meeting your parents."

"Really? You're not nervous?"

"Nervous for what? By the way you've talked about your parents, they seem like really nice, loving, and supportive people. Besides, you've met my mom a long time ago, before me and you started dating, so this is probably overdue. I'm sure they'll love me." John looked at me and smiled, then turned serious. "I do have one question, though."

"Shoot," I said.

"What do your parents think of my being married before and having two kids already? I only ask because you never know how people will react to things like that."

"Sure. Well, I admit that I haven't really talked with them a bunch about that part, but they do know that you were married before and have the girls. I'm sure they know that you can't help being widowed."

John nodded his head as he took the last bite of his sandwich and crumpled the paper in his hands. "Well, they raised a wonderful woman that I'm blessed to have as my girlfriend, so I trust them. I'm sure it will be fine." He leaned over and gave me a kiss, then stood to leave. "Mind if I meet the kid before I go?"

"Sure thing." I packed up my things and John and I walked across the yard to the parsonage. Derek was still where I'd left him earlier, sprawled out on the living room sofa, his nose in a thick book. "Derek, this is my boyfriend John. He wanted to meet you."

"Hey Mr. John," Derek said.

"Nice to meet you, Derek. *Ready Player One* huh? Have you read *Snow Crash* or *Neuromancer*?"

Derek eyes lit up. "Not yet! There on my list, although I'm not sure if the library by my house has them."

"I have a copy of both of them at home just collecting dust. They're great books. How about I bring them to church tomorrow and you can have them? I don't need them anymore."

184

"Wow, thank you!" Derek said. He jumped up and shook John's hand.

As they chatted more about books, John glanced at my shocked expression and winked. I was sure there was nothing this man couldn't do, and I was happy that my parents and family would get to meet him tomorrow.

I woke early the next morning, more so from an inability to sleep than a desire to be well-prepared. Even though my entire family would be in the congregation listening to me preach today, I was confident in myself and the sermon I'd prepared. Still, having Derek and the family here today was enough of a wrinkle in my normal routine that I woke up one hour before my alarm was scheduled to sound, and could not fall back to asleep. I got up and fixed Derek breakfast before leaving him to get dressed and walked over to the church.

William was at his usual post, early and sitting in front of the piano, going through the songs for today's sermons. William's preparation was like that of a professional athlete. I knew that he'd already practiced these songs several times this week, as he did every week. But every Sunday he arrived earlier than anyone else to run through the selections one more time, all of the week's practice culminating in a near perfect execution during each service. I was grateful for his dedication to Covenant and our music ministry.

I spent some time in my office going over my sermon one more time, then went out into the sanctuary to greet the congregation as they arrived. Derek came over and sat in the pew closest to where I stood by the door, and when I saw my parents' and Tom's cars pull into the parking lot, I took a minute to sit down beside him to make sure he was okay and ready to face his parents.

"Hey bud," I said, sitting down beside him. "Looks like everyone is here. Are you okay?"

"Yes, Aunt Annie, I'm fine. Ready to get it all over with."

"Okay," I said. "I love you, and even though the circumstances were a little nerve-wrecking, I'm glad we got to

185

spend the last few days together. Maybe we can do it more often, minus the running away part."

Derek's eyes locked in on someone behind me, and I turned to see Debbie and Tom coming into the sanctuary. Debbie immediately spotted Derek and made a beeline for him, wrapping him in a long and tight hug as his siblings, Carson and Maddie, squealed in excitement and ran over to Derek. I could only imagine the relief and joy Debbie was feeling finally seeing her son and knowing that he was okay. Tom stood back as they embraced, then nodded and gave me a gentle pat on the arm before walking over to Derek just as Debbie let him go, wiping tears from her eyes.

"Hey son," Tom said as he gave Derek a quick hug, then let him go. "Glad you're okay."

"Thanks Dad," Derek said, looking down at the pew in front of him.

My parents were next, first hugging me, then walking over to Derek. Finally, my younger sister Janeen and her husband Joey came over and completed the family reunion. After I finished greeting everyone and they'd taken their seats, I made my way up to the pulpit just as William started his opening selection. As I sat down and looked out over the congregation, I felt very grateful to God to have both of my families at Covenant today: my blood family, who, during good and bad times, were still my family, something that a lot of people didn't have. And the Covenant family, who had, one day over two years ago, invited me to preach for them, then welcomed me into their circle with open arms.

With the family theme so prominent in my mind and thoughts this past week, I preached from Colossians 3:13: *"Bear with each other and forgive one another if any of you has a grievance against someone. Forgive as the Lord forgave you."*

"Normally when we hear that verse," I said from the pulpit, "what is the one word that rings loudest and the one word we tend to focus on? That's right: 'forgive.' We are taught a lot about forgiveness during our lifetime as Christians, and we should listen to that teaching. Forgiveness is crucial if you're going to make it through this life, because you will be wronged at some point. It's just the nature of humans that no one is perfect except our Lord and Savior Jesus Christ, and we all fall short of His glory. We all make mistakes, and whether we want to admit it or not, we all have done something to hurt or offend someone else. Maybe by something we said, or how we reacted to something *they* said, or something more serious. We all need forgiveness and we all need to *be* forgiven. But for the purposes of my message today, I want to focus on the beginning of the verse, specifically the first four words: 'Bear with each other.' Because in these words are the real key of being able to go on each day dealing with people. If some of us could have our way, we'd completely withdraw from the world and not have to deal with anyone. But God didn't design us that way. He designed us to need each other, and to live in communion with each other. When one person is down, there is someone else there to pick them up. God said it was not good for man to be alone. But what are we to do when we have relationships that are strained, or when people you can't necessarily disconnect yourself from, are doing their best to work your last nerve as my grandfather used to say? Bear with each other. God is asking us to hold on, to have mercy, to show grace, to have perspective and think of our own shortcomings, and most importantly, to forgive."

After I finished preaching, William sang "What a Friend We Have in Jesus" and I saw Debbie dabbing her eyes with a handkerchief with one hand, then reach over and grab Derek's hand with the other. I hoped the sermon was an encouragement to my family, and a reminder to all of us to hold our loved ones dear and always treat each other with love and respect. I couldn't really read Tom's face, as every time I'd glance at him during the sermon, his head would be down.

"Good preaching today, sis," my brother-in-law Joey said, the first person to greet me after the service. "I told Janeen we should move to Charlotte so we can come hear you more often. I think she's open to it," he said with a wink. From day one, Joey had always been supportive of me being a woman preacher in a denomination where I wasn't welcome. I was always grateful for his support, even if I'd wished the same support had come from my blood family instead of my in-laws.

"I think Charlotte's a great city," Janeen said. "Just not the one for us, dear. Great sermon today, sis. I'm proud of you."

I was a little embarrassed at the blush that spread across my face at my little sister's compliment. I thought Janeen and I had a good relationship, although we didn't get to see each other much now that we were both adults, and she had Joey and their kids, and I had the church. We'd never had the extremely close relationship that a lot of my female friends had with their own sisters, but our relationship had never been contentious either. But it meant the world to me that she'd come to Covenant to see me in my element, doing what I feel like was God's calling for my life and my life's work, and that she was proud of me.

"Hey there."

I'd somehow forgot all about John, and his voice startled me. He, Edna and Emily and Ella stood behind me. "Mom and Dad, you've already met Edna on your last visit," I said. "This is her son John, and his daughters, Emily and Ella."

"Hi girls," my mom said to the girls as my dad shook John's hand.

"So, you're the lucky guy, huh," Tom said, extending his hand and looking John up and down. "Nice to meet you. Annie says you're a lawyer?"

Mom must have told Tom about John's profession, because I certainly had not. It seemed that I hadn't been able to have a decent conversation with Tom in years.

"Yes, at a firm in Charlotte," John said. "I got a chance to hang out with Derek here a little bit yesterday. Sweet kid." John handed Derek the two books he promised him.

"Yes, he's a good kid," Tom said, eyeing the books. "We have some things to work on-," Tom paused as the words came out of his mouth—, "or maybe just me. But we're figuring it out."

That was the first time I'd heard firm confirmation that Tom was indeed thinking about himself and really considering how he'd contributed to Derek's running away and his frustrations. I knew the change in Tom wouldn't happen overnight but seeing the beginnings of what I hoped to be a fresh start for him and Derek—and my own relationship with Tom—made me happy on the inside.

"Well, while we're all together, we might as well eat," my dad said. "John, do you, Edna, and the girls care to join us at the diner here in town? Annie says they have great specials on Sundays."

"I can confirm that everything at Mary's Roadside Cafe is excellent," Edna said.

"And we'd love to join you," John added.

After I'd finished greeting the last remaining congregation members, we all piled into separate cars and headed over to Mary's. The small cafe was just the right size for Bakerstown. It was one of those small-town diners that served traditional southern meals and hadn't changed the menu in over forty years. There were people in Bakerstown that ate at Mary's three meals a day, and it was very popular on Sunday's after church. When I didn't want to cook my own meals at home or didn't care to drive outside of town for something fancier, or when I simply wanted a good old, home-cooked meal, I always found myself at Mary's.

The place was packed as usual, but there were several open picnic tables outside, so we all ordered our plates to go, then sat outside in the warm sunshine and enjoyed a nice Sunday dinner with family and good food.

Chapter 34

The kickoff day for the garden had finally arrived, and I got up early to dress and walk over to the church to meet Edward before the volunteers started to arrive. Of course, as I locked the front door to the parsonage, Edward's car was already in the parking lot. It was seven in the morning. I walked over to the west side of the church and found Edward and his wife Mai separately walking around the large space where the gardens would go. Mai had her arms in the air, palms out, and her lips were moving.

"Good morning, Reverend," Edward said with a low voice. "We thought we'd come over and pray over the site before the construction starts today. Care to join us?"

"Of course, I would." How thoughtful it was for them to cover the area in prayer before we began work on the project. God was constantly keeping me in awe at the spiritual knowledge and power that resided inside the members of Covenant Baptist church. I separated from Edward and drifted off to the middle area where the gazebo was supposed to go and began to pray silently. I asked God to bless the entire land, to bless our efforts in creating the space, and for His spirit to rest over the area and the church. I prayed that it would be a place of peace, growth, life, new beginnings, and fond memories of our loved ones who had already gone Home to be with Him. I also prayed a more practical prayer for funds for the gazebo, even though Edward was confident it would all work out somehow. We still had not been able find a prebuilt gazebo or someone to build it within the budget range, and I was starting to worry that maybe we'd have to go without one. Edward was still standing in faith, believing in God for provision, so I asked God to help my unbelief and give me the faith that Edward had to believe that He would provide it if was really meant to be a part of the garden.

Ben was the next person to arrive, and I stopped walking to chat with him. His court date was coming up in the next week, and I wanted to make sure he was still in a good mindset to be here today.

"Hey Ben. Good morning," I said when he walked up.

"Morning Annie. I'm okay." Ben gave me a teasing glance. "I know you're wondering whether I'm still up for this today, and the answer is yes. I can't shut down my life while this custody stuff is going on. Besides, it helps to keep my mind busy and working on something. I fully believe God led you guys to ask me to help supervise this project so that I could focus on helping His people and doing His work down here, and let Him focus on the things I have zero control over. It's a trust exercise. So yes, I need and want to be here."

"Sounds good, Ben. We need you too. I think Edward asked the volunteers to be here at nine, and if I know this group like I think I do, they will be on time and ready to work."

I left Ben and Edward to their last-minute discussions and went to find coffee. I still needed to ask Ben about officiating Heather and Dawn's wedding but had decided to wait until after the upcoming court date. If Ben didn't get a favorable decision about custody of his kids, I wasn't sure what state of mind he would be in.

By 8:30, the parking lot really started to fill up, and I helped Mary LeBlanc set up a breakfast table with fruit, muffins, breakfast bars, water, orange juice, and coffee. Lunch was also being provided today with sandwich boxes donated from a local eatery in town. By nine, just as I predicted, there were thirty-five Covenant members lounging around the build site, and several more at the donations and materials area organizing the pile. People had bought plants and seeds of all kinds, some already in bloom or starting to grow: azaleas, tomatoes, Snowmaiden, lilies, roses, peppers, collards, cabbage, onions, Calendula, and many others.

There were also small trees, even a Japanese cherry blossom. It was much too early to plant some of these, like the tomatoes, so Edward and Ben had gotten together with a small group of four people to determine what plants and seeds they had, what could be planted now and what needed to wait until it warmed up. Finally, they made a schedule for when each variety was to be planted. All the plants sat next to piles of two by fours and other various sizes and colors of wood, bags of mulch, garden tools, gloves, twelve benches, decorative stones, and lines of black hoses for irrigation. Edward had produced a supplies list for each of the members, and a lot of them had taken the initiative to go out and buy items on their own to donate to the cause. Once again, I was overwhelmed at how blessed I was to get the opportunity to lead this wonderful congregation.

I looked around at the faces in the waiting crowd and was happy that I recognized almost everyone that was there, and that they'd all come out to support the project: Mary and her son Damien LeBlanc, Elizabeth and Lucille Smith, Harry and Earlene Williams, Fred, Edith and Belinda Miller, Vivian Artz, Heather Artz, and Dawn Fisk, Elena, Julio and Carlita Alvarez, Wayne and Anita Fleming, Elinor Bisgby, Alan and Faye Emerson, Danny and Erin O'Reilly, William Owens, Pete Stoudamire, Jesse and Lorraine, and of course, Edna and John. Every church has a core group of members, that support the church day in and day out, and I realized that this group standing before me was Covenant's core, it's heart.

I beckoned for Ben to blow his whistle, and everyone fell silent and walked over to us. "Good morning everyone," I said. "I want to officially kick off this garden build today by saying thank you for being here as we build what we hope will be a place that all of us will be able to enjoy as a family for generations to come…"

Chapter 35

"I'm nervous about tomorrow," Ben said as he sat in a camping chair at the garden site. He'd come over before his shift at the grocery store this afternoon to get a few hours of work in, and I'd stepped outside during a break in my day to check on him. The group had worked for seven hours under Ben's supervision on the kickoff day and gotten a ton of work done. The garden had already taken shape, and I could envision how great it would look once it was finally finished.

"That's understandable, Ben." I almost admitted to Ben that I was a little nervous for him also, but I didn't think that would help him feel more confident, so I kept it to myself. "I think it's normal to be nervous with your big day coming up tomorrow. Just try to think positive and keep your faith in God, and trust that He will work everything out for the best of all parties. I know that's easier said than done."

"Yes, easier said than done, but still the correct advice," Ben said. "Thank you, Annie. You know, of all of the pastors I knew and fellowshipped with for years in my 'old' life, their isn't one left that I can call on now as a friend. Not one. All I have is you, and I'm so thankful to God for pointing me to you and Covenant. When I was living out on the street and in that homeless shelter, I couldn't see anything in my future. It was just blank. Now that I'm a little more stable and back on my feet, I can start to envision a new and different life for me, where I'm fully living in my truth and finally being myself. So, in a way, this all happened for a reason, I guess. Like Roman 8:28 says, all things work together for our good. *All* things."

"All things indeed," I said to Ben. "You'll do fine tomorrow, just be yourself and tell the truth. And prayerfully God will give you favor in the eyes of the judge. I'll be there for support, and no matter what happens, hold on to that Romans verse. He won't fail you."

The next morning, I arrived at the courthouse early, as I wanted to beat the morning traffic heading into downtown Charlotte and wanted to find a legal parking spot so I didn't risk getting a ticket. Although Ben's instructions that he'd received in the mail stated that he must arrive and be checked in by 8 a.m., that didn't mean his case would be heard at that time, and he should be prepared to be at the courthouse all day. I'd cleared my schedule for the day, telling Edna where I'd be, and brought along a romance novel that I'd picked up in the grocery store. I met Ben, John and Mark in the parking lot, and we all walked into the courthouse together, first passing through a long security line, then catching the elevator up to the fifth floor and finally taking a seat in the back of Courtroom 5B. An African American woman— Judge Whilemina Reed—sat down on the bench. Lawyers and people shuffled in and out of the courtroom as cases were heard back to back and out in the open for anyone in the courtroom to hear.

I'd taken a seat on the row directly behind the three men, opting to give them some privacy as they prepared for the hearing. As I looked around, I realized that this was my first time sitting inside a real courtroom, and hopefully my last. The place was serious and intimidating yet set up exactly like every courtroom you see on television. To John and Mark, this more likely felt like a second home. The fate of lives was decided here within these four walls every day, and the realization of this caused me to pray for favor in Ben's case like never before.

The door to the courtroom opened behind me, and when I saw Ben quickly glance at the woman who entered with her lawyer, then immediately look down into his lap, I knew the woman must be his wife Hannah. The woman sat down on the opposite side of the courtroom, listening as her lawyer whispered something to her, then nodded and stared straight ahead. It wasn't polite to ever tell a woman that she looked tired, but in that moment, Hannah Merriweather definitely looked weary. Her eyes were puffy, and her shoulders slumped as she sat. I could not imagine being in her shoes, having been married to a man for so long and created a family with him, only to have her world shattered and turned upside down with Ben's sudden revelation. There were truly no winners in Ben and Hannah's situation, and I felt deep sympathy for her, despite her attempting to keep Ben away from their children.

194

I listened as cases were heard by the judge: one woman who was denied custody of her daughter because of several arrests and previous drug abuse; a young Hispanic couple who was there to have their child support agreement adjusted now that the father had a higher paying job; and a lesbian couple who had adopted a daughter together but had recently separated. When the two women and their lawyers were presenting their case before the judge, Ben turned around to me and raised his eyebrows in surprise. As he was turning back around, someone who had entered the court room caught his eye, and Ben suddenly stood and looked at an older couple now standing in the aisle like he knew them. The couple looked at Ben with serious faces, then turned away and sat down on the bench beside Hannah. Ben's face turned red as if he'd been struck, then sat down and stared straight ahead as John whispered something to him. "They're my parents," Ben whispered back.

"Merriweather vs. Merriweather," the court attendant called out. We'd waited just over two hours.

John, Mark, and Ben stood and waited for Hannah and her attorney to walk to the front first, then followed them down the aisle and through the low, wooden door-gate that separated the main court area from the benches in the back. They all sat down at the table on the right side of the court, opposite where Hannah and her attorney sat on the left.

"This is a hearing to determine a custody agreement between a Hannah Merriweather and a Ben Merriweather, correct?" the judge said, her eyes skimming through the documents handed to her by the court attendant.

"Correct," both lawyers replied solemnly.

"Are the two still married?"

"The plaintiff, Mrs. Merriweather, has filed for divorce your honor," Hannah's lawyer said. "It has not been finalized yet."

"So, the parties are separated."

"Yes, your honor."

"And I see that Mrs. Merriweather is asking for sole and permanent custody, on the grounds of 'emotional abuse and religious beliefs.'" The judge raised an eyebrow from the papers she just read and looked at Hannah, then over at Ben.

195

"Yes, your honor." Hannah's lawyer shuffled on his feet.

"What evidence do we have to support the plaintiff's claim, Mr. Abernathy?" The judge said, as she shuffled through the papers again. "Am I missing documents here?"

"There should be a written statement there your honor, from Ms. Merriweather, detailing the events that lead to the Merriweather's divorce filing."

"I see it." The courtroom was silent as Judge Reed read the statement. I could see Ben's leg shaking under the table as they all waited for the judge to finish reading. Finally, Judge Reed finished reading the document, re-stacked the papers into a neat pile and looked out into the courtroom. "Mr. Abernathy, am I correct that the 'emotional abuse' the plaintiff is claiming—and I guess for that matter, the religious beliefs also—is based solely on Mr. Merriweather's changing, or discovering rather, his sexual orientation?"

"Your honor, we believe that Mr. Merriweather's sudden change of sexual orientation and his abandoning of his family represents mental instability, and that he is not in any healthy state of mind to be able to have any contact or custody of the two children—'

"Your honor," Mark stood and interrupted his counterpart. "Mr. Merriweather did not 'abandon' his family. He was asked to leave by Mrs. Merriweather after he confided in her about his true sexual orientation, a request that he immediately granted her for the sake of his family's mental health. He was also fired from his job as a pastor at Woodmont Baptist Church, which we admit temporarily left him without a place to stay and a steady job to provide income. He has since been able to secure a job at a grocery store in Bakerstown and has had his own apartment for six months."

"Mm," Judge Reed said, looking through the papers again. "And religious beliefs, I take it since Mr. Merriweather was a pastor, that you both are Christians, correct?"

"Yes," both Ben and Hannah said almost in unison.

"And you're both still Christians?"

"Yes, I am," Ben said.

The judge looked at Hannah. "And you?"

"Yes," Hannah said.

"So," Judge Reed, setting down the stack of papers and removing her reading glasses. "It seems that there are really no real differences in religious beliefs here, despite homosexuality being a controversial subject within the Christian faith. The court will not get into who is right or wrong in that debate. Not this court, anyway. So, what we're left here is the issue of emotional abuse, which I have no evidence of, and seems to be related to Mr. Merriweather's coming out as gay. Mrs. Merriweather, the court can't deny Mr. Merriweather his parental rights simply because of his sexual orientation, and you haven't presented any other evidence that proves he has been abusive to you in the past during your marriage. In fact," —Judge Reed picked up the personal statement and slid her eyeglasses on—, "you state here in your statement that during your marriage, he was a great father and husband to you. Is that correct?"

"Yes ma'am, he was. I just think it will be best for our boys if he didn't have visitation. I don't want them to be influenced—"

"Mrs. Merriweather, again, by your own admission, your husband is not a murderer or an abuser. He's simply gay—or whatever his preferred label is—and your children are his children too. Unless you can prove he has physically harmed you or the kids, or emotionally harmed them, or is a danger to them, he has a right to custody and visitation. I will grant you as the *physical* custodian of the two children, which simply means that they live with you full time, but Mr. Merriweather is granted visitation every other weekend and during the summers, as requested here in his counter-filing. Holidays will be split between the two of you, and a schedule can be agreed upon in advance with the help of a court appointed arbitrator, if you two should need it. Mr. Merriweather is also granted joint legal custody, which means he retains his decision-making rights for the needs of the children, as do you." Hannah nodded her head as her lawyer Mr. Abernathy leaned over and whispered something into her ear.

"Mr. Merriweather, when is the last time you've seen you children?" The judge asked Ben directly.

"Um," Ben looked over at John and Mark and then back at the judge. "I guess it's been since I left home, fifteen months ago.

I've tried calling to get them, but," Ben looked over at Hannah, who dropped her eyes to her lap.

"Mrs. Merriweather," Judge Reed looked directly at Hannah, a bite in her voice now. "Please present Mr. Merriweather's children to him within twenty-four hours for a brief three hour, unsupervised visit, with his every-other-weekend visits beginning on this Friday at five o'clock p.m., lasting through Sunday evening at the same hour, five o'clock p.m. Is your client prepared to present the children to Mr. Merriweather this evening, Mr. Abernathy?"

Hannah's lawyer looked down at her and shook his head to confirm. "Yes, your honor," he said.

"Excellent," Judge Reed said. "Anything else?"

"No, your honor," both Mark and Mr. Abernathy said.

Hannah and her attorney exited the courtroom first, and I could be wrong, but the look on her face looked more like relief than anger, like she was simply glad this entire ordeal was behind them somewhat. I wondered if she'd ever really wanted to keep the children from Ben, or just had been receiving bad advice from someone. Or if she initially thought it was the right thing to do, then had a change of heart. I hoped that she and Ben could now start a new reality and a new relationship, one that was cordial and respectful and centered on their children and both their healings.

Ben was all smiles and tears, and he shook Mark and John's hands profusely before they all walked back down the aisle towards the exit. After he was on the other side of the partition, he stopped walking as his mother made her way past the couple sitting at the end of the bench she and her husband were sitting on and out into the aisle.

"Mother," Ben said.

The original Mrs. Merriweather walked up to her son and started to hug him, then stopped herself and clasped her hands in front of her. "I am so sorry, son."

Her words were like a dam breaking to Ben, who hunched over and wrapped his arms around his mother—who was at least a full foot shorter than Ben's 6'2 frame—and the two sobbed quietly in the aisle before a court attendant quietly motioned them out into the hallway. Ben's father stood and watched without saying a word or attempting to approach Ben, then slowly followed his wife and son out into the hallway.

Outside the courtroom, I waited off to the side while John and Mark huddled with Ben by the large floor-to-ceiling windows that overlooked downtown Charlotte. I could see all types of people down on the street walking or driving to their various destinations. It had been over two years since I'd moved to Bakerstown to be the pastor at Covenant, and sometimes I missed the hustle and bustle of living in the city, and being within five to ten minutes of any type of food or convenience that I wanted. But I knew that Covenant was the place for me at this time in my life, and that maybe one day I'd live in a city again.

They all shook hands again, then broke their huddle as Mark walked down the hallway toward the elevator and Ben and John walked over to me.

"Thanks again for being here, Annie," Ben said. "Even though I ended up not needing you to testify for me. Looks like I'm going to be able to see my boys tonight for a couple hours!" The elation on Ben's face was contagious.

"That's wonderful Ben. I'm glad I could be here with you for moral support. Looks like you have pretty good lawyers," I said.

John lightly nudged me on the shoulder with a closed fist. "Not really," he said. "I think Ben's character speaks for himself and beat us to the courtroom today. They really didn't have much of a case to begin with, but it's always good to be overly prepared just in case."

"Well, I'm grateful for you guys," Ben said. "I would have been lost without you both. And you gave me back one of the few good things I have going right now, which is my boys. So, thank you. I'm just glad we got a judge that understands my situation."

"Yes, Judge Reed is a good judge, but it's not about understanding in most cases. It's simply about the law. And being gay is not a crime in this country, contrary to popular belief in some circles," John said.

"Well, thanks again," Ben said. "I'm gonna head on over to the boys' school and wait for them. The agreement for today is for me to pick them up from school and spend three hours with them, then drop them off back at Hannah's. I'm gonna take them to one of our favorite burger places here in the city, then maybe to an arcade or something. I'll see you guys back in town." Ben waived again as he walked down the hallway toward the elevator.

"I have an hour or so before I need to be back at the office," John said to me after Ben disappeared behind the closing elevator doors. "Want to grab a bite to eat?"

"I'd love to."

"Great. There's a hole-in-the-wall sushi place that's pretty awesome only a few blocks from here. Shall we?"

John grabbed my hand as we walked through the courthouse. I was first shocked at his public display of affection: I'm sure John was a regular here and that many people here had possibly known his wife. But us holding hands didn't seem to bother him as he said goodbye to people as we left, so I tried to quiet my mental thoughts and not let it bother me, either.

Chapter 36

Now that Spring had arrived, Ben had won his court case, and the garden was taking shape, my spirits were on a natural high. Mom had even told me that things seemed to be getting better with Tom and Derek. Things with John were still great too. The change in seasons was truly bringing about new beginnings everywhere I turned.

I had worked on finalizing my Sunday sermon all morning, then took a break at eleven to run to the grocery store, because when I'd looked in my fridge that morning to pack my lunch, it was completely empty except for a carton of eggs and a bag of fresh spinach. My plan was to only grab a few items to hold me over until Saturday morning, when I'd pick up my full grocery list while out running errands.

I grabbed two microwavable dinners, a loaf of bread, sliced turkey from the deli, cheese, and a frozen tray of lasagna. I loaded the grocery bags into my trunk, closed it, and climbed behind the wheel. I'd just buckled my seat belt and put the car in reverse when my cell phone rang in my purse beside me. I shifted the car back in park, grabbed my purse and dug inside until I found the ringing phone. I didn't recognize the number on the screen, and I had half a mind not to answer it, but as the pastor of a church with members who sometimes needed me, I didn't really have that luxury. I pressed the green circle and answered: "Hello, this is Annie."

"Reverend Annie? This is Belinda Miller."

"Belinda, hey. How are you?"

"Not so good right now. I'm at the Forrest Brothers chicken plant on Highway 33. ICE just raided the plant."

"WHAT?"

"Yes." Belinda sounded jittery and out of breath. "There are ICE agents all over the place, and they've pulled a big white school bus into the parking lot. I think they are going to take people into custody. Annie, if I had to guess, there are a lot of undocumented immigrants inside, and this is also where Julio and Carlita Alvarez work."

"What? NO! NO, NO, NO!" I banged my hand on the steering wheel in front of me and screamed. How could this be happening? I've seen these ICE raids—Immigrations and Customs Enforcement— on the news a few times, but never imagined one happening in Bakerstown and with people I knew. I was paralyzed with fear for Julio, Carlita, and all the other workers in the plant. When Belinda and I had visited their home last year, Julio had expressed to us that he and his family were not citizens, and that their worse fear was being deported and sent to a country that was not their home. He'd expressed his love for America and his desire to stay and continue to build a life here for his kids. My heart raced with fear as I imagined the terror Julio and Carlita must be feeling at this very moment.

"What do we do Belinda?" I said, now desperate. "Is there someone we can call? Wait, I'll call John, maybe he'll know what to do. What is the address of the plant? I'm coming down there." My mind was racing a mile a minute as I sat in the car. I'm sure I was only adding to Belinda's stress as opposed to helping dissolve it like a good pastor would.

"The address is 902 Highway 33 South, Bakerstown. We've called the media and a group in Charlotte who works to stop ICE raids and informs undocumented immigrants about their rights. They should be here soon."

"Okay. I'm not sure what help I can be but I'm on my way."

"Thanks Annie, I'm sure your presence and prayers will go a long way."

I hung up with Annie and immediately dialed John and activated the Bluetooth in my car so I could head toward the plant.

"Hey baby," he said when he answered, his voice surrounding me in the car.

"John."

"What's wrong?"

"The chicken plant here in Bakerstown is being raided by ICE agents as we speak. I'm on my way there. A family who occasionally visits Covenant works there."

"Oh my. I'm not an immigration lawyer, but I know one down the hall. I'm not too busy right now. I'll see if I can grab him and head down."

202

"Thank you, John. I'm sorry to keep calling you as my lawyer friend."

"It's okay, I'll never complain about a call from you. Is it the plant on 33?"

"Yes, Forrest Brothers."

"Okay, on my way."

"Okay, love you."

"Love you too. See you in a few. And hey, calm down and drive safe. And don't talk to the agents. They can be a bit chippy."

"Got it."

I hung up the phone and started praying, which I figured was the only effective weapon I had to use at the moment. But before I could start, I realized that I didn't quite know what to pray, and that I was actually torn between two thoughts. The first thought being that I didn't want to see Julio and Carlita or *anyone* rounded up like animals and separated from their families, kept in cages or detention centers and not properly cared for, especially people who weren't criminals or a danger to society in any way, but who simply wanted to create a life here and give their kids opportunities that they never had. The opposing thought was that the United States was a country of laws, like any country, and there were processes in place that everyone should do their best to abide by to become a legal citizen of this country. If immigrants didn't abide by those laws, was it right for our government to detain them and deport them? I didn't know the answer to my wrestling thoughts, and this was a debate that had been discussed for longer than I'd been alive, and more intelligent people than me had still not come to a definite conclusion about what side was right. So, I decided to do what always seemed to be the best option: not try to determine which side was right or wrong, but pray about the situation and allow God to do what only He could do—love and protect everyone involved and guide me to always try to do the right thing by His people.

"God," I finally began, "I don't know what to do or say right now. I know everyone at that plant is terrified right now, and I know that there are people there like Julio and Carlita who have a relationship with You and are depending on You for their deliverance and safety. Please be at the plant right now Father. Be with the immigrants and their families. Calm the fears of Your people and make a way for them. Send them resources to help them in their fight to stay in this great country. And yes, also be with the ICE agents that are there just doing their jobs Father. Soften their hearts toward Your people, help them to be kind and gentle, as if the people they are detaining were their own loved ones. Your will be done. Lastly, give me the courage to stand up for Your people, and guide me, Covenant, and everyone else in the community as to what You would have us do. In Jesus name I ask these things. Amen."

I was still rattled with fear and uncertainty after I finished praying, and I did my best to calm down as I got closer to plant. When I was only a few minutes away, several police sirens wailed behind me, the sound getting louder and louder as they approached, and I pulled over to let them pass. I only made it one more mile before I was forced to pull over and park on the right side of the road. Traffic around the plant was at a standstill, with news vans and vehicles of all kinds pulled over on the grassy shoulder on both sides of Highway 33. I made sure that I'd pulled my car fully out of the way of passing traffic, then hid my purse in the backseat and hopped out, careful not to get hit by any passing cars. There were several people walking to the plant as I was, and some held signs of support for the immigrants and against ICE. The police had taped off the Forrest Brothers parking lot, and the protestors could only stand on the opposite side of the road to express their concerns. Two news reporters that I recognized from television both stood with their backs facing the plant, their cameramen's eyes glued to the camera as the reporters held a microphone and spoke directly into the lens.

I walked behind the cameras, careful not to walk into a live television shot. The last time I was on television for an interview to promote the Family Day event at Covenant two years ago, it didn't go so well. I wasn't eager to be caught on camera again. I scanned the growing crowd of people for Belinda. I had less distance to travel than John, so I was sure I'd beat him there. I estimated that there were already about one hundred people in the group of supporters.

"Annie!" I heard someone yell behind me.

Belinda grabbed my hand and pulled me away from the crowd further into the open grassy land opposite the plant. When we were far enough away from the chants of the crowd and could hear each other, Belinda dropped to her knees and buried her face in her hands, unable to hold her sobs in anymore. Seeing Belinda so distraught broke me down also, and I couldn't do anything but drop down to the grass with her and wrap my arms around her as she shook.

"I can't believe this is happening!" Belinda yelled through tears as she looked at the plant. "Some of those people may never see their families again!"

"Is there anything we can do, Belinda? John and possibly his immigration lawyer partner are on the way."

"Now that ICE has already raided the plant, there isn't much we can do besides make sure everyone has good representation when their case is heard before a judge. The power of the people in the immigration fight is *before* ICE shows up, where we teach people their rights and what the agents can and cannot do under the law. Then, they are more knowledgeable about what is legal and what is not, and not so prone to just believe anything the agents say. And they can stop themselves from being detained in the first place. Once you're detained, it's super hard to get out again and not be deported. I'm not sure what John and his friend can do at this point, but it's always good to have as many lawyer minds here as possible to hopefully cover all the bases and plot out next steps."

The crowd had started to chant, and the ICE agents waiting across the street looked over at the group and shook their heads. There were family and friends of the plant workers now arriving and joining the group also, and I tried my best to comfort anyone that I saw crying or with a worried look on their face. As we continued to wait, I noticed the priest from St. Michael's—a small Catholic Church here in Bakerstown where a lot of the Hispanic community worshipped—walking through the crowd and hugging people he recognized.

"Annie! Belinda!"

John came running across the grass, his navy-blue tie loosened around his neck and flapping against the sky blue collared shirt he had on. A man who looked much younger than John jogged a few steps behind him, glancing over his shoulder at the commotion going on at the plant.

"We got here as fast as we could," John said. "This is Timothy. He's our resident immigration lawyer at the firm."

"Hi Timothy," I said. "Please tell me there is something we can do to help them."

"I'm not sure there is at this point, besides making sure they have representation for their hearing and making sure no one who has the proper papers is detained. I'm gonna go see if I can get some info from them." Timothy peeled away and jogged across the street. A police officer blocked his path, then after a few moments of talking with Timothy, stepped aside and allowed him to pass.

We waited as more and more people showed up to support the immigrants, and even with John there, I still felt pretty powerless. I was in constant prayer—whispering prayers under my breath for the people inside and for anyone I saw in the waiting group who looked distressed or was crying—but the prayer didn't feel like enough. Barring a bona fide, Old Testament miracle from God, anyone who was undocumented in that plant was going to be detained and based on the latest news and the current political climate, the majority of them would most likely be deported to somewhere they hadn't seen or lived in in years. In Julio and Carlita's case, ten. My faith at the moment that Julio and Carlita would be released was tiny, almost non-existent, but I knew that tiny faith was all I needed for God to work.

When the crowd erupted in yells, we all looked across the road. Two ICE agents—muscular men with black vests with "ICE" on the front in white letters—led a long line of people out of the plant and toward the waiting white school bus. Men and women of all ages, and who all looked to be of Hispanic decent, walked in a single file line behind the two officers as more agents emerged from the building, flanking the line on its sides. Chants of "LET THEM GO! LET THEM GO!" rang out from the angry crowd as others called on the names of their loved ones as the line continued to emerge, soon snaking from the school bus door to back into the building. I followed Belinda and John to the curb to get a closer look. Seeing the line of people walk to the waiting bus broke my heart, but the women's faces were what really drained all the emotions I had out of me. Most of their faces were red and puffy, their eyes swollen from crying. Screams erupted from the crowd around us as people recognized their family members in the line. At that moment I felt so helpless, so powerless to do anything to stop what was happening to them. Many families would be destroyed, and I couldn't help but wonder what would happen to them and their children and what long term effects this would have for generations to come. I couldn't imagine being separated from my parents when I was a young child. I wanted to be angry, but I didn't know who to be angry at.

"Julio!" Belinda yelled, waving frantically. "Carlita!"

I searched the line for a familiar face, and finally found Julio, his shoulders drooped, and his head hung as he walked, a look of sadness on his face. Behind him was Carlita, whose head was high and her eyes searching as she peered in our direction for the person yelling her name.

"Carlita!" Belinda yelled again, louder this time.

Carlita's eyes found and locked on Belinda's. "¡Lleva a mis hijos a Elena!" she yelled.

"¡Claro, ya me voy!" Belinda yelled back. "¡Ya voy!"

"What did she say?" I asked.

"She asked that her children go to Elena, her cousin," Belinda said between sniffs as she wiped tears from her eyes. "I think she is a member of Covenant."

Elena *was* a member; she had spoken to our church group one night when we'd invited members of the community who the church has traditionally shunned to speak to us. They talked about their feelings about church in general and how Covenant could better serve them. Because of her, Julio and Carlita had come out to our Family Day event and then occasionally visited Covenant when they weren't attending St. Michael's.

The crowd waited until the last person had entered the bus, and someone announced that they counted roughly fifty-five people in the line that had been detained. Timothy was still across the road, speaking with a female ICE agent. He finished his

207

conversation with her, then looked both ways as he trotted back toward the road and walked over to a waiting group of family members who stepped toward him, then began speaking to them in Spanish.

"They're taking them to the detention center in North Charlotte for now," Belinda translated for John and me, "and anyone who doesn't get out will be taken down the road to the big facility in South Carolina."

"We need people to go to the schools!" Timothy yelled out over to the rest of waiting protestors in English. "There are going to be kids whose parents won't be there to pick them up in a few hours. They'll have to stay at the school until a loved one picks them up. If you are a relative of someone who has been detained, please go to the schools. They will release the children to a relative if the parent has been detained. Bring food for the children! If you are a counselor or know any, please go to the schools!"

The crowd suddenly split in all directions, with people pulling cell phones from their pockets and dialing numbers and running to their cars.

"Yes, you heard right," a man said walking next to me. "Twenty extra-large cheese pizzas."

"Hey bro. Bring the truck over to Bakerstown Elementary now," another guy said to his phone as he held it out in front of him. I could see the person's face on the phone screen as he walked. "The Feds just raided the chicken plant and fifty people got caught."

"What? ¡Mierda!" the person responded.

"Looks like several people are getting food," John said. "How about water? We can get some from the grocery store a mile back on the corner."

"That's a great idea, John! I bet they'll also have a case of those Hug juices we used to drink as a kid."

"Actually, John," Timothy said. "You and I need to follow that ICE bus and make sure the people have representation as they enter the facility."

"Gotcha. Annie, can you and Belinda get the drinks and go over to the school?"

"Yes, you guys go on," Belinda said. "I'm trying to get Elena on the phone now for Carlita. Annie, can you get the drinks and meet me at the school?"

"I'm on it. See you at the school."

John waved goodbye as he ran to catch up with Timothy as they rushed to John's car. I waved back, then reached my car fairly quickly, but with all of the cars trying to pull back on to the road and make U-turns in the middle of Highway 33, I found myself waiting for all the cars parked directly around me to leave first. While I waited, I called Elizabeth back at the church, briefed her on what was going on, and informed her that I would probably not be back this afternoon. It took about a full ten minutes, but I was finally able to make my own U-turn and head to the local grocery store, Adams Grocery. I bought five cases of water, and just as I predicted, they had the signature yellow boxes of assorted Hug juices that I'd drink as a kid growing up in Mississippi. I grabbed five boxes of those also and loaded them into the buggy and pushed my cart up to the cash register. The owner of the store, seventy-five-year-old Mr. Hawk Adams, took one look at the cart and held up his hand. "I'll come around and scan them, save you and me both some hassle," he said.

He walked around the counter, reached back over it and grabbed the scanner, then slowly and meticulously began to scan each one. "Having a party?" he asked, bending over to reach the Hug boxes.

"I wish, but no," I said. "Headed over the elementary school to feed some kids that may be there for a while."

Mr. Adams stopped scanning and stood upright. "This about the raid at the chicken plant?"

"Yes sir," I said hesitantly as I tried to read his face, unsure of what his response would be. These days, you never knew what side of the coin people fell on when it came to hot-button political issues, and even though it was good manners to not talk about politics or religion if you wanted to keep a friendship or a conversation cordial, due to the nature of my job, I always seemed to gravitate toward the fire instead of away from it.

"Go on then," he grunted, jutting the scanner towards the door then setting it back on the counter. "On the house."

209

"Mr. Adams, that's a nice gesture. But are you sure?"

"I'm sure," he said, now back behind the counter. He took a seat on a tall black stool that sat directly in front of the cigarettes. "Had a nice young fellow that worked for me a few years back before those boys caught up with him. He was a hard worker and never bothered nobody. I wish they'd just leave those people alone. Go on, get to the kids."

"Thank you so much sir!" I wheeled the cart towards the door.

"You're welcome. Trey there will help you load them in your car." For the first time I noticed a teenaged boy with shaggy hair standing by the door with a red apron on. He took the buggy from me and wheeled it outside, and I stopped in the doorway to find my keys.

"And now that I know you're legit," Mr. Adams called after me after I pressed the key fob to unlock the car, "I'll be sure to stop by your church sometime."

I turned to Mr. Adams, who tipped an imaginary hat. I was floored. "Thank you for your kind words Mr. Adams, and I'll be waiting to see you at Covenant whenever you'd like to stop by."

Mr. Adams nodded again, and it was all I could do to keep myself from crying as Trey loaded the last package of water into the backseat and shut the door. I gave him a $10 tip, which was the least I could do since I hadn't paid for the beverages. Then I hauled them over to the elementary school.

It was 2:30 p.m. when I arrived, and traffic was once again backed up leading to the Bakerstown Elementary. I wasn't sure if this was normal end-of-school day traffic, or if some of it was people coming to support the kids. The school also shared a campus with Bakerstown Middle School, and I could see two Mexican food trucks already lined up between the two schools, with several adults carrying what looked to be pizza boxes and walking into a set of open double doors on the side of the school.

As I inched closer, I could see a school crossing guard directing traffic, talking to drivers through their rolled-down windows and doing her best to determine where cars should go.

"What are you here for, ma'am?" she asked when it was my turn at the front of the line.

210

"I brought drinks for the kids who may be waiting a while for someone to pick them up."

"Straight up the hill all the way to the back. Don't block the bus lanes."

I did as I was told and followed the cars in front of me to the back of the campus, then parked in the first available parking spot I saw, which was nowhere near close to the open double doors I saw people carrying food into. I thought about getting back into my car to drive around to the door, unload the water, then park again, but the only available lane that looked clear was the bus lane, and I had no intentions of defying the crossing guard lady. So, I opened the trunk, threw my purse inside—minus the keys—grabbed two boxes of juice and followed the crowd. Once inside, there was already a large pile of donations growing in the corner of the lunchroom and I asked two men if they could help me unload the rest from my car.

"Of course," one of them said. "Let me grab a dolly."

We were able to get the rest of the beverages with one trip by stacking them one on top of another on the dolly, and after seeing them to the donation pile and thanking the men, I scanned the room for Belinda. I found her sitting on the floor of the theater stage that took up one entire wall of the lunchroom, her arm draped over the back of someone who was bent over, their head in their hands. When the person sat up, I could see it was Elena Sanchez. I walked over to them, and when Elena saw me, she hopped down off the stage and reached her arms out wide for a hug.

"Pastor Annie, thank you for being here. Our worse fear has come to pass," Elena said. "I don't know what to do? What am I going to tell the kids?"

"We're going to fight it, Elena," Belinda said, now standing beside Elena. "Try to have hope. All isn't lost yet. Let's see what the lawyers say when you talk to them."

"And Covenant is here for you. As everything settles down and you adjust to having the kids, please let us know what we can do. We will assist however we can."

Elena sat up and stared out into space. "Thank you. And Belinda, you are right. I have to be strong for them, for the kids.

211

Thank God I am an American citizen, otherwise the kids would go in state custody. Family is everything to our people."

The bell rang signaling the end of school, and the cafeteria fell quiet. Counselors and DCS staff—Department of Children's Services—stood among the family members, everyone somber but ready to receive the children and break the news to them about their parents. Laughter, shouts, and the general sound of children playing filled the hallways as the schoolteachers led their students out the front door and to the bus and parent pick-up area. Belinda said the school had been given a list of names of affected students in advance and had gathered those kids—sixty-one in all—in the gym before the bell rang that dismissed the other students. Over the next fifteen minutes, the chatter in the hallway slowly died down, and all the school buses and most of the parent cars there to pick up their children were gone from the parking lot. The doors to the hallway open, and a teacher marched the students into the cafeteria.

"Sit down at the lunch tables," she announced, and all of the students ran over to the long, white, collapsible lunch tables and sat down.

"Look, pizza!" A few of them yelled, their eyes unknowingly wide with excitement.

"Cousin Elena!" A boy waved and ran over to Elena and almost knocked her over when he ran into her leg and wrapped his arms around it. Elena couldn't help but laugh, a fleeting moment of joy in all of the day's sadness, and she squatted down as three more children ran across the lunchroom to her.

"Hey, mis queridos," she said.

"What's wrong," the boy asked, now noticing the sadness on his cousin's face.

Elena shifted to her knees and took a second to composer herself, then flipped her long and beautiful dark hair from her face and pulled the kids in closer. "You guys are gonna come stay with me for a while, okay?"

"Why?" The boy and another little girl asked. "¿Dónde está mami?"

"Mommy and Daddy had to go somewhere. And we don't know when they'll be back."

212

For the first time, the oldest boy noticed me and Belinda standing a few steps behind Elena, then turned around and looked around the room as word spread to the other kids that their loved ones wouldn't be picking them up or waiting for them at all anytime soon. The room fell quiet, then a child's single wail broke the silence, and triggered an avalanche of emotions in several other kids. Adults rushed to the children's side, especially the ones who didn't have any family waiting for them and tried their best to comfort the children and make sure they were fed while they waited.

"¿Volveremos a ver a mami y papi?" the girl asked, tears welling in her eyes.

"Yes, of course," Elena said. "But don't you worry about that now. We're gonna eat, and then I'm going to take you home. We're gonna be okay. Okay? We're gonna be okay. C'mon, there's some good food waiting for us outside."

Elena walked over to the DCS table and stood in line, all four of the kids flanked around her legs like they were afraid to leave her side. After she'd confirmed with the worker behind the table that she was indeed the kids' relative, she signed some paperwork and walked out of the door with them. The kids all ran toward the taco truck parked outside the double doors.

Other kids in the lunchroom weren't so lucky: after the kids with relatives already there were accounted for, twelve children still remained who had no family members there to claim them. My heart sank for them, and Belinda and I decided not to leave until every child had been picked up for the night. One older looking boy in particular, dressed in a Dragon Ball Z t-shirt and khaki shorts, sat at the end of the lunch table, bent over with his head resting on his arm. He looked to be writing in a tablet—maybe doing homework—so I walked over to him to see if he needed some help or wanted company.

"I'm just writing my spelling words." he said. "Is this how you spell 'Shouldn't'?"

I leaned over to look at the word he'd written. "That's the correct spelling, but you need an apostrophe between the 'n' and the 't'," I said.

The boy—named Marcus I'd discovered from reading the top of his worksheet—leaned in close and peered at the word as if he was sure the apostrophe had been there before he showed me the paper, then shook his head and added the apostrophe with his pencil. When a DCS worker walked over and asked if he wanted something to eat, Marcus shook his head again and continued working on the worksheet. I sat beside him and watched silently.

"I knew this was going to happen," he said after a few minutes.

"What?"

"My dad getting taken away. He told me what to do just in case."

I wonder what that conversation must have been like, having to sit your children down and prepare them for the possibility that one day, someone may knock on the door and take their parents away. And what to do if that happened. It all sounded surreal, like something out of a movie, and I couldn't imagine having the same conversation with my future children.

"What did he say you should do?" I asked.

Marcus shrugged. "He said that they couldn't kick me out because I was born here," he said with defiance, "so no matter where I went, be a good boy and finish school, and come find him when I got older."

I reached over and rubbed Marcus's back. "Well, I hope you see him again a lot sooner than that, Marcus. But in the meantime, that sounds like great advice. Your father loves you and wants you to succeed, no matter what happens to him."

"Right," Marcus said.

I decided to stay with Marcus until someone hopefully came to take him home, and after another forty-five minutes, an elderly woman wearing a flower-print housedress and leaning on a cane slowly shuffled through the open doors.

"Mi bisabuela," Marcus said, standing up. He placed his notebook into his black bookbag, then slowly walked over to her and carefully hugged her. He then took her by the hand and helped her over to the waiting DCS person. The sight of Marcus patiently escorting the woman to the table made me tear up, and although I didn't believe it was fair nor right that Marcus could possibly lose his father, I knew from my short time with the kid and from watching him care for this woman that his father had prepared Marcus well, not only for the father's absences, but for life.

More children started leaving one by one as people got off of work and made it through rush hour traffic to the school. There were more hugs and tears as relatives served as proxies for their detained loved ones, but little relief, and every child still left with the fear that the life they'd always known was now forever changed.

As we continued to wait, the priest from St. Michael finished up a conversation with the school's principal, then made a beeline for me. "Reverend Adams, my name is Stephen Cooper. I'm the Priest over at St. Michael's." Father Cooper extended his hand.

"I know who you are, Father, and it's very nice to meet you," I said as I shook his hand.

"Likewise. Thank you so much for coming out to help today. A large portion of this community attends St. Michael's, and my heart has been truly broken with today's events. But of course, that is nothing compared to what these families are about to go through, and I know a few people attended your church also."

"That's correct, Father, although I think the one family that I know sometimes visited Covenant also was a regular at St. Michaels. Julio and Carlita Alvarez."

"Ah yes, I know them also. Were they detained today also? It was hard to keep up over at the plant, and they won't officially give me a list of names."

"Yes, I saw them in line being loaded on the bus. Belinda Miller worked to make sure her kids were place with their relative."

"Okay good. Thank you." Father Cooper ran his hand over his balding head. "I'm just so overwhelmed at the moment. I'm a solutions-oriented kind of guy, but I'm afraid there is no quick-fix for this situation, and it's sort of eating me up right now. So of course, I've been walking around praying about it, and although we are very limited in what we can do now, I decided to start thinking about long term, maybe a fundraiser of some sort to help out the families. I was speaking with Principal Marks over there,

215

and she reminded me that this was not only a loss of a family members, in some cases multiple family members, but also a loss of income, maybe two incomes, as in Julio and Carlita's case. A lot of these kids may be placed with family caretakers who are elderly and unable to work."

"I didn't think about that," I said. "And children are expensive."

"Indeed. So, although a fundraiser may not help a lot of these families long term, it could help temporarily fill some gaps until the families can determine a more permanent solution to see to their needs. Anywhoo, I'm telling you all of this because I'd like to invite Covenant to possibly partner with St. Michaels on the fundraiser. Of course, this is just me talking out my ideas, but if it's something that you think your members would like to be involved in, maybe later we can get together to discuss and make it official."

"I think it's a great idea. I'd of course need to run it by our deacons, and we have a meeting coming up. We have another project we're working on at the moment, but members at Covenant have a habit of juggling and successfully executing multiple projects at once. They like to stay busy."

"Well, that sounds like a fun group to me," Father said. "I'll talk with my own board and give you a call later in about two weeks after we've had a little time to settle down a bit."

"Sounds good, Father. I'll go ahead and float the idea around to the group and get their wheels turning."

Father Cooper left me with another handshake, and I sat down to consider what we'd just discussed. In the past, I would have been worried about the Covenant group taking on too much at one time, but I'd since learned from experience that there seemed to be no such thing with the group, and that this was something I'm sure they'd want to be involved in, even with the continuing construction of the garden. And this time, if they indeed said yes to partnering with St. Michael's, I truly wasn't worried at all. I knew we'd all pull together and do what needed to be done to help out these families, just as Covenant had always done.

Soon it was nighttime, and at around nine p.m. there were only two children left. A DCS worker told me the two girls would be taken to a safe foster home for the night. When they left, Belinda and I helped the remaining workers pack up what was left, and the school custodial staff watched as we left the building.

"Belinda," I said as we walked to our cars, "I just wanted to say thank you for being here for Carlita and Julio and Elena and the kids today. What a tough and emotional day, and you handled everyone so well. You could be a pastor you know."

"Thank you, Pastor Annie. And thank you for coming so quickly when I called you. I was truly terrified and didn't know what to do. I know all of the things you've had to deal with at Covenant since you arrived, and I think having you here today somehow gave me the confidence I needed to take action and help however I could in a tough situation."

"Well, you did a wonderful job being there for others today. Let me know if you ever want to get into the ministry."

"I don't think I ever want to go *that* far," Belinda said with a laugh. "But you know what? Now that I think of it, this *is* ministry. There was a time when Mary and Joseph were on the run from the government also, right?"

"Yup, they were. And thankfully they had people like you to help them, even way back then. Maybe this is your ministry. Your calling." I said.

"I think so too. Thank you. You be safe getting home, okay?"

"Yes, it's been a long day. Get some rest."

"Thank you, ladies!" A teacher yelled to us from across the parking lot. "Pray for the kids!"

On the short drive home, I did just that: I asked God to reunite and heal all the families that had been wounded today. I was so exhausted when I got home that I was too tired to even shower. Instead I stripped off my clothes and climbed into bed.

217

"Reverend Annie, this is Lucille Smith. I have an urgent matter that I need to talk to you about as soon as you are available. My phone number is 342-555-7620"

"Oh boy," I said to myself as I instinctively grabbed a pen and wrote down the number, even though I'd called Lucille several times before. I didn't know what the urgent matter could possibly be, but before dialing Lucille back, I looked at the ceiling and said a quick prayer "Lord, please help everything to be okay with Lucille and her family," then dialed the number back. "Mrs. Smith? This is Annie over at Covenant, returning your call."

"My husband's tools have been stolen, and I know exactly who did it."

"I'm sorry, Mrs. Smith. Did you say your *husband's* tools have been stolen?" I knew Lucille's husband to be deceased, so I wasn't sure if I was hearing correctly.

"Yes," Lucille said. "My late husband. He kept a tool shed out back, and I keep my gardening tools in there also. Today, I planned on putting down some mulch, and when I went out there to get some gloves and the wheelbarrow, I noticed my husband's weed eater was missing from the wall. I know it was that boy of Mary's, the ex-con that my granddaughter has been seeing."

Oh no I just kept thinking over and over in my head. *This could not be happening.*

"I've already asked both Mary and Damien about it, and they've both denied that he took it. But who else could it be? Since his mother's been staying here and he's been dating Elizabeth, I just *know* that he's been waiting and watching for the perfect time to strike. Even though I allowed him to come over and see Mary sometimes, I have still had an uneasy feeling about him. He used to sell drugs! He may have my granddaughter and everyone else convinced that he's turned his life around, but not me. And Elizabeth had the nerve to yell at me this morning! I guess Damien told her what happened. After all I've done for that girl."

Elizabeth had yet to make it into the church office for her shift; in fact, now that I glanced at my watch, she was a little late, which was unusual for her. I hoped nothing bad had happened to her as a result of being upset with her grandmother.

"Mrs. Smith," I said, "let's try to calm down for a second. I know you're upset about the missing equipment, but we don't want to accuse anyone without knowing for sure."

"But I *do* know for sure! All of these years living in Bakerstown and I've never had one break-in at my house or shed. And now that Mary's been living here, and my granddaughter's been dating her son that's been in jail before, *now* I have a break-in? You surely cannot think this is just a total coincidence Reverend Annie."

"I'm not sure what it is, Mrs. Smith. I just want to caution against running away with accusations without evidence. It could cause a lot of hurt feelings if it turns out to be untrue."

My mind immediately thought back to two years ago and my very first crises of sort at Covenant Baptist Church. One of our former deacons and a teacher at the middle school, Cliff Burnside, was falsely accused of molesting a student. The entire ordeal turned his and his family's life completely upside and led to a deep division within the church as some people chose sides and labeled him as guilty before the full facts came out. Later, when the accuser recanted his accusation toward Cliff and revealed the real person who had been molesting him, it was a relief, but the damage had already been done, and Cliff and his family had to work very hard to heal themselves of the trauma they'd experienced because of one false accusation. I did not want to see anything similar to that happen again with Mrs. Smith, Elizabeth, and Mary LeBlanc and her son Damien. Damien was one of the people the church had reached out to participate in a panel and speak about how the church could better welcome and support groups of the people like him who church has traditionally shunned. As an ex-con, he'd spoken to our group about the mistake he'd made in his young life after he and his mother Mary had moved to Bakerstown after being displaced from New Orleans during Hurricane Katrina.

"I suppose you're right, but I don't know where else it could be. It's clearly missing, and I've never mowed a yard in my life. Surely, I didn't lose something as big as a trimmer. Unless someone shows me otherwise, I'm standing on my gut. Do you think you can come out here this afternoon, Annie? I'd like to talk more in person. And maybe you can talk more to Mary. She's off today from the restaurant. She's been a little cold with me since I asked them about the trimmer."

I was glad Mrs. Smith couldn't see me shaking my head on the other end of the phone as I consulted my appointments for the afternoon for an open time block. "I can come by there around four, if that's okay with you. I know that's a little late in the day, but I have some appointments I need to keep."

"Four is fine. See you then." Lucille hung up the phone.

"Wowzers," I said out loud to myself. What was I going to do? I don't know how I could fix this situation. And although I tried to deter Lucille from jumping to conclusions, what if Damien *had* taken the weed eater? A lot of people who had gone to jail and been released did end up relapsing, and I remember Pete Stoudamire had specifically asked Damien how the church could help him not be one of those statistics. Damien had responded that he thought it would help if he had someone to talk to when things got rough, to help him not resort back to his old life. But could I be so sure that Damien hadn't done just that? He'd seemed to be doing well the last time I had spoken with Elizabeth and Mary about him. He was in school at Central Piedmont Community College and had secured his own apartment. Had something changed? And where was Elizabeth? This wasn't the first time she and Lucille had disagreed about Damien. Elizabeth had already made some poor decisions romantically in life, which had led to her having two children that she was now raising on her own. And Lucille had not been happy when Elizabeth had revealed to her that she and Damien were seeing each other. Lucille had eventually come around after hiring Mary to help her around the house and allowing her to move into the guest cottage, but this latest development threatened to undo all the good that had been done since then.

As if on cue, there was a knock at the door. "Come in," I called.

Elizabeth burst into my office and stopped in front of my desk. "I can't do it anymore, Reverend Annie! Do you know what my grandmother just did?!"

"Believe it or not Elizabeth, I've heard. I just got off the phone with her about ten minutes ago. She was pretty upset."

"*SHE* was upset? Damien did NOT steal that weed eater!"

"Okay, okay. Come sit down and try to calm yourself," I said as I tried to coax her into the chair.

Elizabeth sat down and sat her purse on the floor. "I just cannot believe she would do something like this. And everything was going so well with her and Mary! Now Damien's mad at her and questioning his relationship with me again. And Mary's in an awkward position too: she needs that money Grandmother is paying her, and her living in the guest cottage was helping her out a lot! But who would want to stay there when someone accuses your son of something he didn't do. It's just a big mess."

"I'm sorry this is all happening, Elizabeth." I sat down in the chair beside her. "Your grandmother asked me to come to her house to speak more about the situation, and I'm going there this afternoon to see what I can do, which I'm not sure if there *is* anything I can do. I'm surely not a cop who can investigate what may have happened to the weed eater, but I'll certainly pray and ask God to give us a solution to this issue. I don't ever want to see you and your grandmother's relationship strained, especially since she's helped you so much and you don't have a great relationship with your parents. But I also support you if you are confident about Damien and want to stand by him in this situation. You certainly know him better than we do. *Are you* confident that he didn't take the weed eater?"

"Yes. No. I don't know." Elizabeth buried her face in her hands. "Yes. Damien has only been good to me and has given me no reason to think he's returned to his old habits that sent him to jail. He's working hard trying to get his associate degree and has been nothing but a supportive companion to me."

"Well, my advice would be to continue to stand by him unless you discover more information that changes how you feel about him. God always has a way of bringing the dark things to light. But what I'd really like you to do is focus on finishing your classes, so you can graduate. You are *so* close to the life you've been working so hard for over the last few years. Please don't let anything or anyone come in the way of that. Your children deserve the best life you can give them. Don't get distracted by what's going on with Lucille and Damien and Mary."

"You're right. I have to hunker down and focus on the goal only. They call that 'tunnel vision,' right?"

"I think so, yes," I said. "Eyes on the prize."

Elizabeth took a deep breath and released it with her eyes closed like she was doing one of those yoga calming techniques. "Thank you, boss," she said, opening her eyes. "I think I'm going to go work on whatever tasks you have for me, study, and not let any of this distract me anymore."

"Atta girl. I'll let you know if there are any new developments that you should be aware of after I visit your grandmother this afternoon."

Elizabeth closed the door behind her when she left the office, and I slouched down in the chair. I was nervous about this afternoon's visit to Lucille's, mainly because I didn't know how to fix the problem, and I didn't know what Mary LeBlanc's reaction would be to my visit.

I decided food would make me feel better, at least for a little bit, so I ate the turkey sandwich and Golden Flake Barbecue potato chips that I brought with me from home. I downed it with a Coke, and then focused on my afternoon calls and tasks.

When I arrived at Lucille's later that evening, she was sitting on the porch in one of the rocking chairs. I climbed the porch and sat down in the chair beside hers.

"Thank you for coming Reverend Annie. Would you like some cookies?"

"I'd better not," I said. "I just had some chips and a coke a while ago. Did Mary make them?"

"Yes, she came over earlier and cleaned the kitchen and did her daily tasks but didn't say much. I guess I can't blame her, but as my pappy used to say, the trimmer didn't walk away. I've been in and out of the shed since Spring arrived, but I haven't touched the trimmer. I think I'm going to call the police."

"That's certainly your right Mrs. Lucille, and that's what you should do if you truly think it was stolen, but I again caution you from pointing the finger at Damien if you don't have any real proof that he took it. An accusation like that to someone who has

222

been in the system before can make him guilty on the spot, even if he didn't do it. He's working hard to get his life back on track, just like Elizabeth. I'd like to ask you to pray about this and please don't jeopardize his future if you aren't sure."

"I see who's side you're on," Lucille said.

"I'm not on anyone's side, Mrs. Lucille, and I want to help figure out what happened to your husband's weed eater. But I'm not willing to potentially alter someone's life forever without knowing for sure. Not over a lawn tool."

"Well, Mary's in the guest house if you want to go talk to her."

Good Lord, I thought to myself. "I'll go see if she's available. Please let me know how else I can help you, Mrs. Lucille."

I walked the fifty or so yards across the fresh green grass— repenting as I walked for my current attitude and negative feelings toward Mrs. Lucille—and knocked on the guest house door. At that moment, I kicked myself for not calling first to let Mary know I was coming to visit Lucille and ask if it was okay if I stopped by. Mary opened the door, and the look on her face was one of surprise and sadness.

"Reverend Annie. I should have figured you'd be stopping by soon," she said.

"I'm sorry I didn't call first, Mary. I just realized my mistake."

"No worries, come on in."

I stepped into the guest house, which was just as immaculate as Lucille's big plantation-style home, just a smaller size. I sat down, and Mary went into the kitchen and returned with two cups of black coffee, cream and sugar, and a platter of warm beignets. I'd turned down the cookies, but I could not pass up the chance to eat some of these special New Orleans inspired treats. The powdery treat melted in my mouth, and before I knew it, I'd reached for two more.

"Mmm," I said, my mouth full of warm goodness. "These are so good, Mary."

"Thank you. I decided to cook something today that reminded me of home. Today is one of those days where I

223

definitely wish I was back there. I'm guessing Mrs. Lucille called you about the missing weed eater."

"Yes," I said, swallowing the last bite of my third beignet and washing it down with a big gulp of coffee. "Although I'm not sure what good I can do. I'm definitely not here to interrogate you about who took it. Actually Mary, I wanted to check in on you just to see how you were making out in all of this. I know it must be really awkward being in the middle of Lucille and Damien."

"It is Reverend Annie, and honestly, I'm not quite sure how I feel. That is why I've been baking all day. I'm not sure what to do. I don't believe my son took that weed eater, and I was offended when Lucille first asked us about it. But then when I came back to the guest house and was alone with myself, I said to myself 'Do I really know *for sure* Damien didn't take it?' You know he's been in trouble before, but he seemed to be doing well lately, at least to me. I want to believe in and support my son, but I also don't ever want to be the type of parent who is oblivious and blind to their children's unsavory behavior either.

"There has never been a lock on that shed, I guess because here in Bakerstown with nothing ever going on, Lucille's never needed it. So anyone truly could have walked away with that thing. I don't know. All I know is, I asked Damien about it, he said no, and I choose to believe him. I thought Lucille was going to fire me, but she didn't, so now I'm stuck with wondering if I should even continue staying here and working for her. God knows it has been a big help with my finances, and I've quite enjoyed it, but Damien is my son, and I have to stand by him through thick and thin. He told me not to quit, at least not until he finished his degree and got a better paying job where he could help me out some, but I don't know. And that poor Elizabeth. I heard her go off on Lucille this morning. I think Elizabeth's about had it with her, but I don't want to see their relationship strained because of my son."

"I completely understand all of your frustrations," I said to Mary. "And I agree with Damien. I think if you still feel comfortable here, you should stay until a better opportunity presents itself to you. I thought you'd be a great help to Lucille after her first helper Frances retired, and it looks like you have been. Lucille has been looking and moving around like she's younger than ever lately, and I know that is in no small part because of you being here. Helping manage that big house is a lot of work. But I don't advise staying here at the expense of your mental health, your integrity, or your relationship with your son, so if at any moment you feel it in your spirit that you can't do it anymore, don't. As for Damien and Elizabeth, they are two grown adults who have both made some mistakes in life, but who of us hasn't? I think you should leave it to them to figure out if they can continue to be together, despite Lucille being her grandmother. I think they can figure it out."

"What about the weed eater?" Mary asked.

"Well, that one's got me stumped," I said. "The common sense thing to do would be to report the missing item to the police, but I'm afraid if she does that, and shares her fears that Damien might have taken it, it may get him in trouble if the police look at his record and see his prior history."

"Oh no! That would be the last thing he needs right now," Mary said.

"I know. I asked her to pray about it and consider looking around the shed again before she called the police, since she said she has been in and out recently and had been moving things around. Let's pray that it turns up. I know that doesn't sound like much of a plan, Mary, but I'm not sure what else to do."

"That's okay, Reverend. This is truly the most awkward situation I have ever been in. I'm not upset that you don't know exactly how to fix everything. I appreciate you coming out to check on me."

"Anytime. And please tell Damien that I am here for him as well, and that I am rooting for him. Actually, I guess I should probably call him and tell myself huh?"

"Yes, I think that would go a long way with him. This entire incident has both of us a little down now. And he really likes Elizabeth, but I'm not sure what path they have if Lucille is just going to constantly question their relationship."

I prayed for Mary before I left, and asked God to step in and right this situation for all involved, to give her the wisdom and discernment about her next steps with Lucille, and for direction for Damien and Elizabeth's relationship.

Chapter 38

The Tuesday morning prayer meeting arrived just on time. It had only been a few days since I was foolishly and naively reveling in how great everything was going. Since then, with the ICE raid and the trimmer fiasco, it seemed that all hell had literally broken loose. On top of that, the budgeted funds for the garden were getting low, and we still had no gazebo. I'd wanted to start making a Plan B, but Edward was adamant God would come through for us.

"Just keep believing, Annie," he said.

I personally thought we should be believing God for more important things than a gazebo, but I decided to honor Edward's faith and follow his lead.

Mary LeBlanc was already inside the sanctuary when I arrived and turned on the music, sitting about five rows back from the altar. I mouthed *Are you okay?* to her, and she nodded a solemn yes in return. The other regulars arrived soon after: Alan and Faye Emerson, Earlene Williams—with Harry this time, Vivian Artz, and a few others. We all sat quietly with our personal thoughts and prayers for about fifteen minutes. I silently asked God to help me with Mary's situation, and I prayed for each and every one who had been detained in the raid. I also prayed for John, the entire congregation, and my parents, Derek and the rest of my blood family. When that was over, I stood before the group and asked if anyone had anything they'd like to share. Mary LeBlanc raised her hand.

"I'd just like to ask you guys to pray for me and my son Damien. I don't want to share details, but if you guys could just pray for us, I'd appreciate it."

Everyone nodded their heads in agreement to pray for Mary. I felt so bad for her and Damien about everything that was going on and was praying that God would deliver them quickly from this awkward situation.

Someone else raised their hand in the back, and I peered around Vivian to see that it was Elena Alvarez. I motioned to her, and she stood up. "I'm not sure if any here beside Reverend Annie knows this, but my cousins Julio and Carlita Alvarez were occasional visitors here, and they were detained in last week's raid at the chicken plant in town." A few people glanced at me, and Mary LeBlanc, who had gotten to know Carlita personally, started to cry. "So, I'm asking if you can just pray for them please. And their children, who I am now taking care of until we can find a solution. Thank you."

Mary got up and went to Elena in the back, and the two women held each other and cried. Earlene Williams got up and went to them with a box of Kleenex and sat beside them and rubbed their backs. Afterwards, the ladies wiped their eyes and were whispering to each other and encouraging each other.

"Thank you for sharing, Elena. Please know that Covenant is here for you if you and the kids need anything. For the rest of you, it is a possibility that Covenant could be partnering with St. Michael's on a fundraiser for the families of the people who were detained. I have a call with Father Cooper tomorrow afternoon, after which I will be talking with our deacons to get their thoughts. If something comes out of it, I'll let you know."

When no one had anything else to share, I prayed "Heavenly Father, thank You for bringing us here once again to petition You for our needs. We certainly need You, as we do each and every day. Please hear our prayers and identify and help us remove anything that may hinder them. We ask that you be with everyone present in the sanctuary Lord. We also ask a special prayer for Mary LeBlanc and her son Damien. Please bless them and deliver them and be whatever it is they need You to be Father. We also lift up Julio and Carlita Alvarez, that you would wrap Your loving arms around them, protect them where they are, give them favor, and reunite them with their family. We asked that You be with their four children, and also with Elena. Please bless and provide for her, whatever it is she needs to take care of them God. Let her strength be equal to her days as she takes on this responsibility for You and use Covenant to be a resource for her to help meet their needs. In Jesus name we pray, Amen."

Everyone hugged Elena and Mary on the way outside, and although the prayer meeting had been emotional, I felt better knowing that we'd all gotten together and left our burdens and concerns with the only One who was strong enough to carry them.

The next morning before Elizabeth arrived, I called Damien on his cell phone to see if I could schedule a visit to his new apartment to check in on him.

"Sure, Reverend Annie," he said. "I know this is about the weed eater though."

"Well Damien, you're right in that this entire weed eater incident was the catalyst for my realizing that I needed to visit you, but my main objective for coming to see you is to check on your wellbeing and to see if I can help you in any way, not to ask about a yard tool."

"Well, okay then. Thank you. I'm pretty free tomorrow if you want to come by."

The next day, I arrived at his apartment building, only two miles from the heart of CPCC's campus. Damien's apartment was on the bottom floor, and he was sitting outside on the very small, square patio when I pulled my car into the spot directly in front of it. He waved, and I got out and simply walked two steps over the narrow strip of grass that separated his patio from the curb. There was only one chair on the patio, and an upside-down white painter's bucket beside it. Damien stood up and offered me the chair and sat down on the bucket.

"Thank you, Damien," I said. "But don't count me out on sitting on buckets. I'm a Mississippi girl, you know."

If the only sound Damien made was the deep, hearty laugh that escaped from his belly at the sound of my confession, that would have been good enough for me.

"No, Reverend Annie, I did not know that. What brought you to Charlotte?"

"Seminary. But the country never left me. I guess that's why I get along so well down in Bakerstown."

"Yeah well, I'm not sure if North Carolina is the place for me anymore. Don't know if it ever was. Been thinking of going home and starting fresh."

"Oh yeah?" I said. "What about your mom?"

"I think she misses it sometime, but I think whether she takes it or leaves it, it's all the same to her. I think Katrina was more traumatic for her than it was for me."

"I understand. Have you been feeling like wanting to go back to New Orleans, or is it because of the situation with Mrs. Lucille?"

"I've always longed to go home, but yeah, this has kind of pushed it over the edge. I don't know what's wrong with the lady. I did not steal her precious trimmer. Seems like she's had it out for me ever since she found out Elizabeth and I were getting to know each other. I know Elizabeth and I have both had our issues in life, despite how young we are, but you would think Mrs. Smith wouldn't judge me just like she didn't want people judging Elizabeth for having two kids without being married. But that seems to have flown right over her head. Sorry if I'm talking reckless about one of your church members, Reverend, but I've about had it with her judgements of me and trying to pin something on me that I didn't do."

"Don't apologize Damien. You have a right to be upset and frustrated, and you have a right to defend yourself from false accusations. I'm sure I'd feel the same way if I was in your shoes."

"Mind if I smoke?" Damien asked me, an unlit cigarette already dangling from his lips.

"Not at all. This is your place."

Damien lit the cigarette and inhaled, then blew the smoke in the opposite direction of me as a car passed by. "I just don't know," he said. "I really like Elizabeth. She's a really great mother to her kids, and a good girlfriend. I was starting to think that we could really be something together. But now I just think that as long as Mrs. Smith feels that kind of way about me, all I'll ever be doing is holding her back and jeopardizing her relationship with her grandmother. And I don't want to be the fall guy every time something comes up missing just because I've made some questionable decisions in life."

"I think I'd feel the exact same way if I were you, Damien. This truly sucks and I'm sorry you're having this happen to you. And I'm sorry for Elizabeth also. You both deserve to be together if you want to, and I hate when other people's beliefs and prejudices get in the way of love."

"So, what do you suggest I do, Reverend?" Damien asked through another plume of smoke.

"Honestly? I don't know how to fix this, Damien. I wish it had never happened. But if you haven't noticed, this isn't the best world we live in, and I don't think this will be the last time you are wronged, or the last time someone tries to stop a good thing you have going. So, my advice to you is to do what's best for you, if you know what I mean. Choose yourself. I know that doesn't sound very Christlike of me—"

"I was about to say," Damien laughed. "I don't know much Bible, but I know the "put others first part.""

"Yes, putting others before yourself is Christ's way. Humility is a tried and true path to God. So is forgiving people when you have been wronged. All I'm asking you to do is not give up on a good thing that you deserve to have just to make someone else happy. Mrs. Lucille won't die if you and Elizabeth are together, I promise you."

Damien laughed. "You're something else. I appreciate that Reverend, and I'll think about what you said. Thank you for coming to see me."

"Anytime. Remember this, Covenant is always here for you."

I prayed with Damien and headed back to the office to get ready for my call with Father Cooper, already feeling better about the situation between the LeBlancs and the Smiths.

"Father, I know I've prayed about this a million times in the last few days, but please make everything right with this," I prayed once more for good measure.

Chapter 39

I sat outside Brian Stanley's office and waited for his current appointment to end and mine to begin. Just like I'd needed the prayer meeting this week, I also thought it would help if I came to visit and talk with Brian. I hadn't visited him at all since Covenant had been removed from the Southern Baptist Convention, although he'd told me he would continue to advise me if I wanted. With this meeting, along with what had now become my routine Friday night date with John, I hoped by Sunday's service I'd have a better grasp on things mentally.

The office door opened, and a man in a three-piece suit shook hands with Brian, then gently acknowledged me and Evelyn, Brian's secretary, as he exited the office. Brian waved me in and gave me a hug. "Haven't seen you in a while, troublemaker. I would assume that your group down at Covenant had decided to dial it back a bit, but I know that's not the case.

"You know us well, Brian," I said. "No dialing back with this group."

"How's the garden-wedding thing coming along?"

"It's coming. It's almost finished actually, and the flowers we planted are starting to bloom and it really looks amazing. We're missing a gazebo, because we can't afford one, and I have a pretty stubborn deacon who thinks God is going to deliver us one right on time before the wedding. I think he's crazy, and we should make alternate plans. I'm starting to wonder whether he should actually be the one pastoring the church and not me. His faith seems to be much stronger than mine. It's like Elijah and his servant. He keeps sending me to look for rain, and I keep telling him 'There's nothing there,' and he just keeps sending me back."

Brian was tickled and leaned back in his seat. "And how's life as a former member of the SBC?"

"You know? Nothing's changed really. We did have a few members leave the church once it was announced, along with the news of the wedding. But beside that, it's been business as usual in Bakerstown."

"Good," he said. "Well what brings you in for a visit? I know something's bothering you."

"Well, two things," I said. "First, two of my members were detained by ICE, and are in jeopardy of getting deported."

"No way," Brian said.

"Yes, and they left behind four children that their cousin is now taking care of. The priest at St. Michael's has approached Covenant about partnering with them on a fundraiser for the families, as a lot of the Hispanic community in Bakerstown attends his church. They want to have it pretty soon, next Saturday in fact, while the raid is still fresh on everyone's minds. They are handling the majority of the planning and advertising to get the word out, and only asked that Covenant members show up with items to donate to be sold. Of course, our deacons voted to join in and participate."

"Of course. But it sounds like it's for a good cause," Brian said.

"It is. It was truly heartbreaking that day seeing all the people loaded on that ICE bus. From what I've heard, only seven of the fifty-five who were detained have been released. I'm not sure what the future holds for the others, and it's scary to think they could be kicked out of the country and torn apart from their American-born families here."

"I see. I'm not sure what advice I can give you on that one, Annie. Our immigration laws are notoriously tough."

"I know. And I'm not sure I'm actually looking for advice, I guess. Sometimes it just helps to share with someone else, let it all out," I said.

"Right. And the second thing?"

"This one maybe you can help me with. I have a member, elderly I admit, who has accused a young man of stealing one of her late husband's tools from her shed. I'll spare you the details and the long backstory, because it's quite a bit, but I truly don't believe the young man took the tools. In fact, no one involved does except the elderly woman. But she's adamant that he stole it, and the entire situation is starting to make me resent having to deal with the entire thing. It feels like unnecessary foolishness. I have more important things to be concerned about, and it's also putting the young man's reputation and future at risk."

232

"You think this is a case of just old people being old," Brian said.

"Basically. And I know my attitude about the entire situation is not the correct one."

"Well, correct your attitude and your pride. I think you're used to the big grandiose problems that, although they are admittedly difficult, there is a sexiness to them also, and we sometimes unknowingly take pride in the fact that we are God's chosen shepherds who have been entrusted with his people and are called on to help people solve all of their important problems. We often get annoyed with the small minor inconveniences. That trimmer may be small potatoes to you, but it's a big deal to your church member, and her feelings are just as important as anyone else's. I'm not saying her blaming an innocent man is right, because it's not. Just try to remember that we have to ask God to grant us with a special grace to deal with our elderly, our mentally challenged, and our children, and to remind us that those are the people that are near and dear to his heart. It can be trying for sure, but they are God's children also."

"I think that's what I needed to hear Brian, to confirm reality. I knew my feelings towards my church member were not right."

"It's human to be annoyed, Annie. But I think that is one of the few things that you can actually pray away. Ask God to help you see that person as He sees her."

I did just that on my way back home. I asked God to forgive me for my attitude toward Lucille, and to help me to see her in a new light.

Chapter 40

St. Michael's Catholic Church wasn't too far in distance from Covenant, so it only took me about seven minutes from the time I left the parish to reach the parking lot, which was already pretty populated with people unloading their cars. Women held balanced on their purses; pound cakes, custard pies, and other baked goods they'd bought to sell, and a few men wheeled in a cast iron grill and coolers onto the front lawn. If the people of the community actually came out for this event, they'd have a variety of options to choose from.

I grabbed the individually wrapped chocolate chip pecan cookies I made to donate to sell and walked inside the church. Tables and booths were being set up on the outside lawn and inside the parish hall. In the parish it was already busy with activity: people were setting up tables and covering them with tablecloths, then arranging them around the perimeter of the room so attendees could easily navigate around the room and browse. Food wasn't the only thing for sale at the fundraiser: there were books, raffle tickets, art sculptures, paintings, and even an auction for season tickets to the Carolina Panthers and the Charlotte Hornets.

Outside on St. Michael's big green lawn—where a massive Easter egg hunt would no doubt be happening next Sunday—a kid's area was being set up, with a huge bounce house, a marked off area for flag football, a dunk booth, sack race, a giant Connect-Four game, and mini-golf. There was also a small stage set up for announcements and entertainment, and food trucks had started to park along the street. St. Michael's had truly done a lot of work to make this a success, and I prayed that the community would come out to support their efforts to help the families of the detained immigrants.

It wasn't long before I spotted several Covenant members around the church helping out in various areas. Alan and Faye Emerson were inside helping with making price labels for all the items to be sold. William was on stage helping set up the sound system. Ben Merriweather, Pete Stoudamire and Jesse Akin were each donning aprons and manning one of the three grills.

"Well I guess I know who to call on when Covenant finally has a cookout," I said to them.

"We're your guys," Jesse said. "I do this for fun."

The fundraiser started at 10 a.m., and it wasn't long before people started arriving and the entire area burst into life. I walked around and tried to make myself useful, greeting people with Father Cooper, and distributing water to the people outside. God had blessed us with a beautiful Spring day, and the community was out in force to take advantage of it.

"Hey Reverend Adams. Remember me?" I heard someone say as I headed back inside.

I turned and looked up for the voice that had boomed down from behind and above me. It was the Reverend Alexander Jones, whom I had met when I'd first started my trial period with Covenant. When he was a child, he was a member of Ebenezer Baptist Church, an African American church that Covenant had partnered and worshipped with during the Civil Rights movement. Reverend Jones had also received a scholarship from Covenant back then. He was able to complete college in Charlotte because of that scholarship, then move on to seminary. Now, he had been pastoring his own church for close to forty years.

"Of course, I remember you, Reverend Jones," I said. "How have you been?"

"Not too shabby," he said. "And call me Alex. I got wind of you guys' fundraiser while I was in town visiting folks at Ebenezer and some of us wanted to come out and support. I've bought my fair share of lemon cake already, and my wife will be none too happy about that I suspect."

"I think she may let you slide since it's for a good cause. Thank you so much for coming out. I know you know a thing or two yourself about what's going on in the Charlotte area concerning our Hispanic community."

"Yeah," Alex said, looking around at the crowd. "Unfortunately, some things never change. The only change is who it happens to. But I believe if we all come together, like your church has long been doing, one day, we'll get the victory."

"Amen," I said.

"I'll let you get back to it. It's good to see you again."

Alex stopped to talk to a few more people, then rounded the corner towards the back of the building. When I turned to resume my way back inside, I spotted John, Edna, Ella, and Emily walking up from the parking lot, and I stopped again to greet them.

"Looks like we got here just in time," John said.

"Daddy, can we go to the bounce house?" the girls both asked, pulling at John's hands and pointing to the lawn.

"Come on girls," Edna said. "I'll take you."

Although this was a fundraiser, the planning committee had decided that water should be free, so John and I looped around the lawn with the cooler several times offering people bottled water. A lot of Bakerstown's Hispanic community attended St. Michael's and it was great to see them come out and enjoy themselves after the last few weeks they'd been through. I didn't know if Elena had brought Julio and Carlita's kids out, but I hoped that they were there somewhere and having fun.

Our cooler ran out of water, and John and I rolled it around to the back of the church to the command center where the cases of water and other supplies were being kept to refill. Other people were milling about refilling their coolers and chatting amongst themselves, and William and Alex sat beside each other on the curb, both eating a hotdog.

"Reverend Annie," Alex said when he spotted me, "I know this old guy of yours only sings gospel songs at Covenant, but one day when no one's around, ask him to sing some Prince for you." William shook his head and grinned quietly as Reverend Jones bodacious laugh filled the air.

"I'll be sure to do just—"

Before I could finish my sentence, a white, unmarked van sped down the side-street that ran along at the back of the church and screeched to a halt in front of us. Alex immediately jumped to his feet, peered into the van, then turned around and searched the faces of the people standing around the back of the church. Three ICE agents jumped out of the van, and Reverend Jones ran over to a man—the only Hispanic looking man in the area—turned, and pressed his back to him, wrapping him in a backwards hug.

"Everybody, lock arms around him!" Alex yelled.

I didn't know what was going on, but I knew that I could trust Alex, so I ran over to him. John and William followed suit. That seemed to encourage others to move as well, and we had quickly formed a tight, outward facing circle around the Hispanic man, who now had a look of terror on his face.

"Move!" The ICE agent yelled at Alex.

"Do you have a warrant?!" Alex yelled back.

"Get out of the way or I'll—"

"Or you'll what." Alex's voice was low and menacing now. "I'm not afraid of you. This man has rights and you are not welcome here."

"Someone get the Father!" John called out.

Several people took off running around the building. We were in a secluded area, hidden away from the hundreds of people who were around front. The agent clinched his jaw, then stepped away to confer with the other two agents who were with him. Then he climbed into the driver seat of the van and pulled out his cell phone.

"Nobody move," Revered Jones said. "They can't arrest you and they can't detain him without a warrant."

I looked over and realized I had locked arms with William. "Are you okay?" I asked.

"Yes, Annie. This is taking me back forty years."

A young man who looked to be in his twenties immediately pulled out his phone and started live streaming the event, and I recognized him as one of the protestors who had came out to the chicken plant. I could hear him speaking loudly into his phone.

"WE NEED PEOPLE, BODIES, ANYBODY WHO CAN COME DOWN TO ST. MICHAEL'S CATHOLIC CHURCH ON WEST BAKERSFIELD ROAD," he said as he held the phone up at eye level and walked the perimeter of the circle, then pointed it toward the two agents that were standing and watching us. "THE ICE AGENTS ARE HERE TRYING TO ILLEGALLY DETAIN AN IMMIGRANT MAN WHO HAS RIGHTS IN THIS COUNTRY. WE HAVE TO STOP THIS TERRORIZATION OF HARD-WORKING PEOPLE OF THIS NATION."

I glanced around the circle as best I could see behind me. Another outer circle had formed around us as an extra layer of protection. The man—Juan—looked nervous, and was on his cell phone also, speaking rapidly in Spanish. In the fray that had immediately formed the circle, I'd become separated from John, but could see his back on the other side of the circle. He must have felt me looking at him, because he twisted himself around to meet my eyes and mouthed *Are you okay?* I nodded.

"Just hold tight folks," Reverend Alex said. "We just have to wait them out until Juan's lawyer arrives and they know we mean business."

"Por favor, por favor," Juan said, and kept repeating in a low voice over and over.

Father Cooper came running around the church—a shocked crowd on his heels—and immediately rushed up to the two agents who were outside the van. "Get out of here!" he yelled in their faces. "You will NEVER be allowed on this property!"

"I can't believe they would target a fundraiser," someone said from the crowd watching the circle. "No shame."

"None!"

"That's okay, they not getting him today."

Word must have gotten out around quickly, because now it seemed that all of the festival's attendees was packed onto the side street, and the ICE van was suddenly blocked in on both sides by angry people. The agent inside the van looked around and shook his head, then hung up the phone and turned the ignition. The other two agents climbed inside, and the sea of people in front of the van slowly part to let the vehicle leave the church. The crowd burst into cheers, and the circle surrounding Juan broke apart and turned to make sure he was okay.

"Thank you," he said. "Thank you."

"You're welcome. Go inside until your lawyer gets here," Alex said. "They may be around the street waiting for you to leave."

Several of us walked Juan inside, sat down and drank water, and tried to process and recover from what had just happened.

"I was this close to being gone," Juan said, his elbows on his knees as he kept his eyes on the open door.

"You were," John said. "Do you have a pending application for a green card?"

"Yes, but it's taken so long. It's been over seven years. I'm not sure why they were trying to take me because there has been no judgement on my case according to my lawyer. I do my yearly check-ins and everything."

"Well, be careful," I said. "They really seem to be targeting the Charlotte area right now."

"I know it. My cousin was detained in the last raid. I love Charlotte, and I've been trying to do this the right way, but I think it may be time for me to move along to another state. I can't go back to my country. There are dangerous gangs in places, and if I don't join them, I'll be killed. Before today, I still held out hope that my application would be approved. But if they tried to take me without a deportation order, I know when I show up for my next check-in, they will detain me. I really don't know what to do. I've lived and worked here since I was fourteen."

"Hey man," Alex said, looking Juan in the eye. "You do what you have to do to stay alive, short of harming someone else. You hear me?"

"Yes," Juan said. "Yes."

Several of us formed a circle around Juan and prayed over him before his lawyer arrived and safely took him away. Edna had sent John a text saying that she'd heard about the incident and had taken the girls home, so we hung around and tried to help out and enjoy the remainder of the event.

Chapter 41

After the unexpected event at the fundraiser and the events of the last few weeks, I managed to make it to Monday morning without imploding or shutting down. But I couldn't rest just yet as it was Easter week, the biggest week of the year for churches across the world. I was also driving to my parent's tonight to attend a birthday dinner for my dad, spending two nights, then driving back to Bakerstown early Wednesday morning. Covenant didn't have anything special planned beside our regular service, but we were sure to be close to full on Sunday, and I wanted to make sure my sermon expressed the importance of Jesus's sacrifice on the cross but was also relatable and personal.

"Jesus, please give me a word for Your people as we mourn Your sacrifice and celebrate Your resurrection, one that touches their hearts and nudges them toward a relationship with You," I prayed.

Ben had asked if he could stop by the office this morning, but didn't tell me why. I was expecting him at ten, so I left the door to my office open. A few minutes after ten, he peaked his head in the doorway.

"Knock, knock," he said.

"Come on in, Ben."

"I wanted you to meet someone," he said, walking in. Two young boys followed behind him. They both had Ben's face and stood tall and straight and maintained eye contact with him as he spoke.

"This is Jeter," Ben said, pointing to the taller one. "And Zach."

"It's good to meet you two" I said.

"Good to meet you," both boys said sheepishly.

"They're out of school for Spring Break, so they'll be with me all week. We're about to head to Carolina Beach for a few days, but we'll be back for Easter on Sunday.

"That's awesome, Ben. Actually, before you leave, can I run something by you?"

"Sure. Boys, go wait in the car for me. I'll be right out." The two boys quietly left the office.

"You have a beautiful family Ben. I'm so happy for you."

"Thank you, Annie. I'm overwhelmed with joy these days. God has smiled on me once again. And thank you for everything you and everyone else here at Covenant has done to help me get here. What did you need to ask me?"

"Well, it's not me doing the asking this time, for once. Heather and Dawn wanted to ask you to marry them at their wedding."

Ben's face became blank and he took a step back. "Seriously?"

"Yes. They asked me to ask you a while ago, but it was in the middle of the custody hearing preparations and I wanted to make sure everything worked out for you with the boys before asking. They said they'd be honored if a gay minister could officiate the first gay wedding at the church."

"Well, what about you, Annie? Don't you want to do it?"

"No Ben, they asked for you. I agreed to serve as backup, and the way things go around here, I'm sure I'll have my opportunity soon enough. So...yay or nay?"

"Yay! Tell them I'd be honored! And thank you!"

"Excellent. I'll pass on your number to them, so you guys can work out the details."

Ben gave me a hug and left, and I called Heather and Dawn to confirm that Ben had accepted their offer. They were overjoyed, with Ben's yes and the progress of the garden, which was almost complete, minus the gazebo. Although Edward was still holding out hope, Heather and Dawn had quietly planned for a second option just in case. The wedding was just three short weeks away.

When I got back from my parents' house on Wednesday, I asked a few of the deacons to meet me at the church to hang Easter decorations. I particularly needed men to dig three holes and use some of the leftover wood we had to make three huge crosses and raise them out by the road, so all the cars could see them as they passed by. I'd missed the Lenten Season, but planned to drape a black cloth across the middle cross on Friday to represent Christ's death, and a white one Easter Sunday for His resurrection.

Edna and I were hanging out in the fellowship hall, decorating the tables for the dinner we'd have after church on

Sunday, and Edward and Alan sat around waiting on Jesse to arrive, so they could lift the crosses into the ground.

"Hey guys! Sorry I'm late," Jesse said when he finally arrived. "Baby wouldn't stop crying. Where'd we find the money for the gazebo? It's pretty sweet."

"What gazebo," Edward said.

"The one in the garden. I just—"

Both men stared at each other for a moment, before Edward jumped up from his chair and ran out of the door. Jesse bolted behind him, and the rest of us followed Jesse. I caught up with Edward just as he'd made it to the garden.

The gazebo was bathe in the light of the setting sun, it's cedar wood rich with color. It looked like Jesus himself had reached down into a magazine, picked it up, and sat it down perfectly in it's planned place in the garden. There was a built-in bench that hugged the entire interior wall, and flower boxes hung on the outside of the banister. Edward stepped inside and jumped: it was sturdy and sure, and not a mirage.

"What in the world?" Edna said.

"Where did this come from?" I asked, looking around. Everyone shrugged.

"Look," Edward said, reaching up to the inside roof of the gazebo. He struggled with something, then snatched down a white envelope with the word "COVENANT" handwritten on the outside in blue ink. Edward waived it at me.

"Open it," I said.

Edward opened the envelope and unfolded the single sheet of paper that was inside. "'Thank you for helping my nephew,'" Edward read aloud. "That's all it says."

"Nephew..." Alan said.

"Let's check the security cameras," Edward said, already walking away.

Now the group was running again—more so power walking this time—to my office, where the security cameras were located and that I barely ever looked at. There just was not that much going on in Bakerstown, North Carolina for them to be something I needed to constantly monitor. They were just there in case something happened to happen, not to be proactive in anyway. We all gathered around, and Edward pulled up the monitors and pressed the Rewind button. The black and white video was like a backwards time lapse of the last thirty-six hours: Elizabeth and me walking in and out of the church, cars constantly passing by on the main road, going from day to night to day again. The next time it switched to night, we saw it: at the time stamp of one a.m., a pick-up truck had backed up to the garden loaded with wood. Four men got out of the cab, then proceeded to unload the truck and their toolboxes and build the gazebo. They'd finished at five a.m. An older gentleman had written the note while leaning on the side of the truck, then given it to a taller man to tape to the roof. All of the men were Hispanic.

"Well I'll be," Edward said, grinning.

"We just caught angels on tape," Edna said.

"Yeah, I'm gonna go cry now," Jesse said, and walked out.

"How did you not hear them, Annie?" Edna asked.

"I wasn't here that night. I was at my parents."

I sat in my office chair and stared at the monitor. I could not believe it.

"Edward," I said, "I owe you an apology."

"No you don't," he said. "If it wasn't for that stand you, William, and John took at the fundraiser, we still might not have a gazebo right now. You just never know how God will use you to answer your own prayer."

"You sure you don't want to pastor this church?" I asked.

"Positive," Edward said. "That's your job. Mine is to keep you on your toes!"

"Oh, you're very good at that. Seriously Edward, thank you. For your tremendous faith and everything you do for this church. I really appreciate you."

"You're welcome, Annie. I'm gonna go check out the gazebo some more."

I closed the door behind Edward, then sat down in my chair. I needed to call Heather and Dawn and tell them the good news. Before I dialed Heather's number, there was one more Person I needed to apologize to.

243

"Please forgive me for not believing, Father," I said. "Please continue to give me opportunities to exercise my faith. And Thank You."

Chapter 42

On Friday night—Good Friday—John came over for our usual date and had already called to warn me that he just wanted to stay at the parsonage this evening and not go out anywhere, which was totally okay with me since I was exhausted. When he arrived, he gave me a quick peck on the lips. Something was off.

"What's wrong, love?" I asked.

John collapsed on the couch and leaned into me, and I could see that he was truly sad. "I learned that one of the security guys at work that I haven't seen in a while, Santiago, was deported today. He was one of my favorite people."

"John, I'm so sorry."

"Yeah. It's crazy. I'm not sure what ICE is doing, but they are clearly targeting our area now. I hate that I'm talking about him like he's dead, but Santiago was such a great guy. I used to have lunch with him every now and then, and we would discuss our dreams and families. He wanted to have a NASCAR team. When Lucinda died, somehow, he found out, and he would pray for me. Even when I told him I wasn't too happy with God, he still kept praying with me. I let him continue to be nice, and because deep down I knew I needed it. My daughters and other people's prayers are the only thing that kept me alive around that time I suspect."

I wrapped my arms around John and pulled him in close to me. "I wish there was more we could do to help them," I said. "But with stories like Santiago's, it all seems so pointless. They're sending good people back to places where their lives are in danger, and it seems like whether you get to stay or not is all a matter of whether you can stay alive long enough for your application to possibly be approved, or you overstay your visa and it's a dangerous game of whether you get caught or not, like Juan and Santiago."

"Right. But I think there *is* something we can do Annie," John said, turning to faced me. "Me and you. I want to start a foundation. Something that raises funds on a continuous basis to help with the legal costs for immigrants fighting to stay with their families in this country. We can solicit donations from all over the world online, and make sure every cent goes towards organizations

245

that work and advocate for detained immigrants and the reunification of families."

"That sounds like a wonderful idea, John. I support you and would love to start a foundation with you. Knowing Carlita and Julio are somewhere still away from their kids truly eats at me sometimes. Of course, I would trust you to know about the legal parts of it, but maybe I can help when it comes to providing mental health professionals, supplies, and caring for the basic needs of the children of the detained."

"Let's do it," John said.

Chapter 43

Easter Sunday morning, I changed the black cloth on Jesus's cross out by the road to white and waived when a car passing by honked excitedly at me. Jesus had risen, and that was cause to celebrate.

As I walked back to the church, I stopped to take in the garden from afar. It was beautiful, and the colors of the blooming plants on both sides of the gazebo were truly a sight to behold. We would be dedicating it after church—a red ribbon already stretched across from garden to garden—and would next christen it with Heather and Dawn's wedding.

As usual, William had beat me to church, and was in the sanctuary filling the air with worship. I made sure to finalize my sermon as soon as possible this week; since I knew we'd most likely have a lot of visitors in the congregation today. I wanted to skip the time I normally spent in my office before service and spend more time greeting every person who came to service as they walked in. So, I quietly took a seat on the back pew by the door and let the sounds of William's voice and the organ settle over me as I waited for the first person to arrive.

Twenty minutes later, the door opened, and I hugged Pete Stoudamire as he walked into the church. "Happy Easter, Reverend Annie," he said.

"Happy Easter, Pete."

I repeated the same greeting to everyone for the next hour, and just as I expected, by the time William played the opening chords to "Because He Lives," the sanctuary was packed almost to capacity. I was especially excited to see and greet Elena Alvarez and her four cousins, Carlita and Julio's children. Elena gave me a big hug and then guided the kids to one of the last open sections in the middle of the pews.

My Easter Sunday message was rooted in Romans 8:34: *Who then is the one who condemns? No one. Christ Jesus who died—more than that, who was raised to life—is at the right hand of God and is also interceding for us.*

"Now, I know you guys were probably expecting a good old, tried and true, 'Jesus died and rose again on the third day' message from the gospels today. But I'll appreciate it if you bear with me as I venture away from the normal a little bit today. In this verse from Romans, we still have what we all want to hear on Easter Sunday morning. That Jesus, indeed, died and rose again. That is the gospel, that He died for our sins so that we could be saved. Simple as that. But this particular verse goes a little deeper, gets a little bit more personal when it comes to how we can remember on a daily basis not only that Jesus died for us two thousand some years ago, but what He is doing today. At this very moment. As we sit here celebrating His victory over Satan and death, as we sit in our offices at work tomorrow, as we are out and about and going about our lives, Christ is sitting beside God and talking to Him about us."

After I finished, I gave the invitation for anyone who wanted to come down and give their lives to Christ, and a family— a man, woman, and teenage daughter—came down the aisle and stood in front of me. I thanked God for their public decision, welcomed them to the Covenant family, and Wayne Fleming took them in the back to gather their details.

The service ended, and everyone followed each other outside to the garden as we prepared to cut the ribbon. We'd asked the congregation to submit suggestions on what to name the garden, and found one suggestion that we thought worked perfectly, so we asked Fred and Edith Miller and their daughter Belinda to come up front to the ribbon.

"Fred and Edith," I said as the congregation fell silent. "This garden is the result of a lot of hard work by a lot of people here at Covenant. But if it wasn't for you Fred, I'm not sure it would exist. If it's okay with you, we'd like to name this garden after your son Tommy. The Tommy Miller Memorial Garden."

Both Fred and Edith were emotional as they nodded and said, "Thank you," to everyone, then used scissors to cut the ribbon. It fell away, and everyone entered the garden to look around and seemed in awe at the design, layout, and how beautiful it was. I saw people sitting on the benches and kids chasing each other in the gazebo.

Edward found me in the crowd of people and wrapped his arm around my shoulder. "We did it again," he said.

"Yes, Edward," I said. "We did."

Chapter 44

"Damien. Mary. Elizabeth. Reverend Annie. I invited you all here tonight to apologize."

Everyone glanced around at each other but remained silent. It was Tuesday night, and I'd gotten a call from Lucille earlier in the day asking me if had dinner plans for tonight.

"No, Mrs. Lucille," I'd said, keeping Brian's advice to me in mind. "Did you want to meet for dinner?"

"Actually, I'd like it if you came over to my place for dinner, if that's okay."

"I'd like that. What time should I arrive?"

After I'd confirmed what time to come, Elizabeth had walked into my office ten minutes later. "My grandmother just invited me and the kids over for the dinner tonight," she'd said.

"Huh! Me too!"

"What? Oh gosh." Elizabeth had looked faint. "What could this be about?"

"I don't know Elizabeth, but maybe we should just trust her," I'd said.

Now, we were sitting at her wooden dining room table along with Damien and Mary, with fine china place settings before us and wondering what Lucille was about to say.

"As you know, last month my late husband's weed eater went missing from the tool shed, and I immediately blamed Damien for it." Lucille looked at Damien across the table. "Damien, I was wrong, and I want to publicly apologize to you. I have been a complete jerk, and I feel that I do not deserve your forgiveness, but I am going to beg it anyway. You see, somehow, in my old age maybe, I completely forgot that Lee Forrester, my husband Brady's good friend, and his wife, Diana had stopped by around that same time to check in to see how I was doing. They've come by every now and then since Brady passed away, and often Diana will bring me these lovely buttermilk pies that she bakes. The last time they came over, on their way out of the door, Lee asked if he could borrow Brady's trimmer, because his had broken and he needed to finish a job. I told him yes without thinking about it, because he was my husband's trusted friend, and told him that he knew where to find it out in the shed. When I next went to the shed a couple of days later, I had forgotten that I had let Lee borrow it. Two days ago, Lee knocked on my door again to let me know he had put the trimmer back in the shed. I asked him what he was talking about. He said, 'Remember I borrowed Brady's trimmer last month?'

"I sat down on the porch and could not believe that I'd forgotten it. But more tragically Damien, I'd wrongfully accused you for taking it the entire time. What I did to you—and to you Mary—was wrong and stubborn since Reverend Annie warned me about accusing you without firm evidence. You have done nothing to me and been nothing but good for my granddaughter. So, I don't know what else to say but I'm sorry. If you don't want to forgive me, I completely understand, but I had to let you, and everyone here know that I was wrong in what I did."

Everyone at the table sat in stunned silence.

"Elizabeth," Lucille continued. "I'd also like to apologize to you. I have made it a point to be there for you since the little ones were born, but I have also at times been overbearing and untrusting of you. Lord knows I didn't like it when my own mother did that to me when I was a young girl. You and Damien aren't the only people in the world to make mistakes, and you will make more. Hell, apparently, I'm still making them at the ripe old age of seventy-nine. But I apologize for trying to control your life and who you date, and for thinking that Damien was unworthy of you, when he has shown me nothing of the sort. You are graduating next week, and I am extremely proud of you, and I promise not to second-guess your decisions and allow you to experience life on your own without my constant judgement."

Elizabeth wiped tears from her eyes as she bounced Jeremy on her knee, and Damien reached over and massaged her neck and shoulders.

"Mary, I apologize for judging your son. I know that must have been awkward for you. Again, I was wrong. You have been such a help to me since you moved into the guest cottage and started helping me around the house. If you weren't here, I don't know if I'd be able to go on living here. I hope you will forgive me and continue staying here. I need you."

Mary nodded and dabbed her eyes with her napkin.

"Finally, Reverend Annie. I just want to say thank you for rebuking me in the right spirit. You sensed all along that I was wrong about Damien. Everyone else had a vested interest in his innocence, but you did not, and you stood up for him anyway. I suppose that is also the same reason why you're doing such an awesome job leading Covenant. So again, thank you for putting up with my foolishness with grace and care, yet correcting me and gently nudging me in the right direction at the same time."

Now it was my turn to cry. "Thank you, Mrs. Lucille, for bringing us all here today and standing before us here, admitting that you were wrong and asking for our forgiveness. I can tell you right now that the most powerful men on this earth are not humble enough to do what you just did. You stand tall today as a great example for all of us."

"Well, thank you. I felt it was the right thing to do after all I put everyone through."

"Alright," Mary said, standing up. "Shall we eat?"

"Yes, let's eat, but I have just one more thing for Damien." Lucille said. Damien put down his napkin. "Son, you are the person that I wronged the most, and I truly feel bad about that. I have helped my granddaughter over the years, and now I would like to help you, if you will accept it. My husband's lawn tools I accused you of stealing: I have no use for them. I'm not on the best terms with my son because of how he treats Elizabeth, and I hire a company to keep the grass cut and the bushes trimmed. I'd like to offer them to you to start your own lawn cutting business with, if you'd like. Free of charge. There's the infamous weed eater out there, plus two more, a couple of push mowers, three blowers, and a riding lawn mower. I even have a trailer somewhere around here if you have something to hitch it to."

Damien's eyes were as big as I'd ever seen. "Mrs. Lucille, are you serious right now? Because if you are, I know a good opportunity when I see one."

"Indeed you do, son, and indeed I am. I was about to say that if you are going to be seriously dating my granddaughter, you'll need a way to provide for her and the kiddos, but I suppose that's old school talk these days, and I reckon I shouldn't make my gift to you contingent on you and Elizabeth working out. So, if you want the tools, they are yours. My only contingency is that you don't sell them. I'm teaching you to fish, not giving you a fish."

"Yes ma'am! I'll take them! Thank you so much!"

"Thank you, Damien."

Damien stood up and hugged his mother first, who was now crying again, then walked around to the table and hugged Lucille.

"Can we eat now?" Mary said.

We all sat around the table and enjoyed the delicious meal that Mary and Lucille had planned. How God had turned this situation around! In one evening, Damien had gone from being a convicted felon and student to a business owner, and a family's relationship had gone from strained to hopefully much, much better moving forward. All because one person was humble enough to admit that they were wrong. If we could all do what Lucille Smith had done that night, the world would be a much better place.

Chapter 45

The morning of Heather and Dawn's wedding, I woke early, as I was familiar with weddings and the last-minute tasks that always seem to pop up, no matter how much planning was done. I'd already called Heather and Dawn and told them I'd be available before the start of the wedding for anything they needed. Thankfully, I didn't have to travel anywhere, since the event was being held right here in the newly built Tommy Miller Memorial Garden. The wedding was slated to start at three p.m. and an event company was arriving at six a.m. to set up chairs in the open area in front of the gazebo, and more tables and chairs for the outside reception that could comfortably seat 100 people.

I wasn't officiating the wedding, but as backup minister, I still wanted to match the creme color theme, and upon discovering this week that I didn't have anything that looked acceptable to *potentially* officiate a wedding in, I'd driven up to Charlotte at the last minute and found a nice suit at Nordstroms. It would hang in my closet in case of emergency, and I had a nice, navy blue jumpsuit to wear assuming nothing went wrong with Ben.

When I stepped outside, the tent company had arrived, and had backed up a large box truck to the garden. I walked over to see if I could help, and found Dawn talking with a man from the tent company and unfolding chairs.

"Dawn! What are you doing here?" I said.

"Setting up chairs," Dawn said.

"Aren't you paying the company to do that?"

"Yea, I guess so."

Dawn hadn't yet made eye contact with me and had a worried look on her face. I walked over to her and grabbed the chair in her hand. "What's going on?"

Dawn finally looked me in the eye, then unfolded the chair and sat down in it. "I don't know. I think I'm nervous."

"Well, that's normal," I said, sitting down in the chair beside her. "But you don't mean nervous as in cold feet, do you?"

"No, I know I want to be with Heather forever. It's just…scared I'm going to do something wrong or mess it all up somehow. Or not be able to take care of my family. I don't know."

The tent company employees continued to set up chairs around us. "I see. I think you're putting too much pressure on yourself right now. I'm not married, but I can tell you that your marriage won't ever be perfect, and *you* won't ever be perfect. Neither will Heather. And you'd be setting yourself up for failure if you tried to make it so."

"I just want to do right by Heather and the kids," Dawn said. The sun was rising above the treetops and touching our heads with golden light. "Sometimes I second guess myself, and I lose all confidence. Then I feel like I will find a way to screw this up somehow. "

"You guys have been together for several years, now, correct?" I asked.

"Ten."

"By now, I think if Heather thought you'd mess this up, today wouldn't be happening, don't ya think."

Dawn took a deep breath. "Yeah, I guess so."

"If Heather has confidence in you, you should too. Come on," I said and tapped Dawn on the knee. "Leave this to them: you're paying them. Go sit over there in the garden by yourself. Pray, relax, release. Talk to God and allow Him to give you His peace. Today is the best day of your life. Don't mentally ruin it for yourself."

Dawn looked over at the memorial side of the garden. "You know, I think I will. Thanks, Reverend."

As the morning went on, more and more people started to arrive, a mixture of workers and Dawn and Heather's friends and family and Covenant members, and before long, even though this would be a small wedding, the entire campus was buzzing with excitement and activity. I'd offered my parsonage to Heather and her bridal party to get ready in, and they had arrived and were camped out inside while I set up shop in my office at the church. Random women ran in and out to their cars sporadically, taking in things and bringing things back out. Dawn's party only consisted of her father and her brother, and the three hung out in the fellowship hall, already dressed and preparing to go to the garden to take pictures with a photographer.

Ben arrived about an hour before the service was set to begin, and came and found me in the office. He was dressed in a navy suit, had a fresh haircut, and looked better than I'd ever seen him.

"Well look at you!" I said to him. "Are you ready?"

"I think so. Heather and Dawn gave me a copy of the program they wanted to use, so all I have to do is read it."

"Sounds easy enough," I said.

"Hey Annie. Are you sure you're good with me officiating? I don't want to step on your toes or anything, especially after all you've done for me?"

"Ben, are you kidding me? It's fine. Besides, I have a suit standby in the parsonage in case you get cold feet." I said.

"Hey you two," someone said behind us. "Care to get the party started early?"

William stood in the door way, exposing a bottle of whiskey inside his suit jacket.

Ben did a double take. "Wait, what—"

"Don't mind him," I said. "We normally share a shot on tough days."

"Which is why I figured that today we could flip the script and have a single toast to something positive," William said as he stepped inside, closed the door, and placed three small glasses on my desk.

"He's serious." Ben said, incredulous.

"I'm afraid he is," I said.

William poured a tiny amount of whiskey in each of the glasses, and we all raised them high in the sky. "To new beginnings," he said.

"To new beginnings!" Ben and I said in unison.

A small tent had been set up at the end of the aisle to hide the wedding party from the guests as they prepared to make their entrance. John had arrived, and we sat together on the third row and on the end, just in case I needed to move quickly to assist with anything. I saw several Covenant members in the seats, and it made me happy that people had come out to support Heather and Dawn in their union.

The music started, and, as officiant, Ben was first to leave the tent and quickly walked down the aisle alone and took his place in the middle of the gazebo. Next was Dawn, flanked by her father and brother. Dawn was all smiles as she made eye contact with people she knew as she walked.

Vivian Artz was next, her creme and blue floral print dress stopped just below her ankles. She was escorted by Steve Angle and Donnie Medlin, who I was delighted to see again, and both wore creme-colored tuxedo pants with navy vests and white long-sleeved dress shirts underneath. Vivian was all smiles as they walked down the aisle, each of her arms hooked under Steve and Donnie's on either side. Once Vivian was safely in her assigned seat on the front row, Donnie and Steve ran back to the tent and escorted Dawn's mother Cathy down the aisle in the same fashion.

Next were Cody and Kami, Dawn and Heather's children. Cody—thirteen years old and growing very tall—held his nine year old sister's hand, then let it go as they reached the gazebo and stood with Dawn. Heather's two bridesmaids were next—her sister and her best friend—their dresses different from each other but still matching the overall theme.

Heather appeared in the back of the aisle, like a radiant angel in the May sunlight, and we all stood to our feet. Her wedding dress was a soft creme color, a narrow cut, with laced shoulders and a long train behind her. She had opted for the traditional veil, so the tears that had started to well in her eyes as the DJ started the bride's song would not cause a chain reaction throughout the gathering. Dawn stood beside Ben, overcome with joy and struggling to keep it together, and her father passed her a Kleenex and gave her a quick rub on the back for support.

Fred Miller, in his creme tuxedo—*with* the jacket unlike Steve and Donnie—held Heather's hand between his arm and chest as he slowly but confidently walked her down the aisle. I could see the pride in Fred's face: it was because of him that Heather and Dawn and everyone in attendance were able to experience this special moment here at Covenant, all because Fred had found the courage to take a stand for what he knew was right. It reminded me that sometimes all it takes is one person to cause a butterfly effect of change.

Dawn had somewhat regained her composure by the time Heather made it to the gazebo, and Fred handed Heather off to her. The couple stood holding hands opposite each other, gazing into each other's eyes, with Heather occasionally reaching over and wiping the tears from Dawn's cheeks. The time had finally come for them to be able to outwardly share with everyone the love and commitment that they always had for each other.

An hour and a half later, Dawn and Heather were married, and the reception was in full swing. John and I sat a table, watching Heather and Dawn dance on the makeshift floor set up in the middle of the reception area.

"Ben did a great job today, huh?" John said. "I'm proud of him."

"Yes, he did very well," I said. "It's great to see him healthy and happy again."

"So, what do you think about all this," he said.

"The wedding? I thought it was wonderful," I said. "I'm glad we all got to be a part of making this day special for Heather and Dawn."

"Can we step inside the church for a minute?"

"Sure," I said. I thought the ask was a little strange, but I obliged, and we walked over to the church and stepped inside the sanctuary. My parents, Edna, and Emily and Ella were standing inside, forming a little semi-circle that cut off the center aisle. I immediately thought something was wrong, and my heart dropped. "Oh my gosh," I said. "What's wrong?"

"Annie," John said, taking my hand and turning me to face him. "I just wanted to come in here away from everyone, so we didn't take any attention away from Heather and Dawn."

"What do you mean?" I was even more confused now.

John kept one of my hands in his as he reached into his pocket with the other and lowered one knee to the ground.

"Oh my gosh," I said, and looked over at my parents. My father had his arms around both my mother and Edna, who were both trying desperately to hold back tears amidst the joy on their faces. Emily and Ella eyes were big and wide, and they jumped up and down with excitement.

"Annie," John said, "These last couple of years knowing you and being with you have been some of the best times I've had. You have loved me when I was hard to love, you've loved my daughters, my mother, not to mention all the people here at Covenant. I love you, so much, and you would make me a very happy man if you would do me the honor of being my wife."

I had fantasized about this very moment for almost my entire life, and now that it was here, I was so overwhelmed with love, gratefulness, and shock that I couldn't immediately respond like I'd always envisioned. I always thought it a little cruel when women would forget to answer a proposal right away, leaving the man on his knees vulnerable and growing more and more nervous about a possible rejection with every slow second that passed, especially when there was a crowd of people watching. Now here I was, so floored by the proposal that I never saw coming, that I was speechless.

"Annie," my mother said, bringing me back to reality.

"Yes?" John said.

"Yes, John," I said, finally pulling it together. "I'd be honored to be your wife."

"And I'd be honored to be your husband," he said. He slipped the diamond engagement ring over my left ring finger, then stood and pulled me to him, kissing me for a few seconds before wrapping me in a tight hug. I could not stop the tears by now, and John reached into his pocket and pulled out a handkerchief and dotted my face. The girls ran to us and wrapped our legs in a hug. John and my father shook hands, and my mother wrapped me in a long, emotional hug, which was immediately followed by Edna.

"Congratulations sweetheart," my mother said. "Your father and I are so happy for you."

"Thanks Mom. I love you."

"Looks like we have another wedding on our hands," Edna said, elbowing me. "You know you'd have to get the deacons' approval if you want to have it here at Covenant. They may not be keen on their woman pastor having frolicked around with a member of the congregation,"

"HA! Wouldn't that be something," I said.

"Hey gang," John said, "Let's keep this under wraps until next week sometime, huh? I don't want to take any attention away from Heather and Dawn."

"That's a good idea, John. I'm glad to be marrying a man who is so considerate."

"Remember every nice word she says about you, John," my dad said. "You're going to have to remind her about them later."

We all left the church and rejoined the reception, and as the sun set on Heather and Dawn's new union before God, John and I danced under the mason jar lights that had been strung up from the posts of the garden. Two and a half years ago, God had brought me to Bakerstown, unsure if I could ever fulfill my lifelong dream of being a pastor of a church and leading his people. Now, I knew that I could, and if I continued to trust in and lean on Him and the people in my life, there was nothing that I couldn't do.

www.ingramcontent.com/pod-product-compliance
Lightning Source LLC
Chambersburg PA
CBHW061601170626
46811CB00001B/277